GRYPHON RIDER ACADEMY

SECOND CHANCE

Flutterbye Trail Press
797 Sam Bass Road #2541
Round Rock, TX 78681

First edition

Editing by Red Loop Editing
Cover Design by Black Bird Book Covers
Chapter Art by Etheric Tales
Map by Reva Design
Printed Interior Design by Enchanting Covers
Published by Flutterbye Trail Press

ISBN: 978-1-954582-07-1 (E-book)
ISBN: 978-1-954582-36-1 (Paperback)
ISBN: 978-1-954582-32-3 (Hardback)

Feedback: Encounter a problem with this book? Let us know at
elisehennessyauthor@gmail.com

BOOKS BY ELISE HENNESSY

Books in the Altare World

GRYPHON RIDER ACADEMY
Second Chance
Chosen
Storm Front
Wild Flight
Gryphon Rider Academy Omnibus 1: Books 1-4

ROYAL SPY INSTITUTE
The Crown Heist
Five & Chance

Also by Elise Hennessy

BLOOD LEGACY SERIES
Dream Walker
The Winter Key
Queen's Return
Court of Illusions

Shadow Dance
Rule the Night
Dhampir's Wish
Blood Curse
Blood Legacy: The Complete Series

MAP

You can find a full-sized version of this map at: www.
elisehennessy.com / maps

GRYPHON RIDER ACADEMY 1

SECOND CHANCE

ELISE HENNESSY

CHAPTER I
HIS LAST SUNSET

Failure to thrive. Those three words hung like bricks weighing down my shoulders. I'd tried everything I could think of, yet it wasn't enough. The order had come down from High Command; there would be an execution at first light tomorrow. *A mercy*, my father had said.

Yet when I looked at Arimus, I didn't see a combat gryphon past his prime—thus useless to the war effort—but instead the gentle beast who'd let me practice brushing out his coat when I was still apprenticing as a caretaker. Now he barely lifted his beak from the straw nest I arranged for him last week when he was finally moved to this private stable away from his fellows.

I faithfully groomed him every day as the only human he permitted to touch him after his rider's death. When he'd plucked his feathers in anguish, I'd tended his wounds until he was covered in pink patches where tiny quills promised new growth.

His situation was deemed unusual the moment his rider, Alamid Maros, perished without him. Few gryphons survived the soul-level shock of the loss of their rider. That Arimus had lived was both a blessing and a curse, as his suffering reached a level deeper than skin and bone. Such was the nature of gryphons and their subtle magic. They forge unbreakable Links with their riders, sharing emotions, thoughts, and so forth.

With Arimus's Link broken, his emotions hung over him like a thick morass, leaking into the psyche of everyone around him. A black halo of despair sank into my mind every time I got close to the gryphon. It was hard to think knowing, *feeling* how deeply he was hurt. That's why he'd been banished to this stable, alone, to await his death.

"This leg next," I said, tapping his right flank with my brush. It took a second tap before he rolled to his side with a deep groan. I stretched out his leonine back leg, massaging the roughened pads of his paw until it spread to the size of a dinner plate, sharp dagger claws descending from their sheathes.

"Not a spot left untouched," I promised him, feeling my smile waver. He knew as well as I did that this would be the last time I groomed him head to toe.

My fellow caretakers thought I was wasting my time returning to Ari every day and making sure he was comfortable as he lay here day and night. They hadn't grown up around the First Gryphon Flight's beasts as I had. Fifteen in total, I knew their personalities and needs as if they were part of my family. It's how I earned my caretaker job in the first place; I was able to feed and groom the gryphons without fearing for my life and limbs.

Ari loved having his paws pampered, so I'd saved this part for last. Gryphon feet were interesting, representing the split nature of the beasts. Lion paws in back, eagle talons in front, both needing different oils and ointments. His back pads were dry and cracked from disuse, so I spent time massaging them until they felt like tough, supple leather. The claws weren't splitting—I'd just trimmed and filed them to the proper length yesterday.

Before I knew it, I was finished with his other paw and he was rolling to sit on his feet, his beak still ploughed into the hay. A quick brush-down tomorrow, and his body would be as pristine as possible going into the execution. In the low light of approaching evening, his tawny feathers were touched with amber where they lined his stout neck and the grand pair of bird wings hanging loose over his flanks. The feline fur that covered the rest of his body was a cocoa brown and deceptively thick, boasting a double coat to keep him warm in the sky and a gryphon's preferred territory: high and snowy mountains.

I took loud, deliberate steps around to his head. As a male gryphon, he was about the size of a draft horse, though longer and leaner, especially since he'd barely eaten after Alamid's passing a month ago.

Kneeling by his head, I placed my hand on the yellowed curve of his beak and made the same offer as always. "You're all cleaned up. Maybe a walk? Show off those beautiful feathers?"

I may be a girl and thus incapable of experiencing the joy of a gryphon Link, but I prided myself in communicating with gryphons nonetheless. Riders could understand their beasts perfectly, but what I received was a jumble of images and feelings when one of the gryphons chose to communicate with me.

Upon hearing his suffering would be over tomorrow, he'd projected acceptance and…darkness. That sense of emptiness echoed over me now, and I shifted on my knees, uncomfortable.

That was what he could see. Nothing.

The enemy rozash had taken two precious things from this broken gryphon: his rider and his sight. The flight healers had labored over Ari for days and nights to reconstruct his face and allow fine feathers to regrow where rozash acid had burned him. But no force of magic could save his eyes.

They'd been replaced by two painted marbles to support his facial structure. The healers wouldn't have bothered if they'd known Ari would fail to thrive. The country needed every beast, and the hope at that time was that Ari would wake up, mourn, and then pick a new rider. He was a trained adult beast and thus invaluable to the Crown...but only if he would fight.

Recently, Ari communicated "no" easily with a sharp turn of dark emotions. But today, he tossed his head, jerking out from under my hand, and projected the barest pip of something lighter. Anticipation, I think. He drew his body up, arching backward with his front legs stretched. Several bones crackled with the motion.

I sucked in a breath, finally able to smile again. That was a yes, and I wasn't going to second-guess it. I retrieved his saddle, moving in those heavy, deliberate steps as I approached and draped it over his muscular shoulders. It was Altarian law that any tame adult gryphon wear a saddle and harness outside of their living spaces. While I understood that it made the average citizen more comfortable around the beasts, it drew a squawk of protest from Ari.

For a moment, I felt it: that slithery feeling of a cut saddle sliding off Ari's back, taking his rider with it. He projected the memory so cleanly to me that I was left trembling with nerves upon seeing the leather listing on his shoulders with the dancing of his front talons.

"Sorry, sorry," I breathed, catching it before it could fall. He stilled when I balanced it in the right place and hurried to secure it. Ari gave me the same blank void in reply, his head hanging low. He accepted the reins as I slipped them over his beak, but he snapped up the bit fast enough that I could've lost a hand.

"Whoa there," I said. I was lucky I hadn't been about to guide that into his mouth, because there'd been no telegraph in his body language or emotion.

He rolled the bit in his beak, murring a low sound of pain. Lowering his head, he projected a feeling of apology. It hurt my heart to see him posed that way.

"No harm done. Are you ready?" I made it a choice. There had to be more than that despairing darkness in him, some mercurial mood he wasn't projecting. With a shuffle of his feathers, he took the first step toward the stable door. I kept a hand on his reins, guiding him outside one slow pace at a time. It had to be painful to use those neglected muscles, but I hoped it brought him some joy to soak in the warmth of the waning sunlight as we emerged into the Gryphon Yard.

The beasts loved to run and fly, especially with their riders. I knew what I offered was a distant second place, as all caretakers were permitted to do was saddle and walk the gryphons if their riders were unavailable.

Ari lifted his beak to the breeze as it blew sweet autumn air over us both. The overgrown grass of the Yard swayed like a rippling ocean of slowly bronzing vegetation. We walked through it, grass tickling his legs and my calves. I wished he could see the sunset before us, how the sky banded with ever-darkening shades as orange became crimson, which then gave way to the plum tones of early night.

It gave me an idea. I turned to Ari, relieved to feel his mood starting to lift. "Would you like for me to describe what's around us?" I offered. I couldn't share mental images like a gryphon, but maybe this would be just as good.

Ari huffed, scratching his talons into the soft earth. He projected his darkness and a fresh wave of hopelessness. My throat closed up, choking on a reply.

"Is it hard to imagine color and, well, other things?" I finally asked. I could hardly picture being struck blind so traumatically, to the point where he could only share his darkness.

To answer my question, he projected something new: the first hint of color and life from him. It was Alamid's face, a smile drawing kind lines around the creases of his eyes. He'd been well-tanned from years in the sun, flying closer to it than most, his military-short hair highlighted with premature silvers.

It's how I remembered him too. Lean, clean-shaven, and the most caring man I'd met outside of my own father, his best friend. I shared that sense of heartbreak with Ari as the image faded; the wound of the other man's loss was raw in us both. But it helped me understand as well.

"You just see him now," I said quietly.

He pushed another feeling at me: painful, gut-wrenching failure.

"I know. But you did what you could. It's a miracle you survived." At the same time, I knew it was a miracle he didn't want, this proud gryphon who saw his rider's face behind his permanently closed eyes.

Unbidden, I started to tell him about the sunset with my words. If he wanted me to stop, he'd tell me. I glanced to him, seeing his tufted ears lifted, rotated toward the sound of my voice. "And autumn has come while you rested," I continued. "The grass has stopped growing. You know that means the frosts are coming soon."

Without the sun, the air was turning nippy. I rubbed my bare arms, regretting leaving my cloak on a hook back in the stable. My well-worn working clothes didn't shield me well from the wind.

"We're almost to the end of the Yard now," I narrated. It sloped upward to a flat peak, the highest point in the city. It fell away sharply, long terraformed by the legion of mages that'd helped settle Kaiamear. We could look into the windows of the royals' high towers in the southern wing of the palace. The rest of the palace wrapped around the Yard, built in a solid cylinder with high walls in case of a siege. The queen's gardens were a distant plot of greenery from this vantage.

Ari placed his paws carefully at the edge of the Yard's peak before sitting. The ridge was wide enough for a team of five gryphons to take off or land at the same time, as this point was their preferred spot for a running start or stop. Now that the sun had set, there wouldn't be any traffic here. Gryphons *hated* flying at night and would only do it under dire circumstances.

I sat next to him, releasing his reins. The night deepened, and the breeze chilled my skin while a sigh whistled through Ari's beak. He shifted and carefully laid his head in my lap, lids closing over his fake eyes as I ran my fingers through his furry neck to a sweet spot right behind his beak.

I told him about the stars as they winked in, glittering above us like spilled diamonds on indigo velvet. The words were slow and halting at first, as I hesitated to cause him more pain. Ari's emotions were still leaking from his broken Link as I spoke, feeling distinctly of concentration. Was he trying to imagine what I was saying?

"And you can see the main road heading away from the palace. There's torchlight all over the city where folk live," I continued.

Ari clicked his beak and projected another memory: of standing in this very place, saddled and ready to fly. But this time, he was digging his paws into the hard ridge of earth, turning his beak up at the idea of navigating the skies by starlight. It was another crisp night, similar to the one before us.

"Yes," I said as the memory faded. "It looks exactly like that."

He shared his wistfulness, cycling through a more complicated series of emotions and images I struggled to understand. Gryphons usually shared these things one or two at a time, going slowly to better bridge the language gap between us.

"Hmm?" Maybe he'd repeat what he was trying to say.

Frustration. Ari's talons scuffed the earth. With him concentrating hard and me focusing on everything he said, for a moment, I understood his true meaning like he spoke to me with words.

"I don't want to go, Sivana. Alamid would want me to live."

"By the gods," I breathed. I hugged him around his neck. "I want you to live too, more than anything." Gryphons in captivity lived for up to seventy years. His life was about to be cut short by over fifty of those, a true tragedy.

Unless I could do something about it. My thoughts boiled over. I needed to speak with my father right away and share what Ari had said. He could speak to his superior and petition High Command for more time. But would those sour old men even believe a gryphon had spoken clearly to someone he wasn't Linked to? A girl, besides?

I frowned as I scratched behind his ears, finding another spot that drew a pleased murr from him. My life for the past month had been convincing my father to advocate for Ari. One week had become two, and two weeks had become "we'll see."

We would see tomorrow unless someone more important than me heard those words from the gryphon himself.

Too preoccupied with this revelation, I missed the first peal of the city bells. Ari went rigid next to me, his ears flicking upright. Kaiamear had a system of deep-throated bells as part of the city's defenses. I'd touched one of them as part of a trip in fundamental school. We'd learned about every set pattern they rang in, from things as benign as announcing the hour or ringing in the New Year to warning the city of imminent danger.

A second bell took up the message, then the rest, deep booms resonating through the city. Distant pinpricks of fire scattered as the common folk heeded the warning: *take shelter, aerial attack.*

Ari shot to his paws. Surety pulsed from him. His head

tilted in my direction, and he poured out countless images, superimposing the serpentine shape of a flying monster. They came in green, red, or yellow, spewing death on four canvas-like wings. *Rozash.*

The burn of acid. The feeling of a saddle sliding from his back.

Ari flexed his wings and bellowed defiance. Then he knelt and said to me, clear as day, *"Get on my back."*

CHAPTER 2

NO MISTAKE

"B-but—" I cleared my throat, standing and taking a step back. "You know a woman cannot ride a gryphon."

He snapped his beak impatiently, projecting his dark sight. I knew he couldn't fly without a guiding hand, but I was the absolute worst option. Untrained, and female besides. Gryphons were the avatar of the God of Man, Orion, who would frown upon any woman attempting to ride one of his anointed beasts.

A discordant clamor interrupted my thoughts. A shadowy creature had knocked down one of the bells, and its distant fall echoed all the way to where we stood. I muttered a curse. The rozash was already here, and the gryphons of the First would just be waking behind us. It would take time to saddle them and fetch their riders from their supper.

Precious time during which the rozash could rampage across the city, spewing its breath weapon over a poorly prepared area. Ari and I couldn't kill it, but we could be a distraction until the trained riders took it out.

I looked back to Ari, who was still waiting for me to get on his back.

"Surely Lord Orion would understand," I muttered.

Before I could second-guess the decision, I slung a leg over his saddle, picking up the reins. Ari didn't have a riding harness on, a separate system of straps to cinch a rider in place, so I would need to hold on with my legs and a prayer.

Ari took a few steps back. I clung to the barrel of his chest with my legs, feeling the great drum of his heart thumping back against my skin. *It can't be too hard. Father does it all the time.*

Ari shared a few quick memories with me, the most important being how the bit felt in his beak. I could control his speed and aim his head in the right direction, which was about to be vital. Next, even more fleeting, was the feeling of Alamid shifting his weight into Ari's motions.

"Wait, this is stup—" I protested, realizing just how unprepared we were. This beast was going to get us both killed, for he took off running before I could complete that thought. We cleared the peak, and Ari snapped his wings out with a *whump.* My heart tumbled to the vicinity of my lap as gravity lost all meaning.

He flapped, and his whole body lifted with the motion, slapping the saddle against my legs. I white-knuckled the saddle horn with one hand, the other gripping his reins. I wasn't much help as he picked up speed, heading toward the city at an eye-watering pace.

"*Guide me,*" he demanded. His beak was pointed toward the ground, and we were losing altitude. The ground got larger and larger with every passing second.

"Up!" I shouted back over the wind, yanking on his reins. His wings strained to correct, now aiming him above the horizon.

We were definitely going to crash. I struggled to get enough air in my lungs, let alone guide him in any meaningful way. The rozash could've been right beside us and I wouldn't see it, my gaze quivering with a barrier of protective tears.

Ari sighed, a great heave of his body beneath me. *"Don't panic."* His voice was coming clearer now. I felt a tingle in the back of my head, like a feather tickled me there. *"Hold the reins with both hands. I won't let you fall."*

I peeled my spare hand from the saddle horn, latching on to the reins as he'd instructed. The corners of his mouth were sensitive, so he would understand any small tug and the direction I intended him to go in.

"There. Blink hard," he said next. Twin lines tracked down my cheeks, freezing against my cold skin. He slowed, allowing me a chance to look around. He wanted me to locate the rozash and…

Orion, spare me. I was sensing Ari's emotions and thoughts like they were mine; that's what that tickle was. We were starting to forge a Link of necessity, because otherwise, we wouldn't escape this flight alive. Already I was starting to move with him, letting my middle relax so he wasn't bouncing me with every flap of his wings.

I could feel his determination and plan. We were going to reprise his and Alamid's role in the First Gryphon Flight, drawing the rozash's attention and acting as bait to distract it. Ari prided himself on his agility, and I was even lighter than his last rider.

I can't wait to get up to speed, came a thought. I shook my head, realizing it was Ari's, as I didn't have wings to gauge the wind. He was relishing the feeling of air through his feathers. I felt his emotions stronger and clearer as the Link started to solidify.

The rozash roared, and I finally saw it in the distance. "To your left!" I called. We surged in that direction, speeding along too quickly for doubt to take hold. I'd worry about the Link if we managed to live.

"What color is it? One head or two?" Ari asked rapidly.

I squinted, trying to catch sight of its serpentine form against any hint of torchlight. Chills erupted down my spine when we were close enough for me to answer. "Green! And two!" I screamed.

Revulsion and hatred quivered through Ari. He stretched his neck out and *screeched*, drawing the attention of the two-headed monster spewing acid at random. My heart rebounded up to my throat as it wheeled around and headed straight for us.

I understood what Ari was doing a split second before it happened. He lifted hard, grazing past the rozash's scaled body and forcing it to twist around midair to give chase. I spotted the one thing that might save us: one of its four wings hung limp, making the maneuver that much harder for it. "It's wounded!"

"*Good.*" Ari must've picked up on my thoughts or the sudden spike of hope. "*Now we lead it out of the city.*"

Which meant he needed me to aim him that way. I tugged his reins and leaned over his strong neck, feeling how he elongated his body for maximum speed. We sliced through the air; his wingbeats matching the thundering pace of his heart. My heartbeat raced along with the same haste.

For one brilliant moment, we weren't a blind gryphon and a female caretaker, but rider and beast perfectly connected. Was this what a full Link felt like? I only knew I'd never felt so free before, here in the sky with the wind whipping past my hair. Ari pulsed with life, thrilled to be in the air again, doing what he did best.

As for me, I remembered and shared a moment buried deep in my past. This wasn't the first time I'd sat in a gryphon rider's saddle, but at the time, I'd been a girl of maybe four, nestled against my father as he took me up on a joyride with his gryphon, Valtora. The wind had caressed my hair in the same way, but flight was a pure joy then. Father had handed me the reins, and for that moment, I'd felt Valtora's attention as she looked over her shoulder and acknowledged me with a burst of warm emotion.

I smiled like a loon, even though I could smell rozash acid as the creature closed in on us, injury or no. The rancid stench helped me shake off the feelings Ari and I had shared over our Link. *"Hold on,"* Ari instructed. I felt his intentions before he rolled to the side, nearly unseating me in a dizzying whirl of starlight.

He climbed higher as the rozash flashed past and lost momentum when it was forced to turn on its wounded side. We were above uninhabited forest now, and a good thing too as it spat two globes of acid that consumed the greenery below with a vicious sizzle.

"Where is it now?"

I called out instructions as best as I could, and Ari continued his game as he screeched and bolted, leading the rozash on a new chase. He rode invisible air currents, performing hard turns that nearly put us vertical with the ground. My empty belly roiled with nerves as we flew laps around our enemy.

One mistake, and we'd burn in rozash acid...or I'd be flung off. Ari didn't roll again, sensing how I clung all the harder to him in heart-bursting fear when he considered it.

"Just a little more," he assured. My frozen ears perked a minute later, picking up the battle cries of a group of gryphons. Ari bellowed in return.

Even with two heads, the rozash wasn't smart enough to retreat as a team of five gryphons lined up and dove toward it, lances out. With a great *crack*, bones shattered, and its serpentine form tumbled out of the sky. One rider followed to ensure it was dead.

Ari slowed, his great breaths turning into labored panting now that the danger had passed. He was out of shape for such a chase, and it showed.

"It's not that bad," he muttered, responding to my thoughts.

"I wasn't criticizing you. That was amazing." I ran my

fingers through his damp neck fur, unable to stop a titter of relieved laughter from escaping. We'd just saved countless lives by turning that rozash away from Kaiamear. Ari had shown a true gryphon's courage in jumping to the city's defense, even without a...

I felt myself pale as a second gryphon came alongside us. By the scant moonlight, I recognized the gryphon by her golden plumage rather than the armored man lifting his flight goggles to stare over at me.

"Sivana?" my father called. "Is that you?"

Valtora lifted her head and screeched in joy. Ari was her son, after all, and she'd been beside herself during his period of mourning.

My father, Knight-Commander Nathaniel Walker, patted his gryphon's side as she swayed midair, projecting happiness for all to feel. "Whoa, girl!" He tugged her reins to keep her steady.

Unexpectedly, Ari flashed joy back to her. Just a brief snippet, but more positivity in that split second than a month's worth of work. My father's mouth dropped open.

"Father, I—"

I needed to tell him about the Link, but he held his hand up and shouted that we'd talk on the ground. By now, the other gryphons were gathering in a loose formation, waiting for Valtora and Father at the head. He called over Knight-Captain Rudrick and his pure-white gryphon, Snowpoint.

They produced rope from their saddlebags and tossed it to me. I tied both lengths around Ari's saddle horn so they could guide us. That done, we flew home, the other gryphons forming a v-formation behind Valtora and Snowpoint. I was in a cold sweat the whole way. I'd defied Lord Orion's will and ridden a gryphon...worse, Linked with one. I knew the moment this came to light, I'd be explaining myself to less sympathetic ears than my father's.

Ari was quiet most of the flight back, undoubtedly

listening to me think through everything that could happen to us.

"*Just remember,*" he interrupted. "*It was my idea, and I chose you. Gryphons don't make mistakes.*"

It just so happened that I was the first woman selected for the honor. Ever.

CHAPTER 3

HERO OF THE HOUR

"I see," Father had said neutrally as soon as I told him Ari and I were Linked. He didn't break his military-strict bearing through the whole tale, only betraying a tightening of his lips as he turned to where the First's beasts were practically frolicking in the moonlight. Amongst them was Ari, taking it easy and letting the other gryphons express their joy around him.

We stood within a circle of lantern light, while several yards away, the rest of the riders and the flight's caretakers watched the gryphons play like they were half their ages. I'd never seen anything like it, so while I explained, I stared at them too. It was a mercy not to look my father in the eye, to not see his disappointment.

I was my father's little shadow, taking after him in more than just appearance. We shared the same reactions to things and love for the beasts that defended Altare's skies, much to my mother's chagrin. While most girls were pretending to be princesses and having tea parties with their dolls, I'd be following my father to the stables every day, hoping to steal time with the gryphons.

Sun exposure had shot his red hair through with shades of

carrot and blond, and he had a deeper tan than I could ever achieve, but I had inherited his narrow blue eyes and freckles. He squinted in my direction like he did every time he was in deep thought.

"The whole Flight celebrates Ari's return. By Linking to a new rider, he has chosen life," he said, clapping a hand over my shoulder. It wasn't displeasure lining Father's face, but something more complicated. Unlike talking to a gryphon, I couldn't just intuit what he was feeling. People were far more complicated than the beasts, and often dishonest to boot.

If I had to guess, that was pride in his voice, but fear warred with it. He knew as well as I did that the gryphons were celebrating too soon.

I swallowed past a dry throat. "What happens next?" I asked.

"High Command is undoubtedly waiting for a report," he replied with a sigh. "If we're lucky, the king won't also be in attendance. But he will hear about it by tomorrow morn."

King Cortes was quite involved in the worship of Lord Orion. In the end, it was his opinion that mattered most, and we could take a good guess as to how he'd react to a gryphon Linking with a girl.

Father took hold of my chin, forcing me to look at him. "You saved lives today, Sivana," he said. "No one can take that from you and Ari. You should be earning the royal award for bravery right now."

Should be. But instead, I feared the reaction of several powerful men when they learned what I'd done.

He gave me a little shake. "*And* every gryphon rider understands that Ari would've never let you ride on his back if he hadn't seen you worthy of the honor."

I nodded slowly. "Thanks, Father."

Another man's voice raised from the shadows. "Walker!"

I tensed up, recognizing the bellow of Knight-Marshall

Morrison, my father's direct superior. The big-bellied man hadn't been on a gryphon's back for years, not since he'd lost his during a separate war with our enemies to the south. No one was reassigned a new gryphon if they'd lost their first, but they often continued serving the military as logisticians. It was Morrison's mercy that had truly allowed me so much time with Ari; he understood what it was like to lose the other half of yourself.

Morrison sported a bald head and a drooping iron-gray mustache that shrouded his upper lip. It formed an exaggerated frown when he made any serious expression, as he did now. Father snapped to attention and saluted, just to be quickly waved away. Morrison wasn't in uniform, his civilian clothes rumpled from a rough wakeup.

"Good gods, Walker," the Marshall said with his usual gusto, drawing the attention of most of the other riders. "I've got High Command calling for blood. We haven't had a direct rozash attack like this since Owens was in charge."

Father's lips quirked into a faint smile. "Yes, sir. Longest three years of my life."

"Anyway, we've already heard report of a lone rider distracting it away from the city. Which of your lads is getting recognized tonight?" He looked expectantly toward the Gryphon Yard, where the beasts were starting to form up alongside their riders. Valtora walked with her flank brushing Ari's, leading him toward us.

Side by side, the gendered differences between gryphons were obvious. Ari had a narrower build and skinny hips, with his belly sloped upward toward his hips like a prized racing dog. He was the fastest gryphon in the First, able to stretch out his body for minimum drag. On the other hand, Valtora was thicker at the shoulders and broader in muscle, built for strength rather than speed. Once gryphons exited their youngling stage, it was possible to know their gender at a glance.

Father cleared his throat, barely missing a beat as he clapped me on the back. "This lass, sir."

Morrison turned my way, his mustache drooping harder with his frown. "What—" His beady eyes shot to the blind gryphon guided to my side by his mother. Valtora flanked me protectively, the gilt feathers along her neck rising as her beak parted. The Marshall took a step away from her in the classic pose of a gryphon prepared to bite.

He dropped his voice. "Young lady, I know you've been quite involved in the rehabilitation of the maimed bird, but this is too far."

"Ari chose to come to the city's defense and turned to Sivana to guide him," Father said for me. His word would carry a lot more weight than mine, considering his rank. "They've always been close."

"Close enough to Link? Walker, gryphons don't choose girls."

"This one did," Father said firmly.

Morrison rubbed down his bald head, breathing a string of low curses. "So, he also chose life?" He was watching Ari now, who listened with his beak pointed off-center from the Marshall's location.

Still, the gryphon's head went up and down in a definitive nod, and he shuffled closer to me. I touched his wing, feeling his resolve. His sadness hadn't left just because of our new Link, but now it was contained between the two of us. It didn't help the churning nerves in my gut to feel his grief so intimately. However, the sharpest edges were smoothed now that we shared our moods.

"*It is more bearable now,*" he said, sensing the direction of my thoughts. I rubbed his feathers, relieved for him.

"Well, all right then." The Marshall rubbed his mustache as he watched us interact. "I see an angle here. How many of your flight would be willing to stand as character witnesses for your daughter?"

"All of them," Father replied without hesitation.

Morrison waved a pudgy hand. "Bring them along. We can all report to High Command."

Father had made the invitation to report optional for his men, but most of them and their gryphons followed us to a huge meeting room. Three of his men, though, glared my way and made the sign of Lord Orion, touching their fingertips to their foreheads like I was some heretic. The sight of it lingered with me through our walk into the palace. Shivers continued to wrack my whole body as a servant stoked the fireplace.

Despite how Marshall Morrison had spoken of the High Command waiting for a report, the group of elder gryphon riders sure made us wait for them. None of us sat, instead lining up against the wall as magelights floated around the room. I watched them with detached fascination. Most of us make do with good ol' fire at night, but the upper crust of society paid Tulari—the mages—heavenly sums for these floating orbs which never stopped glowing.

The room itself was trimmed with fine mahogany wood, from the carved wall panels to the extra-large meeting table resting on a patterned rug as thick as gryphon fur. All imported, expensive things. There was more wealth spent on this one room than I'd ever see in my lifetime.

While I ogled at our surroundings, Valtora edged toward me. She clucked before starting to groom the nest of tangled knots I liked to call my hair. I winced with each pull; I must have looked like an absolute disaster for my skymother to step in like this.

Valtora was a wild-born gryphon and likely only accepted the taming process because she was brought in with a single egg that would become Ari. She should've been named after her plumage, which shone like the tips of her feathers had been dipped in molten gold, but she was far too proud to allow a human to name her or her beloved son.

Unlike Ari, Valtora was a vicious female who hated most humans by default. Yet to my mother's chagrin, Father had introduced us when I was still a tot and it'd been love at first sight. I was her awkward featherless child, and that hadn't changed even though I'd recently reached my sixteenth birthday.

That she was here today as I prepared to face the judgment of High Command was a double-edged sword. If anyone would defend me to the death, it would be Valtora. However, the fact that I'd been allowed close enough to Link with Ari would be blamed squarely on my father. He'd recommended me for a caretaker position with the First— though I swear I got the job because Valtora let me groom and feed her peacefully—but he'd also advocated with my words to show Ari mercy in the first place.

It was very likely he would be punished for my Link, and that thought soured my belly further. Though many of us, myself included, assumed gryphons just didn't choose women for their Links, it was also highly illegal by the laws passed down from Lord Orion's teachings. Each of the four gods had their own rules. With a devout family holding the throne for several generations, the nobility on down obeyed the decrees.

Lost in thought, I jumped when a guard shoved the door open and called us all to attention. In walked a procession of eleven men in dress uniform, not a speck out of place. Shoes shined, belts cinched, polished medals gleaming on their chests. They put the rest of us to shame in their sky blue and gold, Knight-Generals all with the insignia of wings on their tasseled epaulets.

It was practically the middle of the night. Did they really make us wait for them to don their dress uniforms?

"Probably," Ari answered.

High Command faced the door expectantly. The First maintained their salutes as white-haired Knight-Paragon Hughes walked in. I'd never met him personally, but I knew his name...as everyone who worked with the flights did. Paragon Hughes was in charge of the whole gryphon knight corps, reporting only to the king himself. He cut an imposing profile even at his advanced age, holding a walking cane right under the head as if anticipating needing a weapon.

My heartbeat throbbed in my ears. This collection of elder riders was the entirety of High Command, and even they weren't sitting. Instead, they saluted as one last pair was announced. I sank into a quivering bow, watching the boots of the king and crown prince glide past.

"At ease," a cultured voice intoned. King Alonso Cortes took his seat first, a deep frown burrowing fissures through his toffee-colored skin. I'd never stood so close to the ruler of Altare. He looked...far more tired than I expected. Deep bags sagged under bloodshot eyes, his whole being radiating displeasure to be summoned from his bed, even by an emergency the caliber of a rogue rozash attack.

No one moved a muscle as King Cortes sighed through his nose. His generous lips pinched further as he surveyed the faces of the men at the table. The First and I might as well have been invisible. "We are all in attendance. Report." He gestured to Marshall Morrison, who stepped forward and repeated what I'd already lived: how an acidmaw rozash had attacked Kaiamear. It'd likely been set loose on us by the enemy due to its wounded wing.

King Cortes's jowls quivered as he set his gaze on Paragon Hughes and said, "I don't believe I need to stress to you how disastrous it is that a lone rozash made its way through our defenses. I expect you to personally see to it that we don't have a repeat of tonight."

"Yes, Your Majesty," Paragon Hughes replied crisply.

I glanced to my father, raising my brows. I wasn't aware that Paragon Hughes did anything personally, not when he had a council of generals and a chain of command to pull whenever a necessary task arose. Father shook his head subtly, turning his attention back to the meeting at hand.

"In addition, Your Majesty, I am pleased to share that a lone rider distracted the rozash before it could do much damage to the city," the Marshall continued.

For a moment, King Cortes smiled. It took a decade of stress and age off his face. I knew they were talking about me, but just maybe...this wouldn't be a disaster.

"This rider Linked to one of the First's prime beasts, the one wounded about a month ago. You may recall, Your Majesty."

"How could he forget?" Ari snipped, shifting with a low growl in his throat.

The First was the honor flight, stationed in the capital for the whims of the royal family. King Cortes had used them as an armed escort to and from the fighting front to distribute extra rations from the Crown and to give a speech to bolster the soldiers and knights.

Alamid hadn't survived the flight back when enemy soldiers realized which high-profile figure was within striking range.

"Oh, yes." King Cortes waved him on, saying carelessly, "I thought that gryphon was dead."

Next to me, Ari burned with resentment. *"Alamid died for his stupid mission!"*

I ran my fingers through his wing feathers, nervous he'd bring attention to us. There was so much I wanted to say, but I couldn't do it aloud with the most powerful men in Altare in the same room.

"Despite his blindness, he has chosen life...and a new rider," Morrison was saying. "And we have a new hero to thank for mitigating this crisis."

"Is the lad here?" King Cortes finally looked to the First, his gaze roving over them. Since appointment to the First was usually for life, he had to recognize that all these men were seasoned gryphon knights…except for me.

Morrison gestured for me to step forward. I felt a chill as I made eye contact with the king for a split second before ducking my head respectfully. "Your Majesty, Sivana Walker is the hero of the hour," the Marshall said. The men of the First applauded politely.

King Cortes looked me over head to toe, a crimson band rising up his neck and ears. "A *lass*?" he sputtered.

CHAPTER 4
BORROWED TIME

I PARTED my lips to apologize, but a beak nudged my arm. Ari faced King Cortes with me, his presence solid and unrepentant. There was a reason I treated my gryphon charges like nobility; they had the same level of world-owning pride as the upper crust of human society.

"I can explain, Your Majesty," Morrison was saying rapidly.

The king didn't take his rage-filled gaze off me for a moment as he made the sign of Lord Orion with his fingertips. "This had better be good," he said from between his teeth.

Morrison's bushy mustache bunched as he glanced between me and King Cortes. "Sivana is Commander Walker's daughter and a caretaker for the First's birds. She's had a solid connection with all of them. When Captain Maros died in that skirmish last month, it was Sivana who stepped up to care for and rehabilitate his gryphon."

The Marshall had found his center, speaking without a rush even when our monarch's face pinched like he tasted pure lemon juice. I suppose that's why he was the Marshall and I the caretaker, because that look made me feel about two inches tall.

"Let the girl answer my questions," the king said, making a motion to brush Morrison aside. Cold sweat beaded down my back when he left me standing before the monarch with only Ari for support. The king spared me one word. "Explain."

"Y-yes, Your Ma-M-Majesty," I stammered. All the moisture flooded out of my mouth, and the words rattled in my throat just like I was five again, struggling to form them. The silence was deafening. Not only was the king staring, but I could also feel the High Council and crown prince watching me, their gazes like pins with me as the cushion.

Talons clicked on the fine floor as Valtora prowled forward, flanking me again. I heard my father hiss, but she ignored him. If gryphons were nobility, Valtora was a queen and did as she liked, her beak lifted with pride as she stood close enough for her feathers to brush my arm.

I looked up at her, opening my senses to the push of emotion she shared with me. I'd always understood her best, even if we weren't able to speak the other's language. *You've done nothing wrong. Go ahead, tell them why,* she was saying without words, letting me borrow her solid surety.

I cleared my throat and began again. "Your Majesty, what Marshall Morrison was saying is true. I am a caretaker for the First. I've been around the beasts since I was very young, Arimus included. Alamid Maros was more than a rider for the First…he was a close family friend." I coughed as my voice wavered, tinged with the double-punch Ari and I both felt to speak of his loss.

"Ari has mourned him hardest of all. His execution was supposed to be tomorrow as a mercy, to end his pain," I continued past the lump in my throat. "He and I were in the Gryphon Yard to experience his last sunset when we noticed the rozash. It was his choice that I get on his back to guide him so we could distract it for the rest of the First to arrive and kill it."

Ari nodded in agreement.

The low murmuring of men's voices sounded from High Command. Paragon Hughes said clearly, "Gryphons don't make mistakes."

King Cortes considered me for a piercing moment. "This is an affront to the gods," he snapped in the Paragon's direction. "All I hear is this lass took advantage of the gryphon's grief to forge an illegal Link with him."

"Your Majesty—" Hughes began to reply in a careful tone.

"If the gryphon was meant to die tomorrow, then I say his execution stands," the king continued.

"Hear, hear," one of the generals echoed.

The blood rushed from my head in one quick second, leaving the room to spin. Valtora cried out in dismay, leading a chorus from the rest of the First's gryphons. "Get your beasts under control!" King Cortes bellowed over them. "For shame. These are the best riders in my nation, with their gryphons carrying on?"

Father walked up to pull on Valtora's scruff, staring into her fierce eyes. She looked away first, bowing her head to him in a rare sign of deference. That done, he stood with his feet braced, hands laced behind his back as he asked, "If I may speak for the First, Your Majesty?"

The king waved him on impatiently, his scowl deepening.

"The birds form psychic Links with each other as much as they Link with us. The impending loss of Ari has weighed on all of us heavily. If he is still executed, it would be a huge loss for the gryphons who serve the Crown so faithfully," Father said. "We are all here in support of Sivana and Arimus. Please consider mercy, Your Majesty."

"As a faithful servant of Lord Orion, I cannot allow a girl to spit in the face of his teachings," King Cortes replied without missing a beat. "No matter how much it would hurt your gryphons' feelings. They will get over it."

In the quiet that followed, I turned to hug Ari around his bristling neck, hiding my reaction in his feathers. After all this, I was still losing him, and who knew if the king would punish my father as well? "Look, weakness," he taunted. "The reason we don't have women in the military. Lord Anrathor does not mark women for war, and Lord Orion does not call them to ride his gryphons. A mistake was made tonight, but we will rectify it and put it behind us."

But I wasn't crying, I was furious, and the king couldn't see that defiance when it could make things so much worse. His words were needlessly cruel in the face of a miracle. Ari himself had chosen me and taken the step he needed to continue living in his last rider's absence.

"Father, think of how this looks," said another cultured voice. "Some of the populace undoubtedly saw a lone rider distracting the rozash tonight. They will want to know who it was."

I peered through Ari's feathers. It was Crown Prince Isaac speaking, and the king was listening. "It will not foster good-will with our people when they learn what happened and that the gryphon was put down anyway. Haven't you told me that the answers to our prayers aren't direct action from the gods, but people placed in our paths to help us? This young lady performed a service for the city, and for that, I believe she should be given a chance to train as a proper rider."

"The gryphon chose her," another general added.

I lifted my head once I was sure of my composure. Prince Isaac was smiling my way. He was like a kindly, younger echo to his royal father, bearing many of the same features but with a generous head of glossy raven hair compared to his father's balding. "Thank you, young miss. The country needs every able-bodied gryphon, and it's clear you care deeply for them."

King Cortes's expression was lemon-sour once more, but this time, his wrath was aimed at someone who didn't need to flinch away. Emboldened, a few members of the High Command started to echo their crown prince, offering a hail of modest thanks my way.

"Your Majesty, why not let her attend the Academy? It will be clear whether she will make it as a rider past her moment tonight," Hughes said.

"It will make the Crown seem fair to give her a chance," Prince Isaac agreed.

The king scrubbed at his forehead and pinched the bridge of his nose as if we'd given him the worst headache of his life. "Fine. You"—he pointed to my father—"are given leave to escort your daughter to Fortress Aerie. And you."

Now his bloodshot gaze turned to me. "If you should show a poor performance, it would be because of your gryphon, of course. Blind beast that it is." He sounded somewhat reasonable, but his words were sharp enough to cut. "If you fail this year at the Academy, I revoke the mercy the gryphon has been shown tonight, and he will see the executioner's axe. But *if* you can stand toe to toe with the boys and pass, then I shall permit...this." He waved to Ari and me as he stood. High Command jumped to their feet obediently while the First snapped to attention.

He left without another word. It was Prince Isaac who caught my hand and gave it a squeeze. "Good luck, young lady. Thank you for your heroism." A sea of sympathy swam in his caramel eyes, for he'd heard the same threat I had.

My gryphon lived on borrowed time.

✦

I DIDN'T SAY much on our way to the stables. We bedded Ari down with Valtora, the two gryphons snuggling together for comfort. She projected joy and motherly pride, resting her talons over my hand as I finished fluffing her bed of hay. We made eye contact.

Thank you for saving my son, she seemed to say in that moment. For Valtora, "my son" was always an image of Ari's egg split by a dramatic crack. Her first glimpse of him was his tiny golden eye peeking out of a hole his beak had made.

I hesitated, wishing I could convey all my emotions back to her. I was glad Ari would live past tomorrow's dawn, but what came next terrified me. Father loved talking about his academy days, but during his tall tales, I'd think about how glad I was that I'd never get screamed awake by a drill sergeant or forced to do any number of menial jobs as punishments. I thought I'd never experience a school where everything was a competition and everyone there was already the best of the best. That's where I was going.

To Gryphon Rider Academy, where *my* failure would endanger Ari's life.

Yet Valtora seemed to know. She always did. *There's no one I trust more.* She flooded my doubts away for a few moments with warm trust before lifting her talons.

Bye, Sivana.

I knew the image she used to replace my name all too well. It'd been the same one since I was five and always made my father smile. I'd shaded from embarrassment to acceptance that she still pictured me as a little girl sitting between her front legs, turning away from a colorful book in my lap to give her a gap-toothed grin. My hair was as wild as a mop of red yarn, and freckles dotted my face like the fall of confetti.

At that age, I'd felt most comfortable reading aloud to my mama gryphon, who didn't make pinch-faced expressions when I stumbled and fell over common words. Valtora always listened patiently and told me without words that chicks weren't supposed to fly right after hatching, so why were little humans expected to speak perfectly?

"Bye, skymother," I said quietly. I hoped she was right to invest her trust in me, just like how she coached my little self into having more patience.

Now I needed to face my human mother. Okay, *face* is a harsh way of putting it. But as Father and I returned to our family apartment in the palace, I knew she'd still be awake despite it being well into the midnight hour. Hopefully she wasn't fretting too much.

Father had said that he wanted to discuss what'd happened in the privacy of our rooms. It had to be about the king since he wanted to avoid the ears of any guard or maid we might pass by. Rumors would start spreading soon as the rooster crowed tomorrow, if not sooner.

CHAPTER 5

TEMPLE ROW

"What do you think, Talase?" Father asked the woman I sat across from, who rubbed her bottom lip thoughtfully with her thumb.

"This is concerning," Mother answered now that we'd shared everything in the privacy of our kitchen table. As predicted, she'd been wide awake and waiting for us. She'd probably paced a new furrow in the modest rugs we kept in the living room.

Mother was the picture of prim elegance, even at this late hour. The white robes she wore were pristine by lantern light. Her platinum hair was tied back in a bun, not a strand out of place, and her posture straight. But her lips pinched into a rosebud at about the time we told her that we'd met the king, and I noticed her leaf-green gaze sweeping over me. Unsaid was her disbelief that I wasn't dressed better for such an extraordinary meeting.

Father nodded in agreement with her assessment. "Prince Isaac said the right thing to get the king to back off, but it's not over."

"Oh, Sivana," Mother sighed. I knew that sound all too well. As the ninth child of a minor lord, Mother was trained in noble ways but allowed to choose her own path. It'd led her to the calling of a healer in the goddess Nilara's temples and holy places. She'd nursed Father back to health after one of his first battles, and I came into the world approximately nine months later.

She'd been sighing my name pretty much ever since.

However, I listened as intently as I could with exhaustion weighing down my eyelids. If anyone could coach me in speaking with the king in the future, it would be Mother. "Prince Isaac didn't protect you out of the goodness of his heart," she said. "He's going to want something from you in return."

I raised a skeptical brow. "I've heard that he's as kind as his mother," I replied.

Beautiful Queen Jimena Cortes died nearly a decade ago, but her care for the people was felt to this day. She had guided the king to sign off on an expansive literacy and scholarship initiative. Because of her, I was part of the first generation of Altarians who were all taught to read, write, and learn other things "vital to life."

Her passing was a reminder: the Gatekeeper's gray shroud came for the best of us first.

"That's the reputation he wants the public to share about him." Mother raised her finger. "However, it's unlikely for a crown prince to exist without ambitions."

I blinked slowly, too tired to follow anymore.

"The prince's men will be stirring the rumor mill, sharing the story of a caretaker girl who loved a blind gryphon and just so happened to be the hero who chased away a rozash"— she shook her head in renewed disbelief at me—"but the king, stuck in the old ways, called for the gryphon's execution rather than tolerate a woman Linked to a gryphon. It was kind Prince Isaac's intervention that saved her, and by his grace, she will go to the Gryphon Rider Academy. People are going to eat that story up.

"In fact, I'm sure *someone* will leak the entire story with eerie accuracy to the *Kaiamear Gazette*. It's in the crown prince's best interest that everyone knows he was the hero that saved you both from his father," she finished.

"With the First and High Command all supporting and thanking you, plus the crown prince taking your side, the king realized he looked unreasonable and cruel," Father added.

Well, that's because he was, I thought uncharitably.

"Your existence is now a political game. The king and anyone who believes in the old ways will be waiting with bated breath for you to fail. Some will try to interfere to ensure it." Mother gave me a long look. Fire flashed between us, but for once, we were in perfect agreement. I could not fail and give those people the satisfaction. "And *if* you should succeed, it will be because Prince Isaac gave you grace one time to proceed."

I smacked my palm on the table. "That's not fair," I muttered.

"Now you're understanding politics," she replied, reaching over to cover my hand. Her fingers were soft and gentle. They'd never know the calluses I already had from hard work in the gryphon stables. Still, I held on to her like the anchor she was.

"Go rest, baby," she said. "Tomorrow, we get you ready for the Academy."

THE NEXT DAY, Father left early to make arrangements for our upcoming flight east to Fortress Aerie. I woke to the surreal feeling of another living being's emotions and needs on the other side of our nascent Link. My belly rumbled with Ari's morning hunger. Judging by the slant of the sun's rays, the other caretakers would be feeding the gryphons their morning feast soon.

He'd be okay for now. This was no early rise to bid him goodbye, after all. I was in good spirits even when Mother burst into the room I shared with my sister and made us don our ceremonial robes for a visit to Temple Row.

My sister, the lucky child, had slept through everything last night. She emerged from the bath fresh as a spring flower, already waiting with a brush and hairpins when I came out after a long soak. Clarissa was twelve and already a mini Mother with the same aristocratic lift to her nose and oval, freckle-less face. She'd fixed her straw-blonde hair into a bun, and judging by the determined gleam in her green eyes, I was next.

I sighed and slumped into the chair she'd dragged into the bathroom, letting her attack my head. "It's really true. You rode a gryphon," she marveled, tugging on a particularly stubborn knot.

"Yeah—ow!"

"I can tell. This is a disaster," she said matter-of-factly.

I shot her a grumpy look in the mirror. "The crown prince himself thanked me."

"Too bad neither of the other princes were there," she replied.

Rissa had just discovered boys and the horrible little world of noble matchmaking. I knew she dreamed of debuting and catching the eye of someone rich and, more importantly to her, handsome. I could practically see the daydreams in her head before she shared one. "Can you imagine? Prince Mateo is already at the rider school. He could've been there instead of Prince Isaac and defended you. You could ride your gryphons into the sunset." She fanned herself with the brush.

I rolled my eyes hard. "I'm already seeing someone."

"Yeah, well, he sucks," she muttered.

"*And* he's already at the Gryphon Rider Academy too. He's the most promising cadet there," I said over her. Rissa had never liked Victor but didn't share why.

She'd just set her stubborn face and repeat the same thing, like now. "He's no good for you."

"What does that even mean?" I sighed.

She shrugged. "I don't think it's going to last, sorry. You see him twice a year, and the only thing he talks about is himself and his career when you're together."

"No, he doesn't! Whatever, Rissa." I wasn't about to take relationship advice from a twelve-year-old, anyway, even one who ate up all of Mother's advice.

She managed to tame my hair into a bun, though we didn't have enough pins to handle all the flyaways. It didn't bother me until we rejoined Mother and I saw them together. Rissa was obviously her mother's child, and it'd happened while I wasn't looking.

Our family was growing and changing in a blink. No doubt Rissa would be an apprentice acolyte at Mother Nilara's temple within the next couple years. Our absent brother, the middle child, Nathaniel Junior, had just blossomed with magical talent a few months ago and was shipped off to train as a Tulari mage.

Their paths were set and sure. I was the one being thrown into the unknown. Mother was right to take me to Temple Row, where we would pray to each of the four gods.

Just past the marketplace, a street was dedicated to the four shrines, each majestic in their own way. Today, I got to choose the order in which we visited, as I was the one leaving soon.

I picked the Gatekeeper's shrine first, a building done up in monochrome. No one spoke the God of Death's true name aloud, as it could bring his presence. Still, I knelt before the gray shrouded figure at the heart of his shrine and gave thanks for the miracle that'd forced Ari and I together.

Please continue to hold back the death of this innocent gryphon.

As usual, there was no reply, but still we prayed. Next was Anrathor's temple, God of War, who preferred his black and red. His statue dwarfed mortal visitors, depicting him chiseled from stone, his bulging chest muscles on display. He looked like a young man charging to glory, sword in one hand and war banner in the other.

Usually, I had no business with Anrathor, save to beseech him not to send my father into battles he cannot win. But if I was to be a gryphon knight, I would need his ferocity. For the first time, I prayed he would give me the very things Mother told me a good woman never asked for: the fury and fire of a soldier.

As we walked away from his shrine, Mother smiled toward me sadly. I think she knew exactly what I'd prayed. Her main worship was opposite to everything Anrathor stood for.

"I think we should visit the Mother last," I said, feeling a squirmy sinker of guilt.

I had much to say to Lord Orion, after all. His temple of gold was guarded by the statues of two gryphons, their rearing, fierce faces the inspiration for the Altarian flag's gryphon rampant symbol. His chosen avatars kept us safe against the incursion of Lithos and their rozash to the south and the Rathi pillagers from the north, who rode rare storm birds to war.

The God of Man wore many faces, and I'd spat in one of them by Linking to one of his gryphons, circumstances or no. Our walk to the inner sanctum felt twice as long. I swore the acolytes were staring at us.

Magery was born of Lord Orion and his touch. My brother bore the mark of this god on his face, the one in twenty born with magic in his veins. That meant the god *had* noticed my family before and laid his fingers in approval on my brother's cheek.

Yet when I knelt before the golden statue, majestic with its flowing, gilt robes of state, I felt nothing. I touched my chest and then my forehead with my fingertips. Heart to mind, the sign of Lord Orion.

Ari and I did it to save your people. Please forgive me.

We left the shrine with me simmering in frustration. It must be nice to call out and receive an answer, to see and be seen. Mother picked up the pace to Lady Nilara's temple, knowing she would receive guidance there if she asked for it.

This building was the most familiar, with its silver marble and white-robed acolytes. We were right at home with these women, many of whom greeted us by name. Rissa and I were some of the many faces who'd been underfoot as young children.

We took our shoes off right before the inner shrine, placing them in cubbies alongside a dozen other pairs. The floor around Lady Nilara's white stone statue was reflective silver, much like a mirror.

Unlike with the other shrines, we prayed aloud together. I disliked this part the most: being unable to vocalize everything I felt because Mother and Rissa would hear it too. Still, I bowed my head and let Mother lead. "Lady Nilara, I beseech you on behalf of my daughter…"

I heard of how she worried that I'd pushed myself into a masculine role, the first girl to ever become a cadet at the Gryphon Rider Academy, but nerves made the prayer pass in a blur. "Your turn, Sivana," she said.

I sighed to myself. This was pointless. Lady Nilara wouldn't answer; she never did. Still, I bowed my head and prayed next. "I worry for the life of Ari, which the king has said is tied to my performance at the Academy. The fact that something could happen to him because I don't do well… Lady Nilara, give me the strength to succeed."

After Rissa said her piece, Mother took my hands. Emotion shimmered in her eyes. "When I first held you, I had the same kind of fear as you. It was the price of motherhood, the great weight I bore as the one responsible for another life. Now you're liable for a life of your own." She sniffed, but her composure held. "You're truly a woman now, Sivana. May the Goddess smile upon you."

"May she light the way," I agreed with about half the conviction. I already knew the gods had turned their faces away, leaving me to succeed or fail all on my own.

CHAPTER 6

YOUR PLACE HERE

FATHER AND VALTORA flew us east for the better part of a day, a rope tow line ensuring that Ari could make the journey despite his blindness. Nothing could prepare me for the first sight of Fortress Aerie. It was massive even seen from above, hewn directly into the stone of a mountain. A fine dusting of white covered it, reflecting the glare of watery sunshine above us.

Valtora spoke to Ari, who communicated everything the elder pair wanted to share through our Link.

It was a constant stream of wisdom, making my head ache worse than the glare coming off the bright reflection beneath us. At least I had a pair of tinted flight goggles for that, but nothing could stop Father and Valtora from cramming as much knowledge into my head as possible in the limited time we had.

Fortress Aerie was apparently self-sufficient if it ever came under siege, though it was positioned deep within Altarian territory, crooked in an armpit difficult to reach except by air. The idea was to make it as unideal a target as possible, as it served as a training ground for new riders and the hub for the capture and taming of wild gryphons.

A town had sprouted up in the fortress's shadow, growing extra grain and supplying the Academy with a constant flow of fresh meat for the beasts. We flew over it first. Down below, patches of gold and white were situated next to the silvery ribbon of a healthy river fed straight from the mountains.

Tulari mages had raised the ground to unnatural heights, so that river ended with a huge waterfall. In a few hundred years, nature would fix what man had altered, but until then, even this town was difficult to reach by foot. The people were well and truly a part of the Fortress Aerie system, and apparently it would be a huge treat to fly into town for leisure time if I did well in my training.

"They're saying you shouldn't be afraid to write home with as much detail as possible," Ari reported. I could feel his irritation at being used as a middleman for hours. The good news was the practice had helped us strengthen our Link until I could understand him clearly every time he spoke.

I was also riding better, sensing what he needed from me to be less of a burden on his back. My body was numb from the cold, though, sure to ache by tomorrow despite the fur-lined riding leathers Father had gifted me alongside extra money to afford the uniforms and tailoring sure to be in my future.

"Like that's going to happen," I replied over the Link. I'd also figured out how to respond privately rather than attempt to yell over the wind.

"Do you want me to tell Valtora that?" he asked innocently despite knowing the answer.

"No! Just a thanks." I'd been saying thanks over and over since this started.

"They're both very worried," he said after a few moments. I nodded in agreement. It was why I endured this forced cramming session, because I knew it came from a place of concern.

Gryphon Rider Academy didn't sound fun in the slightest,

and Father had gone through it and emerged as the Ace, the best in class. It would be magnitudes worse for Ari and me.

We circled for a landing at the base of the fortress, which was the worst part of the whole trip. Valtora set down gracefully, countering her momentum with a few well-timed backstrokes of her wings. Even on a tow line a few yards behind her, Ari landed in a scrabble of talons before falling onto his side with wings still extended.

I hit the hard, cold ground at the same time, my legs and middle tied to him with a proper riding harness. Distress flooded from him as he found his footing and turned, beak nudging the knee that'd hit the earth under his weight. "It's okay, nothing broken," I assured him, despite the sudden throb of pain up my leg.

"*I will get better,*" he said.

"You will," I agreed, giving his neck a reassuring scratch before tackling the tangle of leather straps that was the riding harness. I'd freed riders of this contraption countless times, but it was different from this angle. Careful not to rock Ari's balance, I threaded my hips and legs free of the straps and untied the tow line.

Father was there to help me step down from my gryphon's back. "This is where we part, kiddo," he said. Deep lines were furrowed around his riding goggles. He and Valtora had to take advantage of the remaining light to make the flight back. "Unless you want us to spend the night? Make sure you settle in?"

I imagined a future where my father hovered over my shoulder during introductions with the other cadets. "It's fine. I'll be okay!" I replied quickly. Embarrassed heat crept up my neck.

He frowned. "Remember everything we talked about, okay?"

"Okay, Father. I will."

"The post leaves every Sunday evening. I can write you

back, and the letter will be in your hands by the Wednesday after."

"Okay, Father."

"Remember—"

Valtora nudged his hands with a low murr.

"She's saying he's fretting too much," Ari told me.

She pushed her beak into my chest next, ears flicking in clear request. I rubbed them and in the place behind her beak that was so sensitive. *Bye, Sivana.* She lingered on the mental image of young me.

"Bye, skymother. Don't terrorize the rest of the caretakers, okay?" I replied, to a distinct snort from her. "They just want to feed and care for you!"

You do it better, she said without words.

A wistful feeling twisted in my chest. "I'll see you in a couple months," I promised her and Father alike. "I promise to write. It's going to be okay."

After a long hug from Father, I stood there waving to the shrinking outline of him and Valtora as they flew away. When they were an invisible speck, I turned to Ari, who wore my meager belongings in the saddlebags strapped to his hips. "Ready?"

"Someone's been waiting for us," he replied.

I glanced toward the gaping entryway of the fortress, lined with the spiked teeth of a raised portcullis. Standing there was an older teen boy with his hands behind his back, gaze turned up to give us some privacy. He was pale, with the shadow of stubble for hair, wearing an all-black cadet uniform with some sort of insignia standing out yellow on his shoulders.

As we approached, he turned a smile my way. "Hello there. You must be Sivana and Ari. This way, please." I fell into step next to him, glancing toward a burst of motion to the side that was from a team of soldiers lowering the portcullis.

We walked into what felt like a drafty cave, except it had two sets of solid doors with slots for crossbars.

"You're going to be assigned to my flight, so we will be working together pretty closely this year," the boy continued. "I'm a second year. Cadet-Commander Valentic, at your service. And this is my gryphon, Birch."

He gestured to a gryphon joining us and keeping pace by Ari's side. His beast was the size of a yearling, just big enough to be able to carry a person on his back. Pale brown fur shaded to dark brown with black speckles across his feathers.

"Nice to meet you," I said. His smile was infectious, and for a moment, I let myself wonder if this year would truly be as bad as I anticipated if this was my welcome.

"Cadets spend most of the day with their gryphons to strengthen bonds and learn with each other," Valentic told me. "We're going to visit the Commandant first so you can get your schedule, but then it's a busy day ahead learning the ropes. Remember to treat the Commandant with more respect than you think is necessary. He's a Knight-Marshall and in charge of all our futures. That's one guy you don't want to piss off." He shook his head in slow awe.

"Marshall Jamison, right?" I asked.

"Yeah. But you want to call him Commandant or sir."

I nodded slowly, knowing this already. Thanks, Father. "He trained my father. He has a wild-born female gryphon, right?"

"Yeah," he replied, eyeing me askance. "So, it's true? You're the kid of an Ace?"

I fought a proud smile, but he saw it anyway and said, "Word of advice, the trainers pick up on stuff like that like a gryphon with fresh blood. They'll work you that much harder if they think you're bragging about someone else's accomplishments." Well, I didn't like the sound of that.

The corridors were growing narrower as we walked,

branching in several directions off the entryway. There were no signs of the slats Father had said served as windows to the outside world, but sconces burned at regular intervals to ward off some of the chill.

"I won't brag, then," I said, nervous anyway. Word had been sent ahead of me with all the details of who I was. The trainers would already know I was both a girl and the daughter of the Commander of the First Gryphon Flight. My father had a *ton* of talent, plus the advantage of a wild-caught gryphon. They'd inspect me with the same expectations.

Valentic filled the air between us as we climbed to the second level, explaining a little more of how the fortress was structured. The less rank you had, the higher and draftier your place was here. Other first-year cadets like myself were roomed at the top, only crowned by the gryphon stables. The fact the Commandant had a second-floor office was apparently a big deal.

Rugs and paint warmed up the atmosphere of this floor as much as the sconces. While other high-level officials must also work on this level, the Commandant's door had a neat placard beside it at eye level: **Knight-Marshall Elijah Jamison, Commandant of Cadets**.

Before I could so much as swallow with nerves, Valentic knocked on that door and stood back when a voice called, "Enter." He gestured to it with a dramatic flourish.

I went inside, inhaling the musk of gryphon feathers. My gaze didn't fall on the man seated behind a solid wood desk, instead turning to the female gryphon on the other side of the room raising her head to fix me with an appraising look. She was lounging across a nest of cushions and blankets, beak lifted like a queen overseeing an intruder to her domain. As a wild-born female, she was larger than Ari, her bulk stretching close to eight feet long beak to tail.

"Wow," I murmured. She was a rival to Valtora with the same viciousness in the curl of her talons and the distrustful expression she wore. Save for her bright yellow eyes, she was pure black, with her feathers reflecting the sheen of a single floating magelight illuminating the whole room. Such a gorgeous beast.

"Hey, I'm right here," Ari complained.

The Commandant cleared his throat, and I startled. Gods, what an idiot I'd already made of myself. The person with rank was the man, not the gryphon. He gestured for me to sit, and to do so, I had to put my back to his beast. It went against my every instinct to turn away from such a powerful predator, but I lowered into the awkwardly high-backed chair and faced Marshall Jamison for the first time. Ari sat on his haunches next to me.

He was completely white-haired and the picture of a wiry military man who'd erased every ounce of fat on his body and replaced it with grit and sinew. Instead of a uniform, he wore riding leathers like I did. His gloved fingers were laced over his desk as he fixed me with a long stare and said nothing. It became more uncomfortable by the second.

"Good afternoon, Cadet Walker," he said at last.

"Good afternoon, Commandant," I echoed.

His expression didn't change at all, each word delivered serious and sure. "Welcome to the Gryphon Rider Academy."

"Thank you, sir."

"You're a late arrival, thus already behind." He reached across the desk, handing me a single sheet of paper and a book. A quick glance showed a handwritten schedule in neat, blocky print, while the book was twine-bound with bulk between the pages.

I knew a cheaply printed press book when I held it, having consumed them by the dozen back in fundamental school. The cover was thick greyish paper, with the words "Cadet Handbook" embossed above a shield-shaped crest.

There were tiny words around the crest: Courage, Loyalty, Discipline, Integrity. "You are to keep your handbook in good condition throughout your stay here, as it is the only one you shall receive," the Commandant said. "Read it, know it, live it."

"Yes, sir."

"Your arrival caused quite a stir around here. We were not prepared for a female cadet, so you will be lodged with another female resident on the seventh floor. Do not take this as a reward." He stared at me hard. "In the military, we have rules against mixing relationships and work. Under no circumstances should I hear about you starting any kind of drama. Your fellow cadets need to focus on the mission, as do you."

I felt myself flush with anger at the implication. What kind of girl did he take me for? I never said "yes, sir" so tightly in my life.

"He was like this with Alamid, too. Told him not to start anything with a maid," Ari reassured. I supposed it was better to take precautions, but I also wondered if that meant things between Victor and me were over.

"Good. Behave and follow the cadet code of conduct, and we need not meet one on one like this again. The trainers will teach you how to be a rider, and I'm here to keep the order and discipline of the Academy. Do you understand?"

I nodded, earning a slight raise of his brow. "Yes, sir," I repeated.

"You are dismissed. Good luck, new cadet."

I stood, and like a magnet, my gaze was drawn back to his gryphon. "You have a beautiful beast, sir."

She snipped her beak at me, ears pinning back to her skull. "I said you were dismissed, cadet," the Commandant said curtly.

I emerged from his office with my shoulders hunched. Valentic was leaning against the wall, waiting, and muffled a snicker at my expense. He gestured that I should follow him down the hall and hovered his hand over the single sheet of my schedule before I let him pluck it away. "Don't worry, he has that effect on everyone. The man has no sense of humor," he said.

"So, let me tell you about the Academy and your place in it." This sounded like the wind-up to a long speech. I prepared to hang on to every word.

CHAPTER 7

PEA FLINGER

IF I THOUGHT Father tried to cram my head with information, he had nothing on Valentic. He chattered his way through my schedule, telling me far too much detail about my classes and instructors.

"I'm never going to remember all this," I'd complained to Ari. And so far, I hadn't. What really helped was knowing where classes were held—third floor—and seeing certain places for myself.

Ari and I stood on a wide balcony overlooking a special place in the heart of Fortress Aerie. It was truly a cave, lit by bright magelights because otherwise, the space would be worthless. "But how good is it really when there's no drafts or…natural wind at all?" I asked. Flight Training was held here, a massive empty room hewn from the mountain and supported by magic.

"This is just for beginners," Valentic responded, gesturing downward. The light grew sparse around a giant net, leaving the space below it shaded in darkness. Who knew how deep of a pit was underneath? "It's as much for training muscle strength in the gryphons as it is our only safe place to fall off their backs. Once you and Ari pass a basic flight class, there are no more nets."

I had said class on my schedule, back-to-back with a section about gryphon care. It carried over the same instructor, but the first class was for first years, and the second for second years. They'd given me this one advanced class since my gryphon was already a trained adult. *"Hopefully we get on the instructor's good side. I'd like extra time to practice flying,"* Ari said. I could feel his wounded pride to admit he needed practice.

"You're an outstanding flier," I assured him.

"Before my injury, sure."

"Skills don't just go away. It'll just take some adjustment."

Ari projected his emotions, a solid feeling of disbelief, as if I'd suggested some incredible understatement.

"And that's all your classes for this year. I'll show you to your room so you can drop off your stuff," Valentic offered. "I heard you're rooming in servant's quarters on the seventh floor. That means you're going to face a lot less stairs every day than the rest of us."

"How many floors are there anyway?" I asked, recalling him saying that first-year cadets roomed at the very top.

"Twelve, plus the gryphon aerie. That's not counting the below-ground levels, but you'll only see them while serving punishment duties."

Eesh. My fellow cadets were going to hate me for having less flights of stairs to climb up and down. Valentic explained just how many stairs I'd be seeing every day.

We were expected to put in the legwork, from visiting the mess hall and bathing rooms on the first floor of the fortress to bedding down our gryphons at the very top each night. Gods forbid a cadet be late to class, else the trainers will assign them a demerit. Too many demerits meant they'd be assigned a punishment duty on Saturday, leaving only one day to rest and recover for the next round of training.

I followed Valentic up the well-worn steps to the seventh floor. "I'm thinking after this, I drop you off with the tailors for a bit so you can be fitted for uniforms. Then you can meet the rest of the flight over dinner. Sound good?" he offered.

"Sure. Tell me about the flight?" I invited. He had already shied away from the subject a couple times.

"Well, there are four first-year flights, all named after birds. There's Falcon, Kite, Osprey, and Harrier, all led by a Cadet-Commander, a second year like me. We'll get to cadet ranks later. I don't want to overwhelm you too much," he said. I started wondering if he was deliberately being dense.

"And..." he sighed. "We're in Kite Flight. With you, we're only one person down from the rest of the flights. You're going to be the eighth first year in our flight."

I furrowed my brow. "The rest have nine? Before I got here, you were two cadets down from the other groups?"

"Yeah, uh..." He scratched the back of his head. "It's by design. The trainers sort of, well, mess with us sometimes. They want to see what we do when some of us are at a disadvantage."

I shook my head in disbelief. Of course I'd be placed with the group already at a disadvantage; that was just my rotten luck.

"Well, here's your room, I think," he said, stopping abruptly at the first room off the staircase. There were little pink flowers painted on the door, though the seven in the number seventeen hung crooked at eye level.

I tried the knob, and the door swung open on squeaking hinges. "Holy gods," I muttered. The place was a disaster, like someone had exploded a basket of clothes since they lay over most of the space. An unmade bed lay to one side below a slightly teetering shelf full of glass tinctures, unidentified metal bits, and exactly one doll. The lingering smell of something bitter hung in the air.

"Are you sure this is my room?" I asked, panning a wide-eyed look his way.

Both of us jumped as Ari tried to enter the room after us, just to whack his head off the door frame with a *thump*. I rushed over to guide him through the threshold, smoothing his ruffled feathers.

Valentic shrugged. "Pretty sure. There's an empty bed right there." He pointed to the untouched side, with its mattress done up with white sheets and a folded quilt resting on top. A plain chest rested at the foot of the bed, and there was a tiny bedside table with drawers I struggled to pull out as I investigated the meager space. A lantern rested atop the table.

I turned to Ari and removed his saddlebags, letting them rest next to my new bed. I needed to have a discussion later with my new roommate about picking up her stuff.

As promised, Valentic took me to the tailors next and ran off after promising to introduce me to the rest of Kite Flight over dinner. *"He seems nervous,"* Ari remarked. He sat in a corner while a pair of women took my measurements. Somehow, he'd secured a ball of yarn and batted at it like a playful cat.

"He probably just wants me to meet everyone for myself," I reasoned.

"Sounds like you're hoping for the best."

"Should I not?"

"I'd prepare to be underwhelmed, if I were you," he said. He had the grace to look embarrassed when one of the tailors tugged the yarn away from him before he could become entangled in it.

I KNEW what he meant when we arrived for dinner sans Valentic. The moment Ari and I entered the mess hall, obviously a pair, it felt like a wave of eyes turned our way. Their stares flowed over my flight leathers and the guiding hand I had on Ari's wing as we headed toward the line waiting for food.

"They're looking at us," I reported to my gryphon nervously.

"Who?"

The better question was who wasn't? Cadets and gryphons alike sat furthest from the food line, yet I could feel them watching every move I made. The seating was done with tables big enough to support ten people, maybe more if they squeezed. Gryphons of all ages sat behind their riders.

Sitting closer were the soldiers and support staff that were also staring. One of those women was my messy roommate, I thought, scanning their faces for a hint of friendliness.

There was one person I didn't spot in all this, though: the boy I was seeing. My face flamed with heat, gaze turning down rather than face the concentrated attention of so many people at once. Where was Victor? And why wasn't he coming over to say hello?

"They'll get over it," Ari said when I didn't respond.

"Hopefully."

I had to perk up when the line moved us closer to dinner, however. It smelled divine to my mostly empty stomach. A small army bustled around behind a glass partition, and I saw the activity firsthand as I grabbed a tray and got to choose sides and an entrée, plus a ration of fish for Ari.

"Hey Sharde, you trying out to be a lunch lady?" the boy in front of me snickered, looking up at a lanky teen serving food behind the divider.

"You look so good in a hairnet," agreed another boy in front of him in line.

The guy they laughed at tightened his grip on a serving spoon. He turned to me and asked, "Corn or peas?"

"Take a good look at what happens when you're a screwup for too long," the first boy said, elbowing me.

"Part-time gryphon rider, full-time serving boy," his friend agreed.

Sharde clenched his teeth. "Last thing I heard, Harrier Flight is in third place. You're one step from being screwups," he snapped.

The first boy held out his tray. "Can't hear you, lunch lady. More peas, please."

A glint flashed in Sharde's eyes before he scooped up a serving of peas and, in a quick flick, made the two hecklers wear them. I muffled a laugh behind a cupped hand as they sputtered in surprise, leaving green streaks on their cadet uniforms as they brushed off the vegetables.

"Hey!" one of the cooks shouted. "That's another demerit!"

"Move the line along!" another man's voice barked.

"Worth it," Sharde muttered. When I asked him for peas, he gave me a reasonable amount and a wry smile. "Hi, new girl."

"Hi—" I was pushed from behind by a bulky soldier, moving along quickly under his steely glare. Food in hand, I emerged from the line looking around for a place to sit. Valentic waved enthusiastically from one of the far tables. On my way there, I spotted a familiar face and nearly froze mid-stride.

Victor and his female gryphon sat with a cluster of boys feeding their youngling beasts. Was he the leader of a first-year flight like Valentic? I switched my momentum toward him, feeling my palms sweat as his gaze turned to meet mine. There was nothing friendly in the stare he leveled at me.

His gryphon, Sunset, bowed her head with a low sound of dismay. She didn't acknowledge me, which was off from when I'd met her as a yearling. I'd met Victor when he'd caught me fawning over his gryphon, who was a gorgeous beast with red-brown fur and plumage that shaded from a deep maroon around her head, to shades of red and orange toward the tips of her flight feathers. It was like she'd captured the setting sun when she spread her wings.

"H-hi, Victor," I stammered, taken aback at the hostility bristling not just from him, but from the glaring boys surrounding him.

"Cadet-Commander Callan," he corrected.

My mouth went dry. I didn't know what to do or how to respond. This wasn't the same Victor who'd kissed me behind the First's stables and promised he'd write me every week. Yet he stood, motioning me toward a patch of relative privacy behind a carved pillar and the stony wall of the fortress.

Before he could speak, I propped a fist on my hip. "What's with you?" I hissed.

We'd been seeing each other for an entire year, yet I barely recognized the boy before me and his cold, flat eyes. The inanimate words in his letters offered more comfort. "Look, Cadet Walker," he hissed back. "You're not going to come here and ride *my* successes. I refuse to be accused of fraternization with an obvious failure."

My whole self felt like it'd been dipped in ice water. "What?" It was the only answer in my head. Ride his successes? Obvious failure?

Victor was first-generation Altarian, from a well-off family of traders who'd immigrated from the distant Endoline Empire. I'd found beauty in his slanted eyes and spiked hair the color of ink and liked how different he was from the average Altarian. He was well-muscled from his first year of training here, not an ounce of fat on his angular face. When he'd come home to Kaiamear, I'd admired how well he filled in the uniform and how flattering it was against his olive skin tone.

Now he towered over me a stranger. "I don't know you," he replied. "I don't want to know you. You're not going to fit in here, and you're not going to drag me down in the process. Got it?"

A low growl came from Ari as he echoed my emotions. I embraced the fire rising in me, wanting to burn away the ache of the wound burning in my chest. "You're wrong, but I got it," I snapped.

"That's sir to you, cadet," he replied.

I nearly shoulder checked him on my way by, a snarl curling my lip as I headed to the table where Valentic sat. His brow knit as his gaze flashed between Victor and me. No, I wasn't calling him that anymore. Callan would do just fine, since I was supposed to know everyone by their last name anyway.

I imagined how Rissa would crow when she learned that she was right: all Callan cared about was his reputation.

I don't know him, I told the part of me that wanted to break down and cry the moment I sat down, surrounded by the boys of my new flight. It would be the worst possible thing. First day, sobbing in front of the people I needed to see me as an equal.

"Man, why'd we have to get the girl?" one of them said.

I turned a glare on him with more force than necessary. He physically recoiled, putting his hands up.

"Everyone, this is Sivana Walker and her gryphon, Ari," Valentic interrupted.

As he did introductions, I realized two people were missing. But in the meantime, I said hello to the other boys. The first was Jairn Biggs, the Black boy who'd already complained about me, and his youngling gryphon, Echo, who sat in his lap.

"You named your gryphon after the letter *e*?" I asked, referencing the military alphabet.

"I thought it was cool," he said defensively, petting Echo's brown feathers. The little gryphon twittered and nuzzled his hand.

Also present was Juanico Pereyra, who'd lost his right to spend time with his gryphon as punishment for improper grooming. His face was sure to get stuck in its petulant twist. Beside him was Codisius Credell, who raised a tanned hand in greeting and didn't say a peep through dinner except when he asked to be called Codi. He hulked over the table, looking more ready to head out for a day at the farm than ride a gryphon.

Perhaps to make up for Credell, Oliver Feyring rattled on about his family down south and how he had to make his pops proud since he was here on scholarship. The last boy, Benton Korvic, rolled his eyes enough without being noticed that I decided I liked him.

"Weslecker is in our flight too," Korvic said, pointing out a boy with short auburn hair laughing alongside the boys in a different flight. "He's a little too good to sit with us, if you know what I mean."

"You won't see much of him," Feyring agreed.

I lowered my voice. "What, is he a noble?"

"Fourth son of a duke," Feyring said. I whistled low. As far as I could tell, most of us in Kite Flight weren't noble-born, but they'd sure stuck a blue blood in amidst the rest of us to make us feel like riffraff.

"What about the other guy who isn't here?" I asked.

"Oh yeah, his name's Sharde. We don't see much of him either," Korvic said with another eye roll.

I muttered a curse. The pea-flinger was in my flight too.

CHAPTER 8
PRESSURE

I PARTED from my flight on the eleventh floor after dinner, climbing up to the gryphon aeries that gave this fortress its name. The temperature dropped significantly when Ari and I cleared the stairs, cold air whistling through the open-air stables where even now, beasts were returning to roost for the night.

Ari answered my thoughts again. *"We're allowed freedom to stretch our wings here, unlike in your human cities."*

"They don't worry about you getting lost?"

He snorted in derision. *"Bonded gryphons don't get lost. We can sense where our riders are."*

"Maybe one of these days, you could take me with you."

For a moment, he shifted uncomfortably, the discomfort I sensed spoke for him. *"That's something I would do with Alamid."*

I started to apologize, just to startle and glance up when someone cleared their throat. A couple caretakers dressed in thick layers of fur and wool waited to take Ari. I hesitated. Just days ago, I was one of them, accepting gryphons to groom and bed down for the evening. It still felt like my duty to see to everything he needed.

Ari's beak nudged at my fingers. *"Go on. It's going to be a short night,"* he said.

I sighed, giving his neck a scratch before passing his reins off to a caretaker. "He is blind, so you need to help him find his way," I cautioned. "But he doesn't bite. He's a sweet one."

"Got it," he replied, starting to lead Ari away.

"Sleep well," I said privately to my gryphon.

"Have fun with your mess," he replied. A hint of humor floated back to me.

Right, my roommate. I took the stairs slowly to the seventh floor, unsure of what to expect. I tried the door to room seventeen, and this time, it was locked. My heart leapt, knowing she had to be in there, listening as I flummoxed my newly crafted key to the room and dropped it. It bounced away with a tinny *ping*.

I figured my roommate would be expecting me by the time I had the door unlocked, but she was laid out on her bed, resting on her front with her arms folded below her chin. She glanced up and startled, nearly rolling off the crooked sheets below her. "Oh, hey there," she mumbled.

She sat up and closed the book she'd had in front of her. "This is yours," she blurted, pushing it out at arm's length. I carefully side-stepped one of her discarded shirts to take it.

My brows bunched in confusion. "You were reading my cadet handbook?" I asked.

Adjusting a pair of round glasses to rest higher on her pug nose, she shrugged. "It's more interesting than my homework." She tugged a hefty book off a stack resting on her bedside table and showed me the spine. *Advanced Alchemical Reactions.*

I was at a loss for a moment. She was here learning too? This was first and foremost a military academy, not an apothecary.

"There are no regulations for a woman's grooming, by the way. If anyone gives you crap for having long hair, remember that," she said in the awkward silence that followed.

"Um, thanks. I'm Sivana, by the way."

"I kno—" She caught herself. "I mean, we all kind of already know about you."

"Right," I said uneasily.

Standing, she offered her hand and introduced herself as Ellie. She was a petite thing, barely coming up to five feet, with long fingers that gripped my own without much strength. I figured she was about my age, though she seemed younger with her fringe of mousy brown bangs.

In this place where most everything was themed after gryphons or birds, she seemed right at home, as her fidgety movements reminded me of a nervous sparrow. The outline of her limbs hiding in baggy clothing was stick-thin, mostly knees and elbows.

"Of course, I bet they'll add regulations specifically because you're here now," she continued like she hadn't been interrupted by introductions. "Is it a lot of pressure to bend the rules so much you make new ones?"

"Pressure?" I echoed. I thought of King Cortes's angry sneer and shuddered. Ellie waited patiently for an answer, though, curiosity glimmering in her honey-toned eyes. "Yeah. There's been a lot of that already, and I haven't even been here a full day."

Her ponytail bobbed with her nod. "Well, nice to meet you. I better get back to my homework. Wish it was as easy to understand as your handbook." She giggled briefly as she curled back up in the middle of her bed with the textbook.

I went to my bedside, kneeling to untie the saddlebags I'd left behind earlier. "They teach alchemy here?" I asked.

She didn't reply for a long moment, looking up with a "huh?" while I started stacking my smallclothes in the chest on my side of the room.

I repeated my question. "Oh, yeah, sort of," she said, her

gaze slipping back to the words in front of her. "I'm here on an academic scholarship. Do you have any classes with Lord Gadric?"

"Actually, yes. I noticed he doesn't have a military rank," I said.

"He's a mage and my mentor. I'm here to learn engineering." Pride tinged her voice.

"Oh yeah? What does that include?" I asked curiously.

"Well…" She shrugged. "The military can't run without engineers and their innovations. I'm learning how things are made, to suggest ways to build them better. Things like bridges and tunnels, but all of that's theoretical right now." She raised her book. "Lord Gadric's specialties are in magic and alchemy, so most of my focus is on doing the same thing with chemical compounds. He and I are seeing right now if something made with magic, like a magelight, can be replicated with ordinary materials by a non-Tulari."

I whistled, impressed, and considered her anew over the lid of the chest. She'd fallen back into reading when I didn't reply immediately, looking completely engrossed in whatever was on the page.

An academic scholarship was no easy thing to get. The queen's learning initiatives included chances for the very smartest amongst us, common or noble-born, to further their learning past fundamental school.

My mother had told me of Queen Jimena's ultimate vision: a university for the scholars identified through the rigorous tests we took at the end of our schooling. Since she'd passed away before ground was broken for her place of learning, the scholars were scattered to the wind if they couldn't pay for the expensive universities and finishing schools that'd catered to noble clientele for generations.

I had so many questions for Ellie about how she'd ended up in a military fortress deep in the mountains. She'd passed the tests I'd just barely failed, held the dream I'd once wanted.

But after my clothes were secured away, I decided it could wait. I lay down and turned my back to the light from her lantern, wanting to sleep.

Instead, worries boiled up behind my closed eyelids. Tomorrow I'd see for sure if I could succeed here. Ari's life hung on my performance alone. No matter what happened, I needed to go above and beyond. I had to succeed in a place Lord Orion had only meant for boys.

ARI WAS the one to wake me, prodding our Link until I woke mid-inhale. The room was pitch dark, and my limbs went sprawling, my half-awake mind not recognizing where I was.

"Come get me right away," Ari said the moment my bare feet hit the thin rug by my new bed. A chill ran up my soles; cold seeped in from the stone around us.

My heart leapt at his urgency. *"What happened?"* I demanded, moving to rush out in my shift.

"Nothing. Calm down." He seemed to be laughing at my reaction. *"I woke you before the rest of the cadets so you'd have time to come get me and be ready on the field. You need your PT clothes."*

I turned around completely and fished out the proper clothes for a workout. It was the only part of the uniform I'd gotten from the tailors yesterday, as the rest had to be customized to fit my body shape.

PT, the military term for physical training, was the first thing on my schedule. I didn't realize it would feel like starting my day at the crack of dawn. I was still rubbing my eyes when I went out the door, moving quietly for the sake of not waking Ellie.

The moment I put both feet down outside my door, the floor slipped out like a banana peel. I shrieked in surprise while my hips slammed into the ground, a starburst of pain shooting down my legs.

I cursed and struggled to stand while a pair of bare feet pattered to my side. "Are you okay?" Ellie whispered, peering down at my blearily. She fluttered her hands by her sides, fretting while I got my bearings.

"Yeah, fine. This wasn't here last night," I said, bending to pick up the thing that'd betrayed my footing. It was a rag of leather, thin and brownish gray, but someone had ruined the bottom by slathering it in oil. My fall had ripped the middle of the hide.

"Oh, yeah," Ellie said faintly. "That happens sometimes." She reached over to tug it out of my hands.

"This has happened to you before?" I asked, my brow furrowing.

"It's probably discarded from the gryphon aeries. I don't think they meant to get you with it." She shrugged, her gaze downcast.

Ari prodded the Link again, the single pulse feeling like a headache.

I needed to go, but something didn't seem right here. "Who is 'they'?" I asked, staying rather than rushing off like my gryphon wanted.

"It's nothing."

Her sigh said it wasn't nothing, but she was already bundling up the leather and placing it neatly beside our door, like she was expecting a maid to pick it up.

"You probably have to go, huh?" Ellie said, glancing over my PT clothes. "I'll tell you later, okay?"

"I'll hold you to that," I replied.

Something told me she expected me to forget, but it was hard to do that when my hip was still smarting from its sudden acquaintance with the ground. I limped up the first set of stairs before finding my stride, heading to the gryphon aerie just to get in line behind a group of boys all shouting and pushing.

"Too late," Ari sighed to me. This mass was all the first years jockeying to get their gryphons and run downstairs to be on time to PT.

"Sorry. Unexpected fall." Now that I had a moment to think, I pictured the slippery fur as a trap for Ellie. How did she usually leave for her classes? I pictured her carrying that stack of thick textbooks she'd had piled by her bedside, unable to see past her nose.

Yeah, that was definitely meant for her, I thought, lips pinching.

Because of the trap, I was one of the last to get my gryphon. I didn't make the kind of haste as the rest of the boys after Ari nearly went headlong into a wall at the bottom of the first stairwell.

By the time we got to the ground floor and followed the last stragglers outside, I realized most of the flights were assembled and standing at attention. I headed for the first years and their fluffy youngling gryphons, knowing one of the four groups was mine. There was a field even larger than Kaiamear's Gryphon Yard in front of us, the grass brown and crumpled from the passage of feet.

On either side of the field, distant figures were already starting to work out. Those had to be the second and third years, as their fledged gryphons were old enough to fly while their riders ran.

"Psst." One of the boys beckoned to me urgently. I recognized the lanky pea-flinger from yesterday standing at the back of Kite Flight. His gryphon was much larger than the others; nearly a yearling, I would guess. I guided Ari so we fell in next to them. While my gryphon struck the classic "at attention" pose, resting his weight on his haunches like he was about to pounce and lifting his head proudly, I scrambled to mimic the other boys with my fists at my sides.

"Just in time," the boy next to me said out of the corner of his mouth. He went rigid as a burly man approached us.

Even without looking at him directly, I recognized the flat-brim hat that cast a shadow over his face. My heart leapt to my throat when I realized this drill sergeant was heading straight for me, not just my flight.

"You must be Cadet Walker." He spoke sharply, louder than necessary, and I looked up at him. His expression was strict, bordering on severe, though a glint of anticipation lit his eyes.

"Isn't your father a Commander? Didn't he teach you anything?" he barked, drawing a wince from me. I snapped my gaze forward again, realizing I wasn't supposed to be gawking at him while standing at attention.

The drill sergeant loudly corrected my stance until I was properly standing like the others. A flush of heat crept up my neck. If we weren't all at attention, I was sure the other boys would be turning to stare at me just like they had at dinner yesterday.

The boy next to me bent double with a gusty *"Achoo!"*

"Sharde!" The weight of the drill's attention flipped to him immediately.

"Sorry, Sergeant Kobarn! Can't keep it in sometimes!" he responded, also speaking louder than necessary. The other boys snickered. I breathed a sigh of relief when we started warming up with a jog, flashing a look of gratitude to the boy who was now running full pelt ahead of us, chased by the drill sergeant.

CHAPTER 9

STEEL AND FURY

Sergeant Kobarn chased me more than he did Sharde. I was slow and out of shape compared to the other boys, and the man must've smelled blood.

After my PT torture was done, I stuffed a quick breakfast in my mouth upon realizing the women's bath was farther from the mess hall than the men's. With little time to dawdle and chitchat, I instead startled the soul out of several women when I traipsed into the bath trailing my gryphon.

"He's gentle, I promise!" I announced. They gave me dirty looks and him a wide berth when he decided to wade into the water and paddle around. I rushed to intercept him when he nearly ran into the opposite side of the pool.

"So *uptight*," he sighed. "*The boys always bathed their gryphons.*"

"*Well, men actually get to Link and get used to gryphons,*" I reasoned. I gave him a quick scrub and paw rub before we were off to my first class.

The boys all had lockers with a change of clothes connected to the baths. I'd been assigned a locker too but stood out once again as I slipped into the back of a gaggle of cadets heading for the third-floor classrooms. The boys wore the all-black uniform, and I'd put on my riding leathers again. At least I was warm.

I checked my schedule and headed for a classroom toward the back of this floor. The door was already closed, and I swallowed my nerve as I turned the knob to be as quiet as possible. Being late to my first class was a demerit waiting to happen. My shoulders ratcheted up, and then I got a good look at the room and the instructor.

The Tulari mage standing before a grand chalkboard raised a wrinkled hand in greeting and smiled warmly. "Good morning. You must be Cadet Walker. We have seats all throughout. Take your pick," he said.

His umber skin was marked along the cheek with a circular symbol I recognized—the mark of magic, Lord Orion's blessing. If I was closer, I would've been able to pick out runes on the inside and its color, denoting which type of magery he could wield.

Behind him stood Ellie, who spared me a quick wave before returning to writing something on the board. My tension dropped like a limp puppet when I walked in, seeing about twenty individual wooden desks, each equipped with a textbook, loose paper, and a quill and inkwell. Most were already taken, yet there was one available up front that I slid into.

"Just like fundamental school," I said privately to Ari. He settled next to my desk, resting his chin on a cushion provided for just that purpose.

He chuckled. *"Except with gryphons?"*

"Exactly. So, it'll be even better." I smiled, excited to get started.

"Alamid was never excited for school."

Ari and I froze at the same time. We hadn't said his name so casually yet. But with our connection open like this, I felt how the smell of the room and the sound of the instructor's voice brought back an avalanche of memories for my gryphon.

He went silent, withdrawing to his side of the Link and taking that déjà vu feeling with him. He closed his eyelids with a low keening noise, and just like that, my first Anatomy and Physiology class lost its luster. Lord Gadric delivered information much faster than the fundamental school classes I remembered. Everyone else was halfway into studying the venom ducts in the rozash species. I just tried to understand.

The next class, History and War Strategy, was far more straightforward. I sat between Biggs and the boy from my flight I hadn't gotten to talk to yet, Acton Weslecker. The young nobleman barely glanced my way, so I decided to try befriending Biggs instead, passing him my notes when he got behind.

Lost in his own thoughts, Ari sighed and slept through most of the lecture. He moved like a sleepwalker as we changed classes, and I sat with Biggs again in World Cultures.

"Finally, they send me a girl," said the instructor's heavily accented voice. I'd caught her attention from the door, but it was only when I was seated across from her that I realized she wasn't Altarian.

She had a solid build, well-muscled despite her obvious age. Time had taken her beauty and given her wrinkles and a sagging back, but it hadn't dimmed the unusual lilac of her eyes nor altered the ivory white of her hair. Her skin was so fair it was tinged with icy tones, setting her apart as a northerner from the Rathi Islands.

"Yes, ma'am," I said, wondering why she was here. Most everyone knew that the Rathi kept to themselves and viewed Altare as prime pillaging ground.

"Welcome to World Cultures." She nodded and started her lesson. Unlike the other two instructors so far, she didn't move off her stool. I didn't take notes, immediately fascinated by the tale she spun from her homeland. With my attention so fixed on her, it didn't take too long for me to realize her legs were of uneven length, one broad with muscle, the other awkwardly folded behind one of the stool's spokes.

I checked my schedule when it was over, and she dismissed us with a wave. Her name was listed as simply "Instructor Signe."

And my next class was down in the training yard. Ground Combat. I groaned to myself, because all that sitting meant my abused muscles had had time to start complaining. We joined a crush of cadets and gryphons all rushing the stairs. The sudden appearance of a drill sergeant slowed everything back to military precision before someone could get pushed down a staircase.

I tried poking the silent gryphon by my side over our Link as we headed toward the first floor. *"Is there a second stair anywhere?"* There simply were too many people choking the area during class changes.

"No," he replied. I shrugged and looked for my fellow first years as we exited through the front gates. It took him so long to continue his thought that I'd forgotten I'd asked the question. *"When Alamid was here, the system was designed so you're guaranteed some demerits."*

"That's not fair." I balked at the idea of guaranteed demerits and losing rest days regularly.

The other cadets led me around the shadow of the fortress, where a shirtless man waited for us in the middle of a ring of packed ground. Four youngling gryphons were already playing in the tall grass beside it, tumbling together like kittens. Ari sat close by with a sigh. *"That's the thing, Sivana. War's not fair, and that's where we're going once you graduate. It's best to get used to it now."*

I watched a brown youngling start to scale Ari's side, tail lashing in determination. My gryphon laid his head down, his expression full of irritation. He turned and snapped at the small beast, sending it tumbling off his back with a frightened yelp. *"Ari! That's not like you,"* I scolded.

He grumbled back, interrupted by a man's voice close to my ear. "Are you going to join us, cadet?"

I startled, realizing that was the shirtless man talking. The other cadets were taking their pick from weapon racks braced against the fortress's side. Turns out the man was our instructor, and I learned why he was half-naked halfway into the lesson. He had a group of boys teach me the basics of maneuvering a long sword called a cavalry saber, meant to be used on gryphon back. I was sweating buckets in my riding leathers.

"You can never expect your gryphon to protect you from everything." The instructor circulated, shouting the same phrases over and over like a mantra. "You get grounded behind enemy lines, what do you show them?"

"Steel and fury!" a few boys yelled back.

Steel and fury, indeed. By the end of the lesson, my arms felt like jelly. I racked my practice sword and turned, finding Ari afield with a youngling snuggled to his side. Calmer emotions flowed from him through our Link. I went over, muffling a gasp when the gray-white feathers of the baby gryphon caught the sunlight.

"Silverwind?" I called, and she perked up, twittering a smattering of birdsong.

Last Spring, Snowpoint had laid two eggs. She'd been one of the meanest gryphons in the First, but she'd still allowed me to babysit to give her a break. The youngling bounding toward me had been bundled away to the Academy to find her rider at only a couple months old.

I took a knee and held out my arms, letting her jump into my chest. She was a fat little thing now, some of her baby fluff transitioning to the tougher flight feathers she'd need to navigate the sky. I'd said goodbye to her when she was still the size of a newborn human baby, but now she was the size of a hunting dog. She curled her talons to bat gently at my chin, and I practically melted. She radiated pure childish joy to see me again.

"You're getting so big, Silver," I cooed, kissing her on the beak.

Ari made a sound akin to a throat clearing. It was only from his mental nudge that I looked up, noticing the boy heading across the grass straight for me and the gryphon wiggling gleefully in my hold as I tickled her belly.

My heart dropped somewhere in the vicinity of my knees. I recognized him, because what warm-blooded Altarian hadn't memorized the faces of the royal family? Prince Mateo had the bronzed skin of his family line but thankfully hadn't inherited the thick lips and jowls like his father and eldest brother had.

No, he was, as my sister said, "the most handsome Cortes," blessed with a squared jaw, straight nose, and soft mouth currently pressed into a thin line of displeasure.

He stared me down with a cool glare. "What are you doing to my gryphon?" he demanded.

CHAPTER 10
DEMERITS

I glanced down to Silverwind, who twittered a complaint that I'd stopped tickling her. My fingers trembled as I stood and held her out for him to take. "S-so sorry, Y-Your Highness," I stammered. "Silverwind is…was…a part of my flight and…"

He smoothed out her feathers, showing no sign of listening to my stumbling apology. "It's Cadet Cortes. She's not in your flight anymore, and her name is Mireille. We're late to our next class because of you," he said briskly, barely casting me another glance before he walked off, taking Silverwind with him.

I sighed through my nose, trembling in the wake of his presence, as brief as it was. Until this moment, I had forgotten Prince Mateo was a fellow first year and that two younglings I'd helped raise from the egg were here too. If Silverwind…I mean, Mireille…was here and Linked to the prince, where was her brother, Ironfeather, and who was he Linked with?

Ari nudged my hip. *"Less thinking, more walking."*

I checked my schedule and groaned. Basic Gryphon Care, my year-one gryphon riding class, was held in the aeries at the top of the fortress. I was *super* late.

Unless…I glanced to Ari, who turned his beak up at the idea forming in my head. *"I'm not saddled."*

"It's what, a five-minute flight for you?" I was ready to beg as I shaded my face with a hand, looking way up at the twelve-plus-story journey we needed to make with haste.

His beak lifted another inch. *"You could easily get hurt. No."*

"C'mon, it's not far at all."

"You could slip off of me and fall."

Ah, so that's what this is really about. I ran my fingers through his neck fur and fluffed the feathers around the ears he had tucked to his skull. "I promise I'll be careful. Please, Ari?"

He growled low but bowed his neck and wings for me to climb on his back. *"Fine. But stay on my back."* I recognized the tinge of fear he tried to hide as my riding leathers slipped against his feathers.

"I will," I said, holding two handfuls of his neck fur. "Where is your saddle anyway?"

Saddling up the gryphons was a morning chore for caretakers, but the crew here hadn't put one on Ari's back. He didn't answer as he surged into a loping run, gaining altitude with a few booming flaps of his wings. I sweated anew trying to guide him with my fingers in his neck, but thankfully the wide, window-like openings to the aerie were a difficult target to miss.

Unfortunately, I hadn't been up here in broad daylight. Ari didn't slow quick enough to stick the landing, so we both went skidding across hay-covered stone until his flank slammed into a wooden stable wall and I rolled off his back in an awkward sprawl.

Gryphons screeched and called to each other in alarm, filling the air with a cacophony of sound. An unfamiliar man wearing riding leathers loomed over me, his severe frown looking almost comical upside-down. "Good afternoon, Cadet Walker. That's a demerit for potential injury to your gryphon companion and three more for riding without a saddle. Let this be a lesson to you on engaging in something so dangerous." He noted something on a clipboard he held.

Gods above. Four demerits! I'd just been stressing over earning *one*.

"Sorry, sir," I practically groaned as I peeled myself off the ground. I wasn't sure if I ached more from training or that hard landing.

"We'll begin when Cadet Cortes arrives," the instructor said, gesturing for me to join the boys waiting by the stairwell with their gryphons. They'd all seen my arrival, a few still laughing and nudging each other. My cheeks burned as I shouldered my way to the back of the group.

"Nice job. Four in one go. I haven't done that in a while," said the tall boy perched on a crate up against the wall. His legs made a figure-four, and he stretched out with his arms behind his head.

Sharde grinned up at me. In the light of day, I noticed his baby blue eyes and shaggy blond hair for the first time. His hair was undoubtedly out of regulation, as the rest of the boys had theirs cropped short to their skulls, some so tightly shorn that I could catch glimpses of their scalp. Still, he looked impressed with me rather than laughing at my expense, so I spared him a small smile.

"Commander Davis is a stickler anyway," he said, lowering his voice. "Watch what happens to the princeling."

Commander Davis sure looked like a stickler as he waited there at the front of the class, standing with a rigidly straight back and irritated scowl. He was tall and broad-shouldered, with a thick brow that shaded narrow-set eyes. What caught my attention most about him was the leather cord looped around his neck, proudly and openly displaying the symbol of Lord Orion, a gold-plated spell circle with a single rune of protection etched into its center.

I waited, and he chewed Prince Mateo's hide in front of all

of us when he finally arrived with Mireille. Since he wasn't out of breath, I assumed he'd taken his time. It felt good to have some confirmation that the prince was just as much a cadet as I was within these stone walls.

I was a little surprised when the lesson began and I knew it all already. The cadets went to work grooming their gryphons. We learned caretaker basics, the kind of stuff I'd already taken care of, like trimming Ari's nails and oiling his pads. Davis checked on me and Sharde first, who'd barely left his crate to attend to his own gryphon.

"Good work," the man said brusquely to us both. "Save your energy for Flight Training."

"Yes, sir," I said. Sharde shrugged.

Davis left us like he was used to a lack of crisp response from Sharde. The boy scooted to the side of his crate, patting it in invitation. "Heard you were a caretaker too," he said.

"I was." I sat next to him, craning my head curiously to take in his gryphon. She was definitely too large to be a first year's beast, but also too small to belong to a second year, being about four feet long beak to rump and covered with fluffy down. She was primarily white, with speckles of brown and black along her flanks, sure to be a beautiful lady once she was fully grown.

"Also heard what you did to Link up with a gryphon," Sharde said, absently scratching down his gryphon's back with a lean to the side. She raised her parted beak and chirped like a hatchling, her wings quivering happily. "But I don't really believe it was out of ego. That's just a rumor, right?"

I felt my metaphorical feathers ruffle, my eye twitching with a sudden rush of ire. "I didn't Link with Ari out of ego! He was going to be executed the next day, and I was trying to save him."

He put his hands up. "Don't hurt the messenger. I think it's cool. Don't we all dream of saving the day and rescuing those we love at the same time? I'm glad you're in my flight. Name's Noah." He hooked a thumb toward his chest. "Me 'n' Puzzlebox have been around a while."

His gryphon released a friendly chirp. "You named her Puzzlebox?" I asked, raising a brow. That was worse than Biggs and his gryphon, Echo.

"Check this out." He retrieved a toy from his bag, one of those cubes with a different color painted on each side. Its edges were chipped, exposing the wood beneath, but Puzzlebox perked up, reaching to paw at Sharde's thigh with a begging whine. He placed it on the ground, and she pranced around it joyfully. I muffled a laugh as she went tumbling around in the hay with it clasped in her beak.

Sharde didn't quite smile at his gryphon's antics. "She's my big baby. I figured it was best to name her after her favorite toy. You're a former caretaker too. Maybe you'll understand her better than the others, but she's…special. Different. She's a yearling."

"Really?" I studied her anew. She was too small and soft compared to the yearlings I'd tended to, though I figured that was due to a lack of yearlings in the First's stables. Usually, we only saw adolescent beasts when cadets came to Kaiamear on breaks.

"Really. Her egg was wild caught. The idiot who brought in her mother had overlooked Puzzlebox's egg in the nest, so it was taken in by a different tracker a day after her two brothers' eggs."

I pulled a horrified expression that she'd gone a day without a brooding mother in the high elevation climate where wild gryphons nested. "It's a miracle she hatched," I said.

"You aren't wrong. You know how some litters of kittens or puppies have one that's a runt? That's how my gryphon was. None of last year's noble boys wanted her," he said with barely concealed contempt.

Puzzlebox returned from her romp, investigating me since Sharde had leaned back on his hands. She made a happy squeak when I rubbed behind her ears and crawled half into my lap, snuggling to my belly. I'd only expected such behavior from Mireille because she was still very young, but by yearling age, most female gryphons were more likely to take a caretaker's hand off than want to cuddle.

"Rather than watch her get forced to Link with a boy that didn't want her, I 'accidentally' made a connection with her last year," Sharde said with air quotes.

"So, you're a second year," I said, confused.

He stretched and yawned, perfectly at ease. "Nah. I'm a repeat first year. You just gotta be a better gryphon rider than me to be promoted, new girl. That's not too hard."

That at least gave context to the taunts tossed at him yesterday before he flung peas back. *Take a good look at what happens when you're a screwup for too long.*

"Are you implying you're repeating your first year on purpose?" I asked in an undertone.

Sharde grinned, snapping his fingers. "Exactly. What are they going to do, fire me? Links are forever, and gryphons don't make mistakes. Me 'n' Puzzlebox will eventually be demoted to Final Flight and tour the world together, delivering mail. Can't wait."

"Seems he has this all figured out," Ari commented in amusement.

I could barely understand aspiring to be a part of the retirees' flight, Final Flight. I pictured every air courier I'd met, all near-elderly men with gryphons who had the yellowing beaks and skinny hips denoting advanced age. Then I tried to put Sharde and petite Puzzlebox next to that mental image and shook my head slowly.

"I'm glad you saved her from feeling unwanted," I said after deciding not to comment on his lack of aspirations. Puzzlebox was quickly becoming my second-favorite gryphon here, just below Ari, as she nibbled on the end of my braid and got comfortable in my hold.

Sadly, this hour was up far too soon, and we had to head to Flight Training in the heart of the fortress. Sharde and I trailed Commander Davis, who taught this class as well. I felt the anxiety in Ari spike as we approached the massive cavern where we'd learn the basics of flying together with the safety of a net below.

My palms were sweating with sympathetic anxiety as we emerged on the platform wide enough for a class of cadets and their yearling or older gryphons. A group of second years had already arrived, their unfamiliar faces turning to take in Sharde and me coming in together behind the instructor.

I spotted Valentic and breathed a sigh of relief. But on the other side of the room, flanked by leering teens, was Victor Callan, his eyes already narrowing hatefully. "Wow, would you look at that?" he said, nudging one of his friends. "Looks like trash sticks together." The lot of them touched their chests and then foreheads, the sign of the god I'd wronged. Something told me I'd be seeing that gesture a lot.

"There's no need for commentary, Cadet Callan," said Commander Davis, but with a sinking feeling, I realized he was laughing quietly along with that group of boys and touching the symbol he wore around his neck.

CHAPTER 11
LOVESICK PUPPY

I HAD little time to brood, but in the little patches of time between classes, I wondered about Victor Callan. I saw him in a pack of his friends every day for Flight Training, but I kept trying to get him alone to ask, *why?*

Why was he suddenly so hostile? Why did he start calling me a heretic and encourage the boys around him to do the same? How could he turn on me like this?

I followed him after class every day, trying to get him alone. It only took two days before he rounded on me in a nearly empty corridor. "What do you *want*, Cadet Walker?" he demanded. "People are going to see you following me like a lovesick puppy!"

"I-I-I just…" I cleared me throat, trying to get a hold on myself. Being the full recipient of his hostility was still unnerving.

"Y-y-you what?" he asked, deliberately mocking the faint stutter that I tried so hard to keep under wraps.

I burst out, "Stop it!" His expression remained a mocking smile, but at least he was quiet for a moment. "Why are you acting this way? Don't you remember…you and I…"

He stepped closer, dropping to whisper over me. "Can I

tell you a secret? It was all a lie. I never cared about you for a moment," he said. Each word was like a little knife in my back, but I held it rigid, feeling like the worst blow was coming. I needed to know the truth, though. "My parents thought I'd get ahead if I married the daughter of the First's Commander, but now you'd just bring disgrace upon my good name."

I set my teeth, trembling with self-restraint. I wished I could just punch him in the face and forget about him, but that wouldn't solve anything. "You're going to regret saying that to me someday," I replied as neutrally as I could.

He barked a laugh. "Will I?" His dark eyes simmered with something I'd never seen in him before. It made me want to put as many closed doors between him and me as possible.

"You will. Get familiar with this." I turned my back pointedly and began walking away.

Victor was still laughing. "See you tomorrow, *heretic!*"

I bet he made the sign of Orion at me, too. I was simmering for a battle the moment I turned a corner, my hands balled into tight fists. I couldn't let him get to me, but gods, he was good at getting under my skin. No doubt I'd toss and turn tonight, reliving everything he'd said and dreaming of better comebacks than the one I'd uttered.

I charged ahead of Ari, only doubling back when I realized I'd taken my guiding hand from his shoulder and he'd blundered into a wall. He rubbed his beak with a taloned paw, grumbling in irritation.

"Sorry," I muttered, walking at a more reasonable pace as we approached the floor where I roomed with Ellie. His ears perked, and a few seconds later, I heard a flurry of feminine laughter.

Then a tearful voice I recognized exclaiming, "Gatekeeper take you all!"

I peered down the hallway, seeing Ellie bent over a clutter of fallen books. She was cornered by three other girls dressed in maid uniforms, all laughing at her expense, and I saw red as one swiped the glasses off my roommate's face and crunched them against the wall.

"Hey!" I shouted, drawing their attention immediately. Ellie blinked owlishly in my direction as the lead girl dropped her glasses frames and turned toward me, hand on hip.

She was a classic beauty, with a full head of blonde locks, which she flicked over one shoulder. Full, pouty lips turned up in one corner. "Problem?" she drawled.

I didn't know who these girls were, but I suspected. One of these maids had laid an oiled rag out in front of our door, hoping to make my roommate fall. "You'll be paying to replace her glasses," I said, crossing my arms.

The blonde smacked her lips, smirking toward her two friends. "The nerd's got an extra pair. Right, Ellie?"

I scowled. "That doesn't matter. You're still replacing them." Heat rolled over my shoulder, and I noticed the other girls glancing that direction. Ari had drawn himself to his full height, glaring with me.

"Oh." The blonde forced a laugh, but it had a nervous edge. "You must be...the heretic. No wonder you're here coming to Ellie's defense."

I stepped in the way when one of her friends tried to leave. "The money for her glasses first," I said pointedly.

She huffed and drew a handful of coins from her pocket. She barely glanced at them before throwing them at the floor beside where Ellie knelt, quietly listening to this exchange. "See if I clean *your* room," she snapped, pushing me out of the way in her haste to leave with her friends.

I took a deep breath, counting up to ten and then back down, before kneeling to help Ellie gather her books and new money. "You didn't have to..." she muttered, blushing up to her ears. I realized she was nearly blind and placed her things directly into her hands. "I really do have a spare pair of glasses."

"It's the principle of the thing," I answered.

I DIPPED the quill into ink and scratched out the first two words: *Dear Father*. Only a week had passed, and I needed the advice of an Ace who'd gone through all of this and emerged a hardened gryphon knight.

A little gryphon paw reached out to bat at the quivering tip of my quill. Ironfeather turned quizzical gray eyes up at me, his childlike emotions flaring with the desire for attention. "Sorry, boy," I said, scratching him behind the ears.

I'd found Mireille's brother by complete accident after being invited to Kite Flight's "roost." It was a common area all the boys in my flight shared, connected to their quarters. But this was Fortress Aerie, where everything had to be named after birds apparently.

I'd come here first to hang out with Biggs and Sharde in the short couple hours of free time we got between dinner and lights out. It was kitted out with several desks for homework, plus plush seating and cushions for gryphons and their riders to share. The boys had snacks hidden in little alcoves which they shared, so they knew how to get me to come back.

Despite smelling like teenage boy, it was the most comfortable space in the fortress outside of my own room. It was also the best place to be to get to know the more reluctant members of the flight, like Pereyra and Credell, who usually stayed in the rooms unless intercepted on the way there. There was really only one boy who didn't spend any time with us...Weslecker.

On his way out the door to spend time with his real friends, he'd had Ironfeather shadowing him. The little gryphon had been beside himself to see me, repeating the same effusive greeting as his sister. Weslecker had taken a good look at us and sighed. "I guess you should look after him for a while," he'd said.

Tonight was the second time I'd gotten to babysit Ironfeather, who hadn't been renamed after ending his stay with the First. With feathers that gleamed a solid blue gray in sunlight, it was probably the most appropriate name he could have. I cooed over him quietly, my eyelids starting to droop. I went back to writing before I lost all my energy for the task.

It's a Saturday, and I've just gotten off my first punishment duty. I've been cleaning pots and pans all day. Some of those things were as big as I am!

I'd thought I could get through Gryphon Rider Academy without sharing every tiny detail of the experience with Father, but I was wrong. I told him about my classes, most importantly about Commander Davis, who'd been responsible for twenty-one of my twenty-three demerits this week. (I didn't write that I'd gotten two in the dinner line when a drill sergeant had witnessed me balling up my fist, ready to hit a Harrier Flight boy for asking why I didn't clean his clothes that morning.)

Ari refuses to fly during Flight Training class. Davis gives me a demerit each time, saying I have no control over my gryphon. But I can feel that Ari's scared that I'll fall off and get hurt. I feel bad because he keeps reliving details of losing Alamid each time Davis tells us that we're meant to fail at first and that's why we have a net.

Some of the boys have taken to making the sign of Lord Orion and then flicking their fingertips at me. They call me a heretic. I'm trying to ignore it, but it feels like it gets worse every day.

I didn't write about the notes. Not yet, at least. There were some things I'd need to take care of myself, especially when no one could really stop the other students from slipping anonymous notes into the desks I sat at every day or sneaking them into my locker in the women's bath. They called me heretic and worse, to the point I took to immediately balling up any strip of paper rather than reading what it had to say.

I had a whole section of my book bag dedicated to crumpled-up notes. I snuck a look at it, nearly full with dozens of scraps of paper all bearing insults. It was like a personal shrine of how disliked I was. At some point, I needed to find a place to securely throw them out, since I'd received a few badly wrinkled notes that I swore I'd read already.

My gryphon was currently resting by the desk I'd claimed, Puzzlebox draped over his wing, grooming his feathers lazily. I smiled to myself, switching to writing about Kite Flight and the individual personalities I was getting to know. When I got to Sharde's name, I hesitated. Something told me Father would advise I stay away from the boy at the bottom of our class, even if I shared why he was failing on purpose. Instead, I skipped to Weslecker.

Lord Acton Weslecker remains standoffish not only to me, but our whole flight. He sits with his friends from before the Academy, which are a cluster of nobles who were all assigned to Falcon Flight together. He's best friends with Prince Mateo and seems to think he's an honorary member of the Falcons rather than the flight he's really in.

I'd scribbled a couple pages of information before turning my attention to the last piece of news, the sight of which still turned my stomach.

The Commandant had called me to his office earlier this week and offered me a copy of the *Kaiamear Gazette*. "Explain, Cadet Walker," he'd demanded.

My soul had felt like it'd left my body when I read the headline: "FIRST FEMALE GRYPHON RIDER TAKES FLIGHT."

I'd apparently said such drivel as, "It's past time a woman joins the gryphon knight corps." Or my personal least favorite quote, "As a devotee of Mother Nilara, I feel it's my duty to bring a feminine touch to the Gryphon Rider Academy." It was otherwise pretty accurate in the details of how Ari and I had first Linked.

I knew Mother was screaming her head off back home. She'd been sure there would be some news about me, but nothing so…icky and girly as this piece made me out to be. I'd sworn up and down to the Commandant that I'd never spoken to a journalist before coming to the Academy.

I don't think he believed me, but he sent me off with a warning to never speak with a reporter from the Kaiamear Gazette *again. Now I worry that I've already fallen in the estimation of the Commandant,* I wrote.

I owed a real punch to the face to the man who'd written that trash, Miles Glimmerwick. What kind of name was that anyway? I didn't doubt copies of the *Kaiamear Gazette*'s special on me were circulating the Academy. Now my fellow cadets had to think I wasn't a girl striving to be their equal who just happened to love gryphons, but instead a female with an agenda.

I hesitated after writing down just the letters "PS". With a sigh, I scribbled the last bit of news in code, knowing my sister would tell the rest of my family exactly what it meant.

PS: Tell Rissa she was right.

As I sealed up this letter to Father, I bid my goodbyes for the night and bedded Ari down. I was ready to go pass out in my room, just to find Ellie standing outside the door, crying. "Don't go in there," she hiccupped when she saw me.

CHAPTER 12
SARGE'S LITTLE ANGEL

Brow furrowed, I did the opposite of what she suggested, stopping dead in the threshold. I'd expected a nasty note slipped under the door, but this was much worse. The stench of fresh paint assailed my nose. "What the…" I took in the destruction with growing outrage, first seeing red everywhere before connecting it to the dripping words glistening on my side of the wall.

"Feminine Touch," the red paint said. Someone had broken the lock and dumped buckets of paint all over our beds, Ellie's textbooks, my uniforms…everything.

Save for the tinctures Ellie kept sealed tightly, all our things were ruined.

"I just got here," she sniffed behind me. "I've been in the lab all day."

"And I was doing a punishment duty," I said, my hands balling into fists. "Whoever did this had hours."

"I'm really sorry." Tears dripped down her thin cheeks as she glanced over my shoulder at the destruction.

I slowly closed the door, turning to her instead. "It's not your fault. Look at this." I thrust my well-worn copy of the *Kaiamear Gazette* at her. She adjusted her fogging glasses and scanned the article about me. "I bet some of the boys got offended."

"A group of cadets would be noticed coming and going with paint," she pointed out. "I bet it was Clara and the others."

"Who?" I asked.

She pulled off her glasses and wiped her eyes with an overlong sleeve. "The maid who broke my other pair of glasses."

I nodded slowly, my eyes narrowing. "You think those girls did this." I wasn't all that convinced. The words on the wall and color choice suggested something else entirely.

"Clara's hated me since fundamental school," Ellie said, keeping her eyes downcast. "She's always playing little pranks. Her favorite is making me slip and fall."

"This isn't a *little* prank," I argued. "You saw the words on the wall. They were targeting me, and your stuff was just there too."

She considered for several long seconds, holding up her finger when I went to say more. "Know what? It doesn't matter," she said finally. "Whether it's my bullies or your bullies, or even both, we have a serious problem. I'm going to go get my secret weapon."

"Your secret weapon," I echoed.

"I'll be right back."

She hustled down the stairs, leaving me to confer with Ari mentally about what happened. The longer I waited, the more dread set in. I'd just gotten my cadet uniforms properly tailored, and my family had footed the bill for them. Maybe some noble's son could replace the whole lot without breaking a sweat, but that wasn't me.

Boot steps echoed from the stairwell, preceding the scowling face of Sergeant Kobarn in full drill uniform. I snapped to a proper parade rest the moment I saw him.

He stepped aside, and Ellie emerged from his shadow. "Right here, Dad," she said, opening the door.

I blinked at the drill sergeant owlishly. Dad? *Gods above.* That was the best thing she could've said.

"What in the three hells?" he bellowed in his too-loud voice from the middle of the room.

"You didn't say that my drill sergeant is your father," I muttered to Ellie, so leery of his mercurial moods that I stayed outside.

She flashed a sheepish smile. "I thought you knew."

"That man yells at me *every day*," I whispered.

Even with them side by side, I couldn't see the family resemblance. Sergeant Kobarn was a tall, broad man who was quite the PT enthusiast—all the better to chase and "motivate" cadets like me—while she was painfully thin and birdlike as she flapped her hands by her side while explaining that we'd been out of our room all day.

"Don't worry, girls. We'll find the human garbage who did this," he said. With his attention on his daughter, his face relaxed into a softer expression. Then his gaze turned to me, and the usual strict mask fell back into place. "But first, you need another place to rest."

"I-I have an idea." I was pretty sure he'd hate what I had in mind and wake up all the girls on this floor going full drill sergeant on me.

I swallowed hard as I met his merciless brown eyes. "There are a few empty bunks in the Kite Flight dorm. Those boys are my friends... I know they weren't involved in... this." I waved toward the room.

The Sergeant glanced to his daughter, a frown pinching the corners of his thin mouth. He gestured for us to follow, and we climbed up to the eleventh floor in silence. I fidgeted with my fingers nervously, never knowing a quiet moment from this man. He entered Kite Flight's roost and closed the door behind him.

We could hear his raised voice on the other side. I couldn't help but inch closer, turning my ear to the door to listen. "You will not touch my little angel, or you will answer to me," the Sergeant announced.

"He always makes such a big production out of things," Ellie sighed. "He doesn't have to yell at them. They're...nice, right?"

"Something tells me they're going to be the kindest, most respectful boys you will ever meet," I answered dryly.

Her father came to get us, revealing the rest of my flight members lined up at attention. "You can come in now." His kind air toward Ellie made me anxious, feeling like he was only talking to her.

"This is my daughter," he said, putting a hand on Ellie's shoulder. "Let me recap. If you touch a hair on her head, make any poorly thought-out comment toward her, or decide you're going to throw paint around her room, I will make your life a living hell. The first thing I'll do is PT you to death, and if you somehow survive that...there are worse things that follow. Understood?"

Ellie's cheeks were bright red.

"Yes, sir!" my flight-mates chorused nervously.

"Get some rest," he said to them. To Ellie, he added, "I'll be speaking to the Commandant. Don't return to your old room. He'll be launching an investigation immediately."

"Okay. Thanks, Dad," she said. He left soon after, but the seven boys that made up my Flight were now paying close attention to Ellie. She seemed to shrink under their focused attention.

Sharde cleared his throat. "So, what happened exactly? Paint?"

I shared what we walked into. Even Weslecker lingered, wrinkling his nose at the details.

"If I were Sarge, I'd PT them to death instead of us,"

Feyring muttered. I glanced to Korvic, who rolled his eyes right on cue. A faint smile lit my face.

INSTEAD OF SPENDING SUNDAY, my only rest day, on leisure, Ellie and I were summoned before the Commandant bright and early to share our side of the story. He looked at me with such disappointment that I wanted to crawl under a rug and stay there.

"You are aware that this is an obvious reference to your little interview?" he remarked.

"Sir, I did not say those things. I swear on the Mother herself," I blurted.

The only thing betraying a deeper reaction was how his fists flexed and his leather riding gloves creaked. He noticed my gaze on them and steepled his hands over his desk, tapping his fingertips together. "Whether you did or not is a moot point in the scheme of things," he said slowly. "The culprits will be found and disciplined. But do be careful, Cadet Walker. You haven't been here a week, and already your presence has caused a stir."

The Commandant glanced to Ellie, his frown deepening. "Young ladies, the flight dorms are not meant to have boys and girls living together. But given the circumstances, I believe the first female cadet should have the closest experience here as possible to a male cadet. I shall permit you both to room with Kite Flight." He gave us both a hard stare. "But should any proof of fraternization surface for either of you, you will prove that I should not have trusted you. Keep that in mind."

Ellie wrung her hands before lifting one. He raised a brow at her. "I'm not a cadet," she pointed out in a faint voice.

"True. But I will treat you like one if you are to live so

closely with some of my boys. You may face some untrue allegations over your virtue as well."

"I'm willing to take that risk," she sighed. "I already feel safer in the Kite Flight's dorms."

"We will find you new accommodations shortly," he promised.

Ellie caught her lower lip between her teeth, holding in a reply. I felt the Commandant's attention shift to me. "I know I'm going to be accused of…things, sir," I said. "I don't like it, but it's better than having my things destroyed while I'm not in my room."

For a moment, something like sympathy lit his expression. "The Academy will cover the costs of your lost clothing and books. Thank you, ladies. You're dismissed."

As we proceeded to spend most of our day with the tailors, Ellie turned to me and said, "Why are all the cadets so afraid of the Commandant? He seems fair."

I chuckled to myself. "Same reason we're afraid of drill sergeants. They can PT us to death, but the Commandant controls our future. Plus, he doles out the extra punishments."

"Is everything about being a cadet ruled by fear?" she asked.

"Pretty much."

CHAPTER 13

FOURTH PLACE

W E RETURNED to our new dorm together, walking straight into Sharde saying, "You don't understand, this is the best thing for…" He glanced up from a conversation with Biggs and Feyring, putting on a bright grin. "If it isn't the girls!"

"Um. Hi." Ellie fluttered her hand as her greeting came out as a squeak.

"C'mon, have a seat," he said. We coaxed her to sit next to me, across from the three boys. "As I was saying, having you a part of the flight is the best possible thing for us."

Her eyes were twice their usual size. "Huh?"

"Because you're a *girl*. You're smart-like." He tapped his temple. "We've already proven that we can't win the monthly competition on brawns, but now we've got us an academic scholarship…uh, owner."

"Scholar," she supplied.

"Apprentice engineer," I added for her.

She sighed. "But you're also forgetting that I'm not a cadet."

"You live in the Kite Flight dorm now. You're an honorary member of our flight," he said, reaching over to pat her slender shoulder.

"Congratulations, I guess," Feyring said.

She blinked rapidly. "Thanks?"

In the meantime, I squinted at Sharde. "What monthly competition?"

"Let's take a walk." He stood and strode to one of the slat-like windows that were currently open, letting in chill air as well as bright sunlight. "See those flags?" He pointed toward the top of the field where we worked out every morning. I'd learned that it was called the Gryphon Green, or simply the Green by hustling cadets. There was a stage area, upon which were mounted several poles. Three colored flags fluttered there too, but we were too far for me to make out the details.

"Every month, there's a competition. First years take each other on in a series of competitive games we can play on the ground. There's dueling, an agility course, javelin throwing, some sports, and sometimes a melee. That's Falcon Flight's flag flying right now. They've won the last two competitions," he said.

I wondered why it seemed like he cared so much when he was also dedicated to getting as many demerits as possible.

"What about the second and third years?" Ellie asked. I nearly jumped. She'd flanked me silently, also looking out at the Green.

"By second year, we keep our flights but get jumbled up into five-person teams called elements too," he explained. "Unlike in the real military, I understand the trainers change around the element teams a lot to make us get used to sorting out our hierarchy and the strengths of our individual gryphons. The elements are given a letter and compete as their teams of five in the monthly competition. Whatever flag is flying for the second years right now just has a letter on it.

"And before you ask, the third years compete as individuals in jousting and other aerial sports meant to mimic real combat. The flag flying for them right now has the heraldry of the current Ace-to-be of their year."

My fingertips tingled. I didn't have heraldry yet, but I already knew I wanted to see it flapping in the wind one day.

"So, you want to win the monthly competition?" I asked, elbowing him.

His expression turned to his usual smirk. "I didn't say that. I just don't want to be last again. The first-place winners get extra leisure time along with having their flag flown, but the fourth-place losers automatically get put on a Saturday punishment duty together. Take a guess where Kite Flight's been for the last two competitions. Go ahead, I'll give you one guess."

I suppressed a groan. "Fourth."

"Yeah, so, I really want a Saturday without a punishment duty," he muttered.

"How can I help with this?" Ellie asked, her hands fluttering nervously by her sides.

Sharde glanced over his shoulder, where Feyring and Biggs were mid-argument about something. He lowered his voice. "I was hoping you could think up some miracle that'll have us actually working together."

While Ellie chuckled, I gulped a nervous swallow. That didn't sound promising.

THE POST ARRIVED WEDNESDAY EVENING, as Father had promised. Last weekend, I'd sent off a small book when the parchment was all folded up, and to my surprise, my family had sent back a box.

I opened it in the Flight roost after dinner, lifting out a lumpy yet feather-light sack first. "Guys!" I practically squealed, already knowing what was inside.

One of Mother's mottos was "Mallows make friends." She made these from a secret family recipe, cloud-like sweet morsels dusted with powdered sugar. I stuffed a handful into my mouth before sharing. We didn't eat them all in one go; that was a great way to get sick. I placed the half-full sack into our snack stash.

I sat down to read the small book my parents had sent back, unsurprised to see my mother's perfect cursive on a new page after my father's advice left off. Ellie sat close by, curiosity shining in her eyes. I'd learned that if I was reading something, she wanted to read it too, but this stuff was personal. I rested the open letter on my chest. "You know how you called your father your secret weapon?" She nodded. "Well, I think I have a secret weapon too," I said.

She seemed to understand, pulling out one of her replaced textbooks to study while I read the letter front to back. My eyebrows slowly crept up. I'd expected kudos and sympathy from my parents, but they'd gone a few steps further. I felt like a blushing Ellie in front of the flight her father had just threatened to PT to death.

Mother's greeting was simple:

Dearest Daughter,

I have taken the liberty to track down this Miles Glimmerwick fellow. Don't worry, I gave him a piece of my mind for putting words in your mouth.

Father, too, had gone above and beyond on my behalf, writing to the Commandant to back me up in saying I hadn't spoken to Glimmerwick and to express pointed concern about my safety in light of the paint incident. Now I worried that I'd be seen as a daddy's girl, that somehow my parents had overstepped while trying to help me.

But…would the other cadets even know?

My parents gave me plenty of advice and strategy. Once I got over myself, I hugged the pages to my chest, hoping I could fix my most pressing concerns by doing as they suggested.

I reached into the box, retrieving a smaller bundle that'd

been overlooked by the mallows. Father had mentioned that everything I'd lost to paint could be replaced, but I'd better take good care of this gift.

I unwrapped it and gasped. Ellie peeked over the edge of her textbook.

"My parents had this custom made," I said, picking up the pair of flight goggles with reverent fingers. The goggles I'd had had been damaged, and the pair the Academy had replaced it with were both made for men to wear, but this one had a smaller, sleeker design. The glass was tinted gray and shaped into two big circles. Shining brass etched with tiny feather designs outlined them, and the head strap was adjustable, buttery leather.

My eyes welled, unbidden. I wasn't an accomplished cadet; I hadn't given my parents any reason to go out and buy me something this nice.

"Hey, I bet you'd look nice wearing those," Ellie said gently.

She helped me adjust them to my head until they clung to my face just right. I had no reason to wear tinted lenses all the time, but an idea occurred to me. I rested the goggles at the ready on my crown, like I was about to go flying at any moment.

By the time we were done, I was on top of the world while gazing into my reflection. I looked more like a proper gryphon rider.

"Ellie?" I asked the girl smiling at my reflection.

"Yeah?"

"Would you mind putting your thinker to work for a problem of mine?"

CHAPTER 14

THE PRINCE'S WARNING

The next day, I was teased or taunted constantly for my new goggles. I didn't expect a group of boys to be so invested in something I was wearing, but here we were.

I set my attention toward the monthly competition happening that Friday. Instead of classes, we'd be playing games and competing all day. And then…they'd post our grades publicly. For the first time, my name and performance would appear on those lists.

Some of my fellow first years seemed excited, but the general attitude was resigned in Kite Flight's roost when Valentic came around to collect us for marching practice. I shared a class with our Cadet-Commander, Flight Training, so I saw a lot of Valentic in the form of an unsure mentor.

Father's letter had given me some insight about how we were ranked, even as first years. Individually. The trainers want to see strong leaders and successful cadets. So, Valentic visited us often and tried to teach us in a gentler way than the permanently unforgiving treatment of the drill sergeants.

Unfortunately, we needed a leader when Valentic wasn't around, and Father asserted that it had to be me. I barely knew where to start. I was still new, stumbling over the marching techniques the rest of my flight had perfected from their extra months here.

I lined up on the Gryphon Green with my flight for my first monthly competition when the sun was still low in the sky that Friday morning. "Remember everyone, every little bit counts. Just do your best," Valentic was saying. Birch bobbed his head in agreement next to him.

They, too, were called to attention by another cadet with a higher cadet rank than them, until the top-ranked third year was saluting the Commandant and beginning a march around the Green to present us to the Commandant and other trainers. We fell in like cogs to a well-oiled machine, and it was thrilling to be one of over a hundred teens and their gryphons marching at once as the air buzzed with jaunty energy.

I'd learned that we were practicing for the end-of-year Pass in Review when we did the same thing with flags, heraldry, formal uniforms, and the King of Altare and High Command on the stage, watching us present ourselves as the future of the gryphon knight corps. For now, the Commandant and his sleek ebon gryphon, Night, watched with steely expectation while the trainers took notes, probably noting mistakes and demerits for later.

Then, the games began.

"You guys are going down," Biggs exclaimed as we lined up against the nine boys of Osprey Flight in our PT clothes. I was nervous because talonball was being tossed out as the first sport we'd be playing. Talonball was a boy's game, with plenty of opportunities to tackle each other as either side attempted to score by kicking the ball into a goal that shifted to a different part of the field with each score.

No one passed me the ball for talonball, and we kept losing because Weslecker was a ball hog. "C'mon!" I ended up yelling at him across the field. "Have you ever played with a team in your life?"

He'd made eye contact for a moment, startled, but nothing changed. We ended up throwing our match to Falcon Flight because of him, and I watched his buddies pat him on the back at the end of the match. "Do you think he does it on purpose?" I asked Biggs as we took a water break together.

A frown crossed the boy's sienna-toned face as he glanced across the field before shrugging to me. "I think he might. You hear he's trying to get the Commandant to transfer him to Falcon Flight?"

I felt myself scowl. Biggs put his palms up, saying, "Hey, I have to room with the guy. He doesn't make much of a secret that he doesn't like any of us."

"I realize why we rank so poorly now," I said mostly to myself. If I wanted to be any kind of leader in this flight, I realized I needed to find a way to convince Weslecker that he needed to be a part of our team. It was nearly the end of October, and I bet he'd had his request to switch flights shot down several times by now.

We had a break as the sun rose to its zenith and the second and third years started competing in the air. I sat in the grass with one arm around Ari, new goggles in place over my eyes so I could stare at the sky and report on the feats of aerial prowess occurring just above us.

"*I miss playing hoops,*" he said, referring to the aerial sport the second years engaged in, where they passed a few weighted balls through the air. Scoring occurred when a ball was tossed through one of the hoops balanced on a fifteen-foot-tall pole and caught by someone from the same team on the other side.

"*Why don't we see if Sharde and Valentic will play a round with us?*" I invited.

He snorted. "*Puzzlebox can barely fly.*"

I'd only seen her in the sky during Flight Training, and unfortunately, I had to agree. She didn't do well in that wind-less training environment, but at least she tried. He, on the other hand, had refused to take wing enough that Commander Davis started overlooking our presence.

"You know why," he said more faintly, picking up on the direction of my thoughts.

I did know. I could feel his fear each time we were asked to fly in there. *"Commander Davis doesn't listen. We have to prove ourselves to him somehow,"* I sighed. Ari obviously knew all the maneuvers, but I hadn't expected how important the wind was to a blind gryphon. Without updrafts and the other invisible, complex currents of air he relied on, he floundered. It was easier to refuse rather than crash.

If he didn't fly in the training area, I also never fell. Flight Training was designed for cadets to fall a few times. We weren't tied down to our mounts yet, so we could get a feel for what was safe to ask of our gryphons before adding that additional safeguard.

"Maybe we can play a pickup game of hoops," I continued when he turned his beak away, heaving a sad sigh.

"Maybe later."

I rubbed his paws for comfort in the meantime. He fell asleep with his head in my lap, giving me a reprieve from the constant rain cloud of negativity he projected over our Link. I watched the third years joust midair while turning over my gryphon's plight.

There was a reason I'd asked for Ellie's help... I needed something made that would help him feel confident to fly in Flight Training. Just like how the Academy didn't have any uniforms or goggles made for a woman, the standard education for flight assumed gryphons were fully able-bodied. I was willing to bet that he was the first and only blind gryphon to ever aspire to rejoin the gryphon knight corps. He had more grit than anyone gave him credit for.

A beak nudged my elbow, and I glanced down, swallowing nervously to see baby Mireille standing there. I lifted myself off the ground as far as I could without jostling my gryphon, not spotting Prince Mateo right off. "Hi, baby," I said, holding my arm out to her. She snuggled against me with a burst of happiness.

"I see your brother all the time, but I miss my little Silverwind," I cooed to her. She looked up at me with shiny gray eyes, uncomprehending but still hanging on every word. I knew her rider was going to feel her effervescence over their Link and come looking for her, but I shamelessly held her anyway. In a few short months, she was going to be a gangly gryphon pre-teen and want nothing to do with me.

I wish it was this easy to make Ari happy, I thought. My gaze flashed to my gryphon still snoozing. I felt a little like a traitor. He was not a baby anymore, with problems that could be chased away with a few tickles of his belly fluff.

When a shadow crossed my path, I was unsurprised that it was Prince Mateo, looking as displeased as ever to see me.

"Are you trying to steal my gryphon?" he demanded, scooping up Mireille so quickly that she yelped and squirmed in his hold. He let her back down by his feet, and she groomed her puffed-out feathers like a miffed cat.

"Not at all. It's a fun day...Cadet Cortes." It still felt wrong not to call him by his title. "Why not let your gryphon make friends?"

To my surprise, he knelt a few feet away, petting Mireille until she stopped turning her beak away from him. "She doesn't need human friends," he said.

Funny, I almost thought he was about to say something decent.

"That's bull, and you know it," I replied through gritted teeth. "You just don't want her associating with the likes of me."

He glared when Mireille padded back to my side, his expression daring me to touch her. I rubbed behind her ears without breaking eye contact.

"You know, my father warned me about you," Mateo said,

his gaze falling to my hand. His lip curled. "I see what he meant now." Ari stirred, raising his head and listening in with a low growl. The prince stood and took a few steps back, eyeing my gryphon warily.

My blood froze in place, goosebumps flaring up my arms. I hadn't had time to really dread the looming presence of his father, but now all I could see was the king in Mateo's bronzed complexion and superior, aristocratic features. "What's that supposed to mean?" I demanded.

He sneered. "You think you're so special. The first girl in the Gryphon Rider Academy. It's past time a woman broke the edicts of Lord Orion and became a gryphon rider, huh?" He leaned in, his expression a careful blank. "I'm going to make sure it's as hard for you as possible."

Mireille's little beak turned from him to me and back before she uttered a small, alarmed peep.

I held in my reaction, letting it shake me to my core. "You're scaring your gryphon," I said tightly.

"Never touch her again," he said, reaching for Mireille. He startled when Ari sat up and held his beak open in clear threat, the feathers on the back of his neck rising.

The prince snatched his little gryphon away quickly before he could get bitten. She reached out a paw to me, but something told me this was the last time I'd get to spend time with her. That hurt far more than anything he had to say.

"Fine. But Cadet Cortes?" I met his gaze, mine sparking with anger. "No more red paint."

Surprise flickered over his face. "I didn't do that," he said, but I was already turning away.

"Sure," I muttered. Someone had, and his hostility put him to the top of my list of possible culprits.

CHAPTER 15

WOMAN'S WORK

I couldn't hide from the last event for first years, the duels, even when Prince Mateo pointed his practice sword at me and won our bout within thirty seconds. My teeth ground together hard enough to send up sparks as I watched the Falcon Flight flag get hoisted as the winners for the month.

Last place? Kite Flight.

Afterward, I went with the crush of cadets to view our posted grades, sure that this was the one area of Academy work I was excelling at.

"Hah!" a Falcon Flight boy exclaimed, making the sign of Orion and pointing me out to his buddies. "The heretic's failing! Look!"

I elbowed my way to the front of the group with a glare his way. "There's no…way…"

Gatekeeper take me. There was my name at the bottom of History and War Strategy with an awful grade. I had to scrub my eyes, drawing further derision as several boys waited to see my reaction.

I was failing Flight Training too, which didn't surprise me at all. But I was at the bottom of the class for Basic Gryphon Care—the same class Commander Davis usually dismissed me from earlier because I knew it all! My face flushed with rising emotion, eyes pricking at the corners to spot a failing grade in Ground Combat too.

You can't cry. You can't let them see that, I told myself. The only classes I was passing were Anatomy, with a lukewarm grade I believed I deserved, and World Cultures, where my name sat at the top of the pack.

I turned to run from this reality, but there was a ring of jeering boys, mostly from Falcon and Harrier Flight, that'd formed behind me while I'd looked at the grade postings. They made the sign of Orion while I looked around, trying to find an easy escape. It felt like they loomed over me, cutting off any avenue except standing there and taking every awful word they pelted at me: heretic, whore, harlot.

Callan stood right behind one of his flight-mates, watching with a grin splitting his face. "Rushing back to the arms of your flight?" he jeered.

"Hey!" an unexpected voice cut through everyone else's. I turned my attention to the burly boy shoving a few others aside for me. Soft-spoken Credell cringed as his outburst drew immediate attention, but he gestured urgently that I leave, which I did. I stumbled up the stairs and stopped halfway down an unfamiliar hall to curl into a ball and cry.

This was so unfair. I knew I was performing well in my academic classes. Sure, I could do better at combat and flying, but that didn't mean I deserved to be *last*. It took me a few minutes to realize I'd lost Ari at some point, rushing ahead in my urgency to see my grades.

I doubled back and swiped at my face, afraid I'd find him off getting plucked by the same crowd that'd taunted me earlier. Instead, my Link kicked in and helped me find where he'd hidden—next to the lockers in the women's bath, belly down, eyelids shuttered with an air of despondency about him. With the humidity and lingering cloud of women's fragrances, it must've been easy for him to find.

I knelt and pet down his wings so he'd know it was me. *"There you are. I thought you'd forgotten about me,"* he muttered.

"Never," I murmured.

"You left me." Now he snipped his beak at my hands, chasing away my touch.

I rocked back on my heels, scrubbing down my face. I wasn't just a screwup at my classes; I'd let my emotions get ahead of me. That split second I'd lost him, my grades had been the most important thing in my life. They were what stood between life and death for my gryphon.

"I'm sorry, Ari. I'll do better," I promised. I'd pass for him, but more importantly, I'd make sure I wouldn't leave him behind again.

Ari's eyelids fluttered upward. Without my touch to clue him into where I was, his beak pointed over my shoulder. *"It's fine."* He stood abruptly. *"I want a bath."*

The warm steam rising from the bathing pool called to me, too. I needed to wash the oily feelings of failure and fear off my skin.

Instead of getting Saturday off, the lot of us reported for laundry duty, sans our gryphons. I was in a particularly foul mood when I saw all the cadet uniforms and male underwear we had to clean.

"Well, we won't get this done by staring at it," Sharde said, the first to cut the tension after a crew of grinning maids showed us to our punishment.

"If anyone *dares* suggest I take care of this because I'm a girl, I'll feed them to my gryphon," I said with a scowl.

"Please. Ari likes me too much to eat me," Sharde replied flippantly. He started divvying up tasks with an air of old familiarity.

I didn't laugh or even look up from my work until I heard the approaching footsteps and deep chortles of a pack of boys. My teeth set to see all the members of Falcon Flight in casual clothes, probably stopping by right before they were flown off for their leisure day.

Prince Mateo came over to my tub, accompanied by the other person I'd pay good money to never see again. Victor—sorry, *Cadet-Commander* Callan—was with his flight of first years, joining in on their success.

They watched me scrub for a half-second, my gaze practically murderous toward them. I wanted to go out and have leisure time *so badly*, and here these two were, going off to collect that prize instead.

"Looks like she's where she belongs," Callan remarked, making the sign of Lord Orion, with an additional flick at the end in my direction. I flinched at the unexpected motion.

"Woman's work suits you, Walker," Prince Mateo agreed, the two of them snickering.

My fingers trembled under the soapy water. I wanted to wipe the smirks off their faces. The rest of their flight were touring around, jeering at my friends bent over their own tasks. Water sloshed. Feyring uttered a loud string of curses.

I reached into my tub. "Sorry, did you need a change of clothes? Here you go," I said, before throwing a balled-up shirt square into Callan's chest. Water sprayed everywhere.

He balled his fists, raising one in an obvious threat. "Gatekeeper take you, here—"

"Hey," barked the most welcome voice. Sergeant Kobarn's angry shouting chased off Falcon Flight before I could start a brawl. I didn't even get a demerit for leaving a wet patch on Callan, though his parting glare promised retribution.

As they left us to our hours of labor, I turned to Weslecker, scrubbing in the tub next to mine. "Those are your friends, huh," I said.

"Yeah."

I was a little surprised he'd deigned to reply. "Some friends they are." I added a good dose of sarcasm. It hadn't slipped my notice that he'd gotten taunted along with the rest of us.

Weslecker's mouth twisted, but he didn't say anything. If only he were a gryphon right now so I could feel his emotional state and figure out what he was thinking.

Still, as my adrenaline faded, it occurred to me that maybe he had nothing to say. If it were me, I wouldn't want to badmouth my friends either. Except I could clearly see that they were perfectly willing to taunt him and take leisure time without him while he struggled alongside the rest of us.

That's it, I thought to myself. The way to bring him over to our side shone before my eyes.

"Hey…you know we're your friends too, right?" I asked, waiting for the scoff. I wasn't disappointed.

"Yeah, okay," he murmured.

"The Academy is a game. I know it doesn't seem like that right now because we're not having fun," I continued. "Being a gryphon rider isn't all about who you know. You, as an individual, have to stand out. I saw you duel yesterday. You're good."

For the first time, I inspired a smile on his prim features.

"You must feel like you've been singled out because you're not in the same flight as Prince Mateo and all those guys you grew up with. Have you ever considered it could be a good thing? You're in a group that has no obvious leader. Kite Flight doesn't have a member of the royal family that we're used to bowing to. Maybe you were picked to stand out."

Just like that, his expression returned to a studious blank. "Look, I have nothing in common with you or anyone else in Kite Flight." His voice was painfully noble, designed for him to lift his nose. Which he didn't. Instead…I saw faint lines of fatigue lining his face. "I'm here because of my family name, not because I'm a lucky caretaker or someone identified for talent in fundamental school."

He shook his head slowly. "I didn't even *go* to fundamental school."

"Personal tutor?" I guessed.

"Indeed."

I bet he had little noble boy playdates, too.

"That sounds…" I drifted off as his expression shuttered. He was ready for an insult, but I just said, "…lonely."

Weslecker bowed his head back to his work in one long nod. "I'm sorry they're so cruel to you," he said more quietly. "You should know it's all Cadet-Commander Callan. He speaks poorly of you every chance he gets."

I sighed through my nose. He spent so much time with Falcon Flight…he would know Callan better than Valentic at this point. "I was seeing him. You know, before all this."

His brows raised. "Really? You strike me as more prudent than that."

I had to laugh. "Prudent? Is that the highbrow way to say smart?"

A faint blush tinged his cheeks. "Callan's a jerk anyway. I'm glad he doesn't lead our flight."

We bumped wrinkly fists to that.

WE SLUMPED BACK to the Kite Flight roost together. My eyebrows lifted in surprise to see Ellie in the middle of our common area, measuring my gryphon's beak with a tape. Ari's patient blankness flowed easily over our Link, but I'd thought he was getting some easy exercise today with the caretakers alongside the rest of our flight's gryphons.

Ellie glanced up from a clipboard filled with scribbles, startling. "Oh, hey guys."

"Whatcha doing?" Sharde asked.

My flight sprawled around or returned to their rooms. I knelt beside Ari, rubbing his beak in greeting.

"I allowed her to bring me here for…whatever this is," he said, butting my palm with a soft twitter.

"You know, engineering," Ellie was saying.

I spoke up for Ari and Sharde's benefit. "I asked her to help me design a new kind of reins so I have a way to send extra signals to him in flight."

The gryphon's shock registered while Sharde nodded along. "Did you know that gryphon reins are designed exactly like a horse's?" Ellie said, glee in her voice to share the research she'd already done. "In fact, traditional gryphon riding is nearly indistinguishable from horse racing."

"Except gryphons have wings," he pointed out.

"Well, yeah. I posit that there's been no need to change traditional rein design because gryphons have a level of independence in the air that horses don't need. Riders don't have to explicitly tell their gryphons how to angle their wings," she said.

Ari's feathers puffed out in offense. *"You think I need that?"*

"It's just for Flight Training. I want to help you work up your confidence." I petted his neck, hoping he would at least give it a try.

"Did you figure out if it's possible?" I asked Ellie.

"I have a couple ideas." She flipped her page of notes over, showing us a rough sketch of a gryphon's head with a second lead attached to two loops of metal designed to rest on the beast's brow. She pointed to it. "These will put pressure on Ari's temples. I'm thinking you could design a few types of tugs for different maneuvers."

I patted my reluctant gryphon's flank, beaming. This was exactly the kind of thing I was hoping she could figure out for me. *"I wanted to let you know that I secured the flight-testing space so we can be there alone. Just you, me, and the net,"* I told him. *"We can practice as much as you need."*

"I can have a prototype made for you this week," Ellie continued. "It'll be a little pricy."

Ari heaved a sigh before putting his head in my lap. His ears flicked for attention, so I gave him a good scratch. *"I'm willing to try it. Whatever gets us out of flying in that dreadful place faster,"* he said.

"Whatever the cost, I'll figure out how to pay it," I said. Ari was worth every bit.

CHAPTER 16

NOT JUST ANY FISH

"Deep breath," I said. Ari and I perched on a shelf in the rock of the Flight Training cave. I eyed the several-story drop to the net below, my palms sweating in my riding gloves. Two sets of leads rested in my hands, and I'd looped the slimmer set between my ring and middle fingers, pulled taut and at the ready.

Ari's nerves and my own blended all too well. I admired how he was willing to throw himself full speed and blind into this drop as we figured out how to navigate with me as his eyes. He was truly hurtling himself into danger, the difference between crashing into solid rock or soaring completely in my control. I didn't fault him for his anxiety.

"Go!"

He jumped, flaring out his wings. I tugged hard left, and we banked until I was nearly horizontal with the ground, descending in a tight spiral.

Falling was the easy part, though. We lurched upward clumsily at the end of the maneuver, his flight feathers brushing rock as I directed him upward in a tight zigzag. He balked halfway up, flinching when I tugged too firmly on the second lead. His wing scraped painfully over the rocky wall of the training room.

"Almost there," I assured him, correcting us hard until he slowed to land on the shelf once more. Sweat poured off me.

He shook himself, wordlessly demanding I get off his back. Drawing himself to his full height, he threw his beak back and screamed, throwing harsh echoes throughout the stone chamber.

"*Why is this so hard?*" he burst out.

I cautiously laid a hand on his shoulder, afraid for a split second that he'd bite me as rage bumped into our Link. "It's okay, Ari. These new reins should help you. We just have to practice—"

"*Stop,*" he demanded. He paced away, drooping his head toward the ground. The pulse of anger turned inward, shading with self-loathing. "*I'm tired of pity. I don't need excuses. What we're practicing is* easy! *I used to be able to do it in my sleep!*"

I clammed up, letting him scream and pace and rail at his disability. Within ten minutes, he slumped to the ground, belly down, beak making a furrow in the dirt. Only then did I kneel by him, rubbing soothing circles into his damp flanks.

"We'll try again tomorrow," I said.

"*Tomorrow won't change anything.*"

I BATHED TWICE a day from the day Ellie and I fitted and adjusted Ari's new reins. Tomorrow bled into several tomorrows, and I kept him going for "just one more day. Just one more practice run."

Our solo flight class had no grades or demerits, just myself and my gryphon developing the nerves of steel and trust level to fly together despite his disability. We started getting called on again to fly in our first real Flight Training class, with the hard stare of Commander Davis and most of the second years practically daring us to fail and dash ourselves against solid rock.

With my second set of uniforms finished, I started feeling like a true gryphon rider cadet upon donning them. They were all-black, with discrete buttons and a collar that tended to ruck up and start pulling against my throat. Despite the abuse I received regularly—the anonymous notes, and the subtle murmurs in a crowd about my heretic status—I was starting to grasp a sense of belonging.

Valentic and Sharde witnessed the successes that followed so much hard work. They also were present for my attempts to bring in Kite Flight, starting with the day I snagged Pereyra on his way to hide in his room and Weslecker right before he and Ironfeather left to spend time with Falcon Flight.

"I think we need to get to know one another better," I'd said, making all seven of my flight, plus Valentic, and our gryphons sit in a circle and talk.

It was the tensest game of twenty questions in my life. No one wanted to go first, so I just started by asking whatever came to mind. "Where are you from?" I asked Credell, the quietest of all of us. He looked the part of a great gryphon rider, with his muscles and bulk, but spoke just above a whisper.

"My family calls it rozash country," he murmured. "We live in the river valley Lithos wants so much. They send the monsters to blight our land. Gryphon riders have saved our farm so many times. I just…really wanted to be one and give back to my community."

"Hey, that's cool," Korvic said without sarcasm for once.

"Yeah." Credell's shoulders rose. It was his turn to ask a question, and he was already looking at Korvic, so he asked him, "How'd you get recruited to be a gryphon rider?"

"Oh." Korvic smirked and was right back to rolling his

eyes. "In fundamental school, I was kind of obsessed with gryphons. The library in my village was very small, but the librarian knew me because I kept asking when she was getting more gryphon books in. When the aptitude tests were announced, I focused on the parts the military wanted and aced them. Got real lucky and was picked for the Academy, Linked to a gryphon…and got put in *this* flight."

"We're going to be the best," Biggs said loudly over him as a few of the boys glared at the sarcastic way Korvic referred to us.

"Yeah, okay," Korvic sighed. "Sharde, when are you going to cut your hair? You get demerits for your appearance all the time."

The other boy laughed. "When Sarge can catch me with a razor!"

Biggs snorted. "Guys, Sarge is going to sneak in here with one just to get him in regulation for once."

We had a chuckle at the idea of the big man himself doing anything quietly.

I was optimistic until Weslecker admitted playing polo was his favorite sport.

"What's polo?" Biggs had asked.

"A fancy rich-boy thing," Sharde answered, rolling his eyes.

Just like that, we'd lost our most reluctant member again, going silent with his arms crossed. At least I'd learned that Feyring had a lovely singing voice when he wasn't busy yapping every random thought he had aloud. Korvic muttered something under his breath, and the boys started squaring up against each other in mutual offense after Feyring challenged him to say it louder.

So, we weren't great at talking to each other. I already knew that.

I'd found a lot more success inviting them all for pickup games on the Green in the evening. It let the boys tackle each other in talonball, really get that aggression out. They even started passing me the ball a few times.

"I don't think we're becoming closer friends," I admitted to Ellie one night after I lay down. My ever-present bruises and sore muscles ached the moment I went still at the end of each day. "Aren't the flights supposed to be bands of brothers?"

She barely looked up from her book. I figured she hadn't heard me, so wrapped up in her studies. After a few long minutes, she turned to me with an odd expression on her face. "The Commandant called me to his office today," she said.

I wondered if she was just as afraid of a random call to the Commandant's office as I would be. "But you're not a cadet," I said.

"Yeah. He just wanted to tell me that he had to close the investigation on our room. No one was able to give him anything conclusive about who'd taken red paint to our things."

"Figures," I muttered.

"He seemed really angry about it. Like, on our behalf. He apologized"—I shot her a look of shock—"and offered me another room so I didn't have to live in a boy's dorm anymore."

My heart sank. "You're leaving?" I'd gotten so used to having another girl around, to be able to share what I was experiencing with someone slightly removed from the situation but who still understood and was on my side.

She smiled and shook her head. "I told him what would make me happiest is if I could stay here, no questions asked. He said yes, as long as I stop making you fail room inspections. I'm staying!"

"You're staying!" I echoed, giggling gleefully with her. Kite Flight would keep its honorary engineer, and I'd still have a female friend to keep me grounded.

We soon had to snuff the lanterns for lights out, but I buzzed with happiness in the dark.

"Sivana?" she said.

"Yeah?"

"I have a suggestion."

I brought her idea to Sharde the next morning. "A prank? Together?" he echoed, raising a brow.

"The mostly innocent kind that won't give us too many demerits," I said.

He grinned. "*C'mon*. Those are the best kind." I gave him a serious look and he put up his palms. "Okay, okay, a mostly innocent flight prank. Who we hitting?"

"I think maybe that should be a group decision—"

"Falcon Flight, you say? I would love to prank Falcon Flight," he said over me.

I'd come to him first, hoping he had ideas, and by dinnertime, everyone knew to meet in our common area. Even Weslecker stretched out his long legs by the door while I snuggled Ironfeather in my lap.

Sharde arrived last, holding a dried filet on a fold of wax paper. "Do you guys know what this is?"

"A fish?" Biggs asked.

Sharde put his arm around the smaller boy's shoulders. "Not just any fish, my friend. This bad boy is a side of greenhead snapper. Plentiful, delicious."

I started to laugh, drawing a few glances.

"The chefs use this stuff for fish fry night. It's really cheap. A lil butter, lil seasoning, boom. Delicious," Sharde continued.

"Thank you for the cooking lesson," Weslecker said, sounding bored.

I was still chuckling. "Hold on, you're going to want to hear this!"

"Every caretaker learns not to give this type of fish to a gryphon firsthand. Don't they, Sivana?" Sharde asked. He was one of the only cadets who still used my first name.

"They sure do. I accidentally stank up the First's stables for days," I said.

"You see, guys, green-head snapper gives gryphons gas. Not just any kind of gas…the worst gas you've ever seen. And the worst part is, they love the fish so much, they'll eat it knowing that's what'll happen."

Biggs pulled his gryphon away from the filet Sharde had dangling by his side before Echo could take a nibble.

"I took the opportunity to liberate the kitchen of approximately ten portions. Who said extra punishment duties weren't worth anything? What say you all to Falcon Flight experiencing the wonders of green-head snapper firsthand?"

I watched Weslecker carefully, but the noble boy was smiling behind his clasped hands, leaning forward with a glimmer of interest in his eyes as Sharde outlined his plan. We could only pull this off if Weslecker was not only on our side, but able to keep his mouth closed about where the fish had come from.

"I'm in. Let's humble them a bit," he said finally. "But not tomorrow."

Sharde raised a brow. "No?"

"The next competition is this Friday. The fish can keep that long, right?" Weslecker rubbed his upper lip, hiding a devious smirk.

Biggs sat up straighter with a gasp. "It's time Falcon Flight wasn't first!" he exclaimed.

Could gassy gryphons accomplish such a miracle? I wondered. We were about to find out.

VALENTIC HAD LAUGHED and refused to help us to have some plausible deniability should we get caught. That meant I had two portions of green-headed snapper secreted in my bag that

Thursday, while everyone else had at least one and a clear target to slip theirs to.

I'd insisted on being the one to take care of Prince Mateo and Callan's beasts, remembering their taunts after the last competition all too well.

That evening at dinner, I took my tray and squeezed into the barest space Weslecker had left between himself and Prince Mateo. "Hey, guys," I said to a wave of frigid looks.

"What are you doing here, heretic?" Callan asked, scowling at me.

While the group was staring daggers at my audacity, Credell snuck up and dropped an extra piece of fish into one of the gryphon's bowls. He flashed me a fleeting smile before hurrying to Kite Flight's table.

I shrugged, popping a bite of black beans into my mouth and gesturing with my fork. "A member of my flight sits with you every day," I said.

Callan frowned toward Weslecker, a flicker of irritation there and gone in a flash. "That's different."

"Is it?" I countered, letting my gaze drift to where Mireille pawed at my leg, her big gray eyes pleading for attention. My fingers itched to pet her, but with her rider watching my every move, I didn't dare. "Does that mean I'm not rich enough, or that I'm not allowed because I'm a girl?"

"Go away, Sivana," Callan said sharply. Unlike Sharde, I could tell he used my first name as an insult.

I leaned forward, reaching into my bag, which I had propped on the side facing Weslecker. "Did you guys know that families from the Endoline Empire give their children two names?" I asked conversationally. "Cadet-Commander Callan once told me it's a language difference. I found it diffi-cult to pronounce his Endolian name."

Callan stared me down with clenched teeth. There was true hatred in his dark eyes, and in that moment, I regretted this distraction technique. Wax paper rustled as I spoke, everyone's attention on my face and words as I put a small filet of green-head snapper in Mireille's bowl and snuck a quick rub behind her ears. Hopefully she could forgive me later.

"But he told me it meant 'A Lifetime of Bountiful Victories' in his parents' native tongue," I continued. "Thus, in Altarian, his name is Victor. It's a lot like his gryphon's name…"

I glanced to the maroon and red gryphon by his side. "Last Light of Sunset, or just Sunset. I thought it was a cool tidbit."

Callan's face had turned red with repressed rage. The color stood out starkly from his olive-toned skin.

"If you're wondering, I knew Victor before the Academy," I said, pressing my luck as I passed the second fish filet under the table to Weslecker. Sharde approached with his food, taking a late dinner since he'd been serving yet another dinner duty punishment.

"Quit lying," he practically snarled.

"So your name doesn't mean—"

"Get away from me, heretic! You and your…flight-mate." He sneered toward Weslecker, who stilled. "Go sit with your trash flight, where you belong."

"Oh, hey, guys. Is this where we're sitting?" Sharde interrupted. He tried to sit next to Callan, who raised his balled-up fists. "Whoa, sorry."

A few of the soldiers on monitor duty shouted at our table, making us all stand up. Weslecker passed the fish behind his back to Sharde, who dropped it discretely into the bowl of Callan's gryphon. Sunset perked up when she saw the green-headed snapper.

We went without complaint to Kite Flight's table from there, though Weslecker's expression was stormy. "I doubt I'll be welcomed back there anytime soon. Thanks," he snipped.

I thought to myself, *Maybe that's for the best.*

The next day, I was thankful that the monthly competition was held outside. Falcon Flight stunk. Literally. My grinning teammates watched Osprey Flight get declared first place for the first time this year. Our rank? Third.

Falcon Flight was second, because some gas couldn't make them worse than us. I almost felt bad for the Harrier Flight boys, who, at fourth place, had a Saturday duty of mucking out the gryphon stables.

CHAPTER 17

An Unexpected Tutor

I EARNED envious looks when Commander Davis declared that I was finished with the Basic Gryphon Care class. That meant the caretakers would saddle Ari up for me each morning, giving me space to breathe before Flight Training rather than running from the Green all the way up to the top of the fortress every day.

I hoped that meant my grade would improve by the next grade posting, but it was a false one. Grades were updated a couple days later, and there I sat for Basic Gryphon Care, at the bottom. I went to speak with Commander Davis himself after Flight Training, swallowing down the dread caught in my throat.

"Yes, Cadet Walker?" he asked in irritation when I ignored the cold shoulder he gave me upon dismissing the class. I followed him out of the training cave, Ari at my side.

"Sir, I wanted to ask about my grades. You said yourself there's nothing else you can teach me for Basic Gryphon Care, but—"

"You earn the grades you deserve. I suggest you not blow off the class." He shot a glare over his shoulder. "You thought you could just skip because the caretakers saddle your gryphon now?"

"But…" I thought that was how things worked in class. He continued walking, leaving me standing there in confusion.

Well, if I didn't like it, I decided I would need to talk to the Commandant rather than Commander Davis. So, I resolved to continue showing up to the class I'd "finished."

Weslecker caught my attention the next day when I stopped before the grade postings again, checking to see if anything had miraculously changed. "I would like to offer you a trade of mutual benefit," he said.

I was pretty used to his prim manner by now, but this was a surprise. He didn't usually talk to me unless it was dinner time, since he'd been turned away from Falcon Flight's table permanently. "Oh?"

He handed me Ironfeather. I'd started noticing the little gryphon was heavier than ever, and a grunt escaped my lips as I hefted his bulk. He twittered, beaming a rainbow of happy emotion to me in greeting.

"See this gryphon? He loves rolling in the grass right before I have to groom him for class," Weslecker sighed. "Will you help me ace Basic Gryphon Care?" He tapped the page, where his name was only a couple spaces up from mine. A failing grade he'd earned.

I glanced between the gryphon, who smelled distinctly of grass, and his rider. "You want me to groom him for you before you get graded on it," I guessed.

"Yeah. But look. I see you struggling in this class." He gestured toward the Ground Combat grades, where he was amongst the top students. "I could give you extra help."

I bit my lip. If Davis caught me grooming Weslecker's gryphon for him, I was sure we were in for a world of demerits and screaming. But I'd seen Weslecker duel. He had the benefits of private tutoring way before he ever came here, while I'd assumed incorrectly for most of my life that I'd never need to learn how to hold a weapon.

"Okay," I said slowly. "But you're not going to become a master caretaker overnight."

Weslecker shrugged. "And you won't be an expert duelist that fast, either. Every little bit helps, right?"

I wondered if that was true in the world where Commander Davis and the other instructors could continue to fail me horribly. But I still nodded politely.

I HELPED Weslecker on the sly, and in return, he and I met when we both had a spare moment to square off with wooden training swords in the circle of packed earth where we practiced in Ground Combat class. "I think I've figured out why you're struggling so much," he said during one session after knocking the sword out of my hand for the second time that evening.

"Oh?" I grumbled, stooping to pick it up. My arm still smarted with the force of his blow.

"I'm going about this wrong," he admitted. "Mateo and I had an Endolian tutor who taught us how to use several weapons, including the cavalry sabers." He indicated the extra-long and skinny fake swords we practiced with, designed to give extra reach for mounted fighters.

"Yeah, yeah," I muttered, assuming he was showing off his family's money again.

He read my expression and put his palm up. "I'm trying to say I learned how to wield a weapon differently than they teach here at the Academy. My tutor taught me Triple-R, the Rushing River Rapids style. Whichever style you're learning in Ground Combat, it's different than mine."

My shoulders started to drop. "So you can't actually tutor me?" I asked.

He smiled reassuringly. "The exact opposite. We'll start at the very beginning and disentangle what you've learned, so you'll know two styles by the time you leave the Academy."

This was the beginning of Weslecker and me seeing each other a lot more. We partnered first in Ground Combat and had a few quick discussions with our instructor, the perpetually shirtless Commander Falirin, who clarified that the Academy taught a style called Gryphon's Extra Talon, though the average cadet didn't need to know that.

Weslecker brightened with excitement at the knowledge and constantly compared the motions. It was like I was seeing a completely different boy when we practiced, as he poured every bit of his passion into mastering both styles and teaching me along the way. I took to Triple-R much easier, as it was a more aggressive style made for solo fighters that could also be used on gryphon back. It had fast, sweeping motions, designed for constant movement and momentum like a river's endless flow.

Weslecker would stand behind me, hands on mine, guiding me through the motions. We fought invisible enemies together, and he heaped praise on me each time I got it right. "I wish you were my actual instructor," I admitted one evening. With the exception of Signe, none of the Academy instructors bothered telling me when I did a good job.

A touch of color lit his cheeks. "You think I could be one day?"

We were practicing against each other again. I tried to push him back with sweeping motions of my practice sword, while he practiced the defensive blocking pattern and quick jabs of the Gryphon's Extra Talon style.

"Absolutely. You're turning me around, after all," I said. It turned out Commander Falirin noticed the changes in me and my poise. My grade was still failing, *but* I wasn't last in the class anymore. Weslecker was basically a miracle worker. If I ever passed Ground Combat, it'd be single-handedly because of his tutoring.

"Well, you're an excellent study." He said it with a smile, even as he disarmed me and pointed the tip of his weapon at my throat. It meant he'd won this round, but in the end, he always did. My fingers were numb with the force of his last blow.

"Thanks," I said on a sigh. "But you're still so much stronger than me."

His expression sobered, and he shared what I was thinking. "That's not really going to change, though. Every man you face will have that advantage." He gestured for me to pick up the sword, assuming a starting position again for another round. "The only thing I think we can do for it are strength exercises and train until our fingers bleed. Technique always beats brute force."

A part of me warmed at the idea of having a training partner stick by my side until I had the technique to actually defeat brute force. Especially one so passionate for the craft as Weslecker.

"Watch out. One day I'll even beat you," I said.

A glimmer of eagerness lit his eyes. "I can't wait."

CHAPTER 18

ARI'S LIMITS

For every two steps forward, there had to be at least one backward. Ari squawked in clear dismay when Davis announced our next maneuver to master: gryphons catching an unseated rider. "Flight Training is the only time you will have a net. It's vital your beasts learn how to safely catch you should your saddle ever be cut or, gods forbid, your restraints break. Falling is the number one cause of death amongst gryphon riders."

In the back of my head, I felt what it was like to have feathers and how Alamid's weight leaving Ari's back had felt so final. *"No. No no no,"* Ari chanted. He'd been blinded by the same spray of acid that'd ruined the saddle. Without his sight, my gryphon hadn't been able to save his first rider.

My shoulders slumped with dismay. I had no doubt Ari would refuse to practice again. No special set of reins would help us here. If I ever fell from Ari's back in combat, it would be the end, just like it was for Alamid.

"It's okay. We figured everything else out. There has to be something that'll help you with this too," I told him.

"There's one gryphon here that's already been educated in

the technique of catching his rider." Davis's hard gaze landed squarely on Ari and me. My gryphon shook his head preemptively. "Perhaps he'd like to demonstrate."

"He wouldn't, sir," I answered a moment later.

"That's yet another demerit for not being able to control your beast," he said without missing a beat, adding the mark against me to his clipboard. I'm sure he had a special tally just for me. He pinned me with an irritated stare. "I don't care what your gryphon says. This is a direct order from one of your commanding officers: demonstrate the technique."

My back went rigid with his tone. He wasn't going to let this go until Ari caught me in free fall. I peered over the edge of the platform to the net waiting far below. A jump from this height would break several bones, so I would need to be on Ari's back somewhere in between the platform and net to land safely on it.

"Bite me," I projected to Ari as I suppressed a sigh and turned to my gryphon. It was the only thing I could think of to get out of this without refusing a direct order.

I reached up to adjust Ari's harness, and without a moment's hesitation, he clamped his beak around my forearm. Shocked cadets shouted all around us…but it worked, and instead of greeting the net firsthand, I went to the infirmary.

ARI DRAPED himself despondently over a cushion in our common area, radiating self-loathing. I rubbed down the edges of the bandage around my bite wound for what felt like the fifteenth time while lost in thought. The entirety of Kite Flight, Ellie included, sat in a circle, brainstorming possible solutions.

"You could tie a line between you and him?" Biggs said.

Valentic shook his head. "The point of the exercise is to teach a gryphon how to catch a free-falling rider before they hit the ground. There are no tethers or lines in the real world, so Commander Davis won't allow them here either."

Ellie's charcoal pencil was flying over a sheet of paper on her clipboard. I figured if anyone could figure this out, it was her.

"What I don't get is why that bastard keeps insisting on singling out a disabled gryphon," Sharde muttered.

"Again, real world. Ari has to be able to do everything an able-bodied gryphon can do," Valentic pointed out.

I bit my lip. No one here knew that the king had threatened Ari's life if we failed out of the Academy. My declining grade in Flight Training was starting to make our place here shaky. I knew it; Ari knew it. If we couldn't think up some solution, the consequences were huge.

"So," Ellie said, putting her pencil down. "We are aware that gryphons rely on their instincts when it comes to wind currents and open spaces. This isn't the first time Ari has struggled in the enclosed space where Flight Training is held, but I think in this case, it will work to his advantage."

A smile was starting to engulf her mousy features. "Did you guys know it's not against the regulations to wear a bell?"

"Really?" Sharde asked.

She beamed. "Yup. It says nothing about bells. I've read the cadet handbook a few times now."

"Unlike you, Sharde." Feyring elbowed him, and the older boy smiled wryly.

"Ari might not be able to see, but it's a known phenomenon that losing one sense means the rest grow stronger," Ellie continued. "If Sivana falls, she could jingle-jangle a bell on her way down. It'll take some practice for him to rely on his hearing to find her midair, but I don't see why this isn't the perfect solution."

"You're brilliant," I said.

"I know," she said matter-of-factly.

"Hold on a second." Sharde held up a finger. "Why did you read the cadet handbook?"

She shrugged, adjusting her glasses. "I was curious."

He tapped his temple. "Girls. They read when they're bored."

ARI WAS NOT THRILLED to practice. *But* he did catch me.

When no one else was watching, of course. I was sure to wear a belt lined with bells, creating a racket each time I flung myself off my gryphon's back. My back and sides were developing crisscross patterns of bruises from hitting the net hard and bouncing. I now knew how deep the hole was underneath the net—a solid fifteen feet, cut jaggedly of dark stone that must've resisted terraforming.

Ari released a frustrated screech in Flight Training after we were called on first...and I hit the net yet again. The outlines of watching heads lined the far-off balcony. One cupped his hands over his mouth, shouting, "Don't worry, Walker! You can be our class mascot until you fail out of this class."

I scowled up at Callan as the net ceased its quivering bounces. The sturdy thing had to be magically reinforced, either to strengthen the net or the bolts connecting it to the wall. Instead of yelling back and disrupting Ari's hearing further, I jingled my belt so he could descend and hover without getting his talons snagged in the net. Climbing back into the stirrups while he waited was becoming a practiced motion for us.

We ascended to the balcony, landing to see Callan and Valentic nearly nose to nose. Rather than taking notes on Ari and me, Commander Davis was in the process of shoving both boys apart.

I glanced to Sharde, who looked a little disappointed. "I was hoping someone would finally punch him," he muttered.

"What happened?" I asked in an undertone as Davis called on a different boy to show off the maneuver properly.

Sharde snickered. "He suggested you lend your bells to Callan, because Sunset hasn't been great at this either."

"Oooh." It had to be salt in the wound that Birch had caught Valentic each time they'd been called on. For once, they'd mastered something before Callan.

"And then Callan said he hoped Birch would drop Valentic if this were real."

"*Oh*," I hissed.

My friend was practically gleeful. "Right? Valentic said at least Callan would hit the ground first, with his fat head. But then…Davis just had to stop them."

I shrugged, not so bothered that they hadn't fought. Despite having so many boys in heated competition, true fights were rare. The last two who'd thrown punches had been given a whole month's worth of punishment duties. Not just on Saturday, but every evening, akin to Sharde and his honorary position in the kitchen when his demerit count overflowed. Callan deserved that, but not our Cadet-Commander.

I felt hot attention on me and glanced up, realizing I was on the other end of an angry stare from Callan. I didn't know what I'd done to earn his ire this time, but I suspected it was related to telling his flight that he and I had history beyond the Academy. He probably suspected we'd pranked his flight too.

But what was he going to do other than throw petty insults around? Maybe grab some red paint. I had my hunches it was either him or Prince Mateo that'd ruined my old room, and I hadn't forgotten, even if it seemed like the Commandant had.

Ari and I returned to practice more after classes were finished. We practiced every evening. I even skipped Kite Flight's talonball night and dragged my sorry, sore self out of bed early that Sunday to saddle up Ari and proceed to jump off his back some more.

In other words, I was desperate. We had to pass Flight Training. I knew for a fact that Ari was an outstanding flier—he'd been part of the First, after all. We just had to overcome this last flaw in his new lifestyle.

The first time I hit the net for our Sunday training session, it wobbled strangely beneath me. I'd slammed my body into this thing countless times, but it'd never groaned like bending metal. A bolt shot from the wall, stirring the wisps of my hair as it just barely missed my head. Another whipped free of the stone, and another.

"Ari!" I screamed, grabbing two fistfuls of net as the whole thing rapidly collapsed. My body bounced once and would've gone feet first into the jagged rock below if it weren't for my handholds.

My gryphon's emotions turned to sheer terror as he heard the sharp echoes of the net's anchors failing. *"What's happening?"* he demanded.

"The net's falling!" I screamed back.

The net tangled up from the force of the violently displaced bolts. It lurched downward another heart-stopping foot as Ari dove, talons out to catch the material before the last two supports shot their way free.

One of my hands slipped as the net spun with the loss of one of those bolts. It ensnared my arm and twisted it all wrong. My cries turned to wails of pain as Ari struggled to lift the weight of the net when the last support buckled. His panic filled my chest as he lowered the mass to the rocks.

Tears streamed down my face as I struggled to stay conscious instead of falling into the white void of screaming agony that'd once been my right arm. Ari shook his paws free of the loops trying to snare his talons. Carefully, he sniffed me and made a low croon of dismay. *"This is my fault."*

"N-no." I fumbled to rest my good hand on his head. "G-go get h-help."

CHAPTER 19

SABOTAGE

Being a Sunday, it would take Ari an agonizing amount of time to find an able-bodied person to rescue me. Our Link faded to nothing as he traveled out of range of our emotion-sharing bond. I lay there nearly out of my mind with pain. My arm was unable to remain still, and each twitch sent spasms of torment through the rest of my body.

I vaguely picked up the sound of stone grinding before new light flashed over my face, blinding with its intensity after the darkness at the bottom of the flight training cave. There was another entrance to this space several yards away, hewn from the rock. Standing in the threshold was a tall, broad-shouldered silhouette that swam in ghostly doubles before my eyes.

"Commander D-Davis?" I croaked. "T-thank the gods."

The man glanced over his shoulder before entering the cave alone and partially closing the secret entrance behind him. A magelight bobbed over his shoulder, its beams focused on me. "You survived," he said flatly as he drew a knife from his belt.

I tried to sit up, despite being tangled with what felt like two hundred pounds of net. His expression was hidden behind the magelight, but I realized it couldn't be friendly, not with his disappointed tone and a knife in his hand as he advanced on me. He pointed the tip at my throat. "Don't move."

I swallowed and tried to feel for Ari, screaming for him over our too-thin Link as he continued looking for help. *"Ari! Ari, come back!"*

"Heretic," Commander Davis hissed, making the sign of Orion at me, with the added flick of his fingertips in my direction. "It'd solve all my problems if you'd just *died* like you were supposed to."

I wailed aloud as his boot came down on the net, further pulling my arm into an unnatural position. Agony fried down my spine, paralyzing me as he loomed with the knife at the ready.

"Ari! Help!" I cried in desperation.

Distantly, I felt an echo of emotion from my gryphon. *"Sivana?"* he called back in a panic. I could practically feel him bumbling blindly into a wall, trying desperately to reverse course.

"I can't believe Jamison allowed you here," Commander Davis was saying. It took me a few seconds to realize he was referring to the Commandant's real name. "It's a good thing a truly devout man is willing to pay to have you removed before you can become a black stain in our country's history."

"W-who?" I managed to ask. He had me pinned without effort with his boot on the net, though I turned my head and neck away from the gleaming tip of the weapon being lowered toward my unprotected flesh.

"Don't worry your empty little head," he said with a chuckle. "You'll be answering to the Gatekeeper for your crimes soon."

I was taken aback by the glimmer of true malice in his eyes as he carved a wound into the skin right below my collarbone before lifting the bloodied tip of his knife toward my face. I quaked in terror as it hovered over my left eye.

"I'm coming. Just hold on a little longer," Ari reported.

"Hurry," I urged. I could feel my heartbeat throbbing in my ears as the knife moved to my forehead to finish cutting what I assumed was the symbol of Lord Orion. In fundamental school, I'd learned that there was a not-too-distant age where heretics and oath breakers were marked in such a way before being put to death in various gruesome ways.

A gryphon's screech echoed through the cave as Commander Davis began to make the mark on my forehead. Wetness trickled into my hairline from the open wound that cut abruptly sideways as he reared back. Rapidly descending like an avenging shadow was Ari's form, his wings tucked tightly to his sides.

"Ari! Here," I said as loudly as I could muster and jangled the bells on my belt. He snapped his wings out and landed heavily on the other side of me. Feathery ruff raising, he loosed a deep-throated battle roar.

Commander Davis backpedaled from me as Ari's talons swiped through empty air. "Hah! He can't see," he exclaimed, just to duck to the side just in time to dodge the heavy *clack* of my gryphon's beak closing where his elbow had been.

Their figures danced before my eyes as I tried to focus on their fight and help Ari nail him. *"To your left…no, right. Straight ahead,"* I said. Ari's frustration raised until his beak closed around the man's leather armor, ripping it up the side-seams.

That must have woken a serious fear in Commander Davis, as he rushed to the secret door and slammed it behind him, sealing me in with my gryphon. "Gatekeeper damn you both," he snarled right before the rock closed seamlessly.

Ari huffed furiously, his hide still puffed out. He lowered his beak to the ground and rooted around until he found me, resting his bulk over my lower body protectively. *"Help is* coming," he said. *"I'm sorry I couldn't be here sooner...and that I wasn't good enough."*

I rested a hand over his feathery wing, my lips poised to say, "You saved me, that's enough." I don't think the words escaped, though, before darkness carried me away.

I WOKE FROM A MAGIC-INDUCED SLEEP, colors blurred to a muddy palette. My heart beat sluggishly, returning feeling and emotions with the speed of chilled honey poured from the bottle.

I hadn't felt this way since I'd underestimated a wild-born gryphon who'd temporarily been stabled with the First. His warning bite had snapped my wrist. If the gryphon had been a female, she wouldn't have warned or telegraphed her attack, just taken my hand off. I was spoiled by Valtora.

For a few minutes that felt like hours, I wondered if I'd hallucinated my whole life since then. Maybe I was still a silly caretaker that loved gryphons so much I'd gotten injured trying to tend to a new one.

But even in the midst of this delirium, I knew it wasn't true. Alamid had left a bouquet of pink "laughodils" by my bedside, his favorite gift to say, "I love you kid, but that was stupid."

There were no pink flowers this time.

Instead, I came back to wakefulness realizing I had gryphons instead. Ironfeather lay on my chest, his concerned face only a few inches away. Mireille sat by my hip, her taloned paw batting at her brother's tail. "Hmm?" I blinked at her presence but couldn't remember why it'd be unusual.

Resting over my legs was Puzzlebox, her feathers nearly blending in with the white sheets. She squeaked excitedly, popping to her haunches when she realized I was awake.

"Not so fast," I rasped. She'd shaken the bed, jostling the heavy and numb weight where my right arm should've lain.

Bandaged and splinted, it was trapped at a perfect right angle in a sling.

How am I supposed to pass Flight Training now? I thought in dismay.

More gryphons chattered around my bed. I recognized Echo's chirrups and the deeper register of Birch's birdsong. I wasn't the only one smothered by gryphon cuddles. Ari had laid himself on the floor by my bedside, flat out on his belly. He'd plucked a few feathers from his wing, leaving a bald patch. I recognized the dejected pose, though now he had several younglings from our flight, plus Birch's more solid yearling presence, to lean on rather than waiting alone in an empty stable.

"Hey, guys," I said slowly, surprised by the turnout and lack of human supervision.

"Ah, you're awake." A nervous Tulari healer appeared close to my bedside in what felt like a blink. She cast her glance over my feathery friends before flashing me a smile. The mage mark on her face wrapped around her left temple, fully invested arcane symbols glimmering in a healer's deep green against her coppery skin. "Will you please call off your flock? The gray one gets nippy."

"Do you mean that one?" I pointed at Mireille on a hunch, earning a nod.

I reached out to pet the youngling, and she twittered while giving me an innocent look. "Don't grow up so fast," I whispered to that face.

I kept Mireille distracted so the nurse could help me sit up and drink slow sips of water. "You've been out for a full day to sleep off the worst of the pain," she said. "Since your injury was not life-threatening, you received a minimum dose of magical healing when we set your arm, and we removed some, ah, cuts before they could become scars."

"Why not more?" I asked. Tulari healers could be miracle workers. They'd restored Ari's facial structure when he'd been hit in the face with rozash acid. But the team in the fortress had left my arm in a sling.

"It's too easy to develop a tolerance to magical healing, young lady. You won't find a Tulari willing to force your bones to mend faster, not if it means one day you experience a more traumatic injury and our magic can't fix you." She lectured me further, repeating herself until my lethargic brain got the message.

"Do you remember what happened?" she asked, concern bleeding into her professional expression.

"I..." It was vague but there. The net, Commander Davis...something about being a heretic. I touched my chest, just to find whole, unscarred skin. "I need to talk to the Commandant about that."

"He has already been told about the situation we found," she said. "You are to rest first, and he'll call you when you're well enough to talk."

I was soon strong enough to get out of bed, so I needed to figure out how to get all my fellow cadets' gryphons back to them. The healer let me take care of it, saying I had the day off from classes.

I won't lie; I definitely did not return my little flock right away. Instead, I took them to Kite Flight's roost and crafted a toy out of a piece of string and one of Ari's loose feathers. My gryphon lay across my lap while I figured out my left arm coordination, flicking the toy around for the younglings and Puzzlebox, who was more than eager to join them.

Birch lingered to groom Ari, the two of them passing emotions and thoughts back and forth privately. I hadn't realized it, but it seemed my gryphon had befriended the speckled male while I wasn't watching. Ari was in a low mood, huffing sadly and retreating to his side of the Link. His beak reached for the bald patch on his wing, but Birch's paw pushed it away.

Prince Mateo walked in to see all of this, his brow drawing in reaction. "Oh, that's where she is," he muttered.

My heart sank. I didn't want him to rip Mireille away again. "Hello, Cadet Cortes."

He nodded. "Walker."

To my surprise, he sat on a nearby cushion, watching Mireille as she ignored him and pounced on the feather toy instead. I itched to say something, but what? This situation was so surreal in the first place. I was pretty sure most injured cadets didn't wake up with their gryphon friends around them.

"I'm sorry about your arm," he said. "The Commandant thinks the net was sabotaged."

I stiffened, waiting for the insult since he was starting off decently.

He sighed. "Commander Davis is gone."

My head whipped toward him. "What?" I blurted.

The prince arched one of his thick black brows. "It's not like the Commandant has *said* this to anyone. But the Flight Training room is barricaded, and the Commandant himself taught Basic Gryphon Care this afternoon. He told us Davis is on 'administrative leave.'"

Ari raised his head as a slow smile gathered on my face. He pushed his confusion toward me over our Link. *"You just had your arm broken, and this man attacked you. Why are you happy?"*

I huffed a little laugh. "He's *gone*. He tried to kill me, and he's gone!"

"I don't know if it was that extreme—"

I met the prince's eye and said firmly, "He tried to kill me. Knife and all." I gestured to my chest and forehead.

Mateo's lips quirked. His gaze read my face in a rare moment of uncertainty. "Is it true..." His dropped his voice to a whisper. "...that my father is going to have your gryphon executed if you fail?"

He laid the reminder over me like a wet blanket and nodded at whatever he saw in my expression. "I understand so much better now," he said mostly to himself.

This wasn't the first time I realized that Mateo had the king whispering in his ear. But for a split second, I felt like maybe he disagreed. His glance went to his own gryphon, something like pity in his expression.

"Now that you're better, I'll be taking my gryphon back. Come, Mireille," he said, snapping his fingers like she was a dog. He left abruptly with her.

I puzzled over this softer moment with the prince before deciding he was still a jerk, even if he must've approved of letting Mireille spend some time with me.

IT TURNED out that the first years didn't have a monthly competition in December. A small blessing, because I knew Kite Flight would be at an even more severe disadvantage since I was forced to sit out most physical activities. Ari lay out beside me most days, as gloomy as a full rain cloud. Nothing I said could convince him my broken arm was anything but his fault.

"We're going to fail Flight Training anyway. It won't matter soon. I knew I wasn't good enough to be here," he muttered.

He was so sure of his fate that he didn't believe me when I read off my semester grades to him. We'd passed every-thing...even Flight Training, though we hadn't had to attend in weeks. By some miracle, I was passing even the classes like Ground Combat.

I scratched behind his ears, hoping to perk him up. "We're

still in the game," I reassured him. I wanted to climb to the top of Fortress Aerie and shout it. *We're still here!*

In the meantime, the flight prepared for a special Pass in Review, which we were only included in on formality. The yearly Cadet Games were approaching, a second- and third-year-only affair that would showcase the up-and-coming talent to at least one representative from each Flight.

Third years would be assigned to squire for a handful of eligible Flights for the second half of their last Academy year. The Cadet Games were their last chance to show off for the best placement.

That meant my father and Valtora were coming to the fortress, and I had yet to hear back from my family since describing the net incident and the aftermath. The silence felt like anger, even though I knew it was only a couple weeks before I would see my parents again for the holiday break.

Kite Flight marched in third place out of four for the first years, meaning Father would see two things: Prince Mateo's flight humbled by their smelly showing in November, marching in second place, and my own flight not bringing up the rear for once. When we saluted the stage, I spotted his red hair where he stood with the other Commanders.

My heart sank. He looked *furious* when he spotted me.

"What's the matter?" Ari asked, picking up my heavy emotions over our Link.

"It's probably nothing, but..." I described the expression. I might prefer my father's even temper, but when he was angry, that redheaded rage made me want to cower unseen behind the nearest couch, no matter what age I was.

Ari tilted his beak up, his emotions flaring with disbelief. *"I will talk to my mother,"* he promised.

I barely heard the Commandant's speech as we stood in our flights, awaiting the Cadet Games. He was mostly addressing the third years anyway. I started wondering how the Academy would feel with so many cadets gone next semester.

"They will throw the second years straight into boiling water. You should pay close attention," Ari said to my thoughts, though he sounded distracted. In my periphery, I could tell he was concentrating hard with his brow bunched up. *"Ah. Valtora says not to worry. There's a lot going on that your father didn't want to write down."*

"Really?" I resisted shifting my weight, restless to know what it could possibly be.

As soon as the Games started, the first years were allowed to sit around. We had a picnic while watching the third years joust. A shadow fell over my towel, and I glanced up, swallowing hard. Usually, it was a bully sneaking up on me, but standing over me this time was Father, with Valtora already bowling a grumbling Ari over in effusive greeting.

"Got anything to share, kiddo?"

He ate half of my bread and cheese, his expression vastly cooled from the lava tide of anger during the Pass in Review. I started wondering if I'd hallucinated it. Valtora sat with her front paws in my lap, her head close and ears pricking expectantly.

She greeted me with a cluster of emotion and mental images. *Humans are stupid,* she seemed to be saying.

"Oh?" I scratched her behind the ears and beak.

Making things too complicated. He should just kill his rival.

"Valtora," my father said with a hint of reproach. She twittered in a sweet register, her golden eyes wide. It was the most innocent face she could make.

I glanced between the two of them. "What's going on?" I asked.

"I'll tell you later," he promised.

"Valtora wants me to tell you that he's gone after Commander Davis in a baffling human way," Ari reported, sounding puzzled.

Rather than killing him, which I supposed was Valtora's first solution.

"*What did he do?*" I asked. Weeks of nerves hinged on this one question.

"*She thinks he's not acting fast enough. He's pushing this up the chain of command and demanding an investigation…and they are not cooperating. It sounds like Commander Davis will be returning if no evidence of his direct involvement is found.*"

My stomach turned. It was hard to find any wrongdoing if no one would look for it.

CHAPTER 20

SECRET SNACK POCKETS

Valtora told us everything as I watched the Cadet Games, numb at the thought of Davis coming back. Father had only a few hunches as to why the Chief of Staff of the gryphon knight corps wouldn't meet with him. Few could sway such a powerful man, save for the king himself.

"That doesn't mean there won't be an investigation. Just that it will be the slowest thing you've ever seen," Ari said. *"By the time they're done, there will be a new net up and no evidence left behind."*

I balled my hands into fists. *"That's so unfair."*

No wonder Father was so angry. I was too…but more than that, a deep squirm of fear was burrowing into my gut. If Davis was working for the king, then there was clear evidence the man who ruled Altare wanted me crippled, or worse, as part of a "training accident."

Months without seeing his red-rimmed eyes had made me complacent. I realized now that he still hated me and would continue to do so no matter what. In his eyes, I had defied Lord Orion's will, and that was a cause for death, no matter the circumstances.

It couldn't be fixed. This wasn't an enemy to kill or a bully to ignore. I could be the best cadet here, but I was still a girl. Did the king think my name's appearance in the *Kaiamear Gazette* was a taunt? Oh, gods above. My "quotes" were nothing but a mockery of everything King Cortes believed in.

But Father didn't seem to notice his gryphon had already shared everything and that I was an anxiety-riddled mess beside him. We discussed my grades. He insisted on meeting my flight. He shook Sharde's hand the longest. "Son, there's an easier way to get what you want."

Sharde gave him a leery look. "I told him about Puzzle-box," I interjected.

"The Academy's designed to torture you if you don't fall in line. I already know that," Sharde replied.

"Let me give you some wisdom from the other side," Father said, leading my friend off to walk a lap around the Green.

I watched them go, a little bemused. *"He can't help himself,"* I thought to Ari.

"When your own kin barely listen to your advice, you share it with those who will," he said.

"I listen," I said defensively.

His beak clicked with a rush of humor. *"Valtora's words, not mine. I am apparently equally guilty."*

We both tensed up when the next jousting pair was announced. I adjusted my goggles to watch Callan joust with a third year high above us. *"Gods above, he's impressive."* I was so grudging to admit it aloud that I gave the whole blow-by-blow of the match to Ari over our Link.

Callan's gryphon, Sunset, was a powerful female who was considered wild-born, though she'd been taken very young from her wild mother's nest. Anyone who could tame and ride a female beast had the tactical advantage of the biggest and strongest gryphon by basic biology. In a heavy-impact sport like jousting, that was where the natural benefit was most noticeable. I shifted uncomfortably as Callan easily won.

"Showoff," I scoffed. The Cadet Games were for third years. It would be sporting of Callan to lose graciously, or at least not embarrass his opponents when they were the ones being judged today. Only a few second years had been taught to joust at this point anyway, depending on how developed their gryphons were.

"Based on how you describe him..." Ari hesitated. The fur on his flank puffed out, and he turned to groom himself. I'd ruffled up the fur of enough cats to recognize the same motion when they were out of sorts.

"Well, it sounds like he's going to be the Ace of next year's class."

My lips turned like I'd tasted something foul. I didn't have a beast in that game—Callan was still a year ahead of me—but I hated that he could be so nasty toward us and still be in the running to graduate with the highest honor. There were other awards we could strive for at the Academy, but the Ace pin...

Well, I'd only really associated Aces with my father and a few of the First. They started with a better placement and rose in the ranks faster. It put the victory in Victor if he were to earn it next year.

I didn't suggest we strive to be Aces. It was a faraway dream I only entertained in the dead of night, imagining my bumps and bruises were payment toward a bigger purpose. Not just surviving, but emerging on top of the pile. I knew it was impossible for us.

"Excuse me," a woman's voice said behind me.

Standing there with a hand on her hip was a maid in full uniform. Her glare practically bore a hole through my skull as she shoved a small box at me. "Here. This is for you."

"Th-thanks?" I spoke to her back. She walked stiff-backed back to the fortress with all the haste of a late first year. With a shrug, I inspected what she'd handed me. It was a display box with a heavy lid, which lifted on invisible hinges. Nestled on a bed of velvet was an oval stone half the size of my palm, its gray face carved with a circular mage rune that was healer green.

"*Well, what is it?*" Ari asked when I'd stared at it for too long.

"*A magestone,*" I said in quiet awe. Anything produced by Tulari hands was worth a small fortune, be it lights or the magic-infused rock I picked up with careful fingers after sitting to rest the box in my lap. The magestone vibrated like a single angry wasp was trapped inside of it. A curl of paper hid in the indent left in the velvet.

"Dear Cadet Walker," I read aloud, holding it open with thumb and forefinger. "I was sorry to hear about your accident. This magestone has just enough power to speed your healing along. Apply it to your wound twice daily for best results. Best wishes…"

I furrowed my brow, expecting it to be signed with a name. "…A friend. Huh."

"*Are you going to use it?*"

I turned the magestone over in my hand before pressing it to my broken arm. The vibrations sent soothing waves of magic out to help my mending, and the rune lit with a faint glow. "I won't tell the healers if you won't." Being pain-free was a blissful sensation.

I SAID my goodbyes shortly after the Cadet Games, more than ready for a break. Next time the Academy saw me, I'd have both my arms back and be well-rested and prepared for the worst.

Ari and I returned to Kaiamear as we'd left it, attached to a tow line. I suppose I should've felt joy to be returning home, but my gryphon and I shared a sense of exhaustion instead.

He was feeling down; I was beaten up. It'd serve us both well to be away from competitions and PT for a while.

"Alamid didn't work out over a vacation once. It was painful to return to Academy-style PT afterward," Ari pointed out. I cut off my fantasies of not PTing with a sigh.

"Fine, I'll still PT. But not before the rooster crows," I said.

I rubbed his neck, realizing he'd just said his old rider's name without a hint of pain. There was hope. Time was closing the gaping, soul-deep wound he'd suffered.

It hadn't changed Mother at all, though. As soon as I was inside my family's apartments, she swept me into a hug before fussing over my riding leathers and inspecting the ends of my blown-out braid. "This needs a trim right away," she announced.

"Can she say hi to me first, at least?" asked someone I hadn't seen in quite some time. I beamed at my little brother, a fourteen-year-old version of Father, if Father were pale as a ghost and had a shoulder-length mane of frizzy red hair. The mage mark on his cheek stood out in the sapphire tones of a budding wizard.

"Hi, Nate," I said, twinkling my fingers. I wasn't sure if he thought it was still uncool to hug his big sister or not.

He answered that unspoken question with a quick side hug on my unwounded side. "You look official."

"It's the goggles."

"Definitely the goggles. I wish Tulari had something as cool to wear."

I poked the center of his mage mark.

"Other than that! I want a great robe with bell sleeves so I can hide my hands in mystery." He clasped both wrists and lifted his head, schooling his expression until only a glimmer of mischief lit his eyes.

"And a cowl to hide your goofy face," I said, ticking off on my fingers. "And a secret pocket in your sleeve for snacks..."

His lips twitched. "This is completely serious, Sivana.

Secret snack pockets aren't something a cool, official Tulari would have."

"Won't the wand be enough?" Rissa asked, poking her head out of our bedroom. I supposed it was her bedroom now, so I prepared myself to see my half taken over by her stuff.

Nate sighed. "Wizards don't get their wands until they've trained for years. Have you seen the books I have to read first?"

He dragged us to his room to view the books he'd come home with. I glanced over my shoulder to see my parents in deep discussion. Mother's concerned gaze followed me.

Nate's textbooks were about five times the size a book should be. He opened a random page to show us how it started blank before ink magically rose to the surface. "It's old, old magic. The Tulari who dictated this had it written on enchanted paper, which a wizard can just..." He flicked his hand like he was casting a spell with a wand. "Whoosh, boom, an identical copy. Lucky me."

"Have you made anything yet?" Rissa asked, clearly disinterested in Nate's magical book.

"Well..." He elongated the word but bent to open one of the crates stacked up by the door. "One of the first things a wizard creates is light."

He retrieved a simple case marked with a single rune. The moment he cracked it, sharp white light haloed the opening, revealing a too bright magelight which jumped into the air with a quick jerk.

"That doesn't seem right," she said.

"Oh, it's not. But I kind of like it. Check this out." Nate clapped his hands. An ordinary magelight snuffed out its radiance at the sound, but not Nate's light. Instead, the orb rotated before shooting toward his face. I moved too slowly to bat it aside.

It bounced off his skin with the same kind of sound a slice

of ham made when it was dropped. He laughed as it went circling around the ceiling, randomly bouncing off the walls. "Don't worry, it's made of magic! I just didn't make it right," he said, clapping again. It zoomed toward him like that was the intended command.

Rissa laughed as he made it bounce off him rapid-fire, but I was seized by a sudden idea. "Nate…can you make me more like it?" I asked. "I know a group of rich kids who'd just *love* to have a couple, with a few adjustments…"

CHAPTER 21

EXCLUSIVE INTERVIEW

Yule was Mother's time of year. I fell into old traditions like I'd never left, like negotiating Mother away from picking out the biggest snow pine from this year's selection and trying to trick Nate and Rissa to eat an unsweetened cranberry as we strung them dutifully to make garlands.

They were getting older and wise to my tricks, so I eventually said, "I'll eat one if you do too."

Mother came by to collect our garlands, raising a brow at the stone faces we were making. My cranberry was under my tongue, while my siblings stared at each other with their lips sealed, waiting for one or the other to start chewing. She shook her head and said, "Rissa, baby, come help me hang these."

I swallowed mine whole like a gryphon during the momentary distraction, while Nate ended up pulling a face at the berry's bitterness. "Those are only good for decoration. Bleh!"

I didn't have much free time until the pine was properly balanced in a bucket full of water in the middle of our living room, its silvery branches decorated liberally with cranberries and red ornaments. Silver for Mother Nilara and red for

Father's main worship, Lord Anrathor, with a huge glass sun balanced on the top to symbolically call back the sun from the longest night of the year.

It was nice to put on casual clothes and go shopping in Kaiamear on my small cadet salary, which my parents had been saving in my absence. For once, I was unremarkable, just a girl with a little money to burn for gifts. I realized quickly that I had too many people to buy for, a sharp difference from past years.

Still, I bought everyone at least a small something, even the friends I'd be seeing again after the holiday break. The corner of my room piled up with boxes, forming a precarious tower I hoped would fit in Ari's saddlebags.

The morning of Yule, I went down to the docks to pick up a package wrapped with heavy white paper. A fisherman had promised me his best catch of the day if I paid in advance, and the whole fish I hauled back the Gryphon Yard made me glad for all the excessive PT at the Academy… It was a hefty catch. With the palace healers wanting me to keep my arm immobile for another couple weeks, I wheeled the fish uphill to my gryphon in a child's wagon.

"I have a gift for you," I sent ahead to Ari, inordinately proud to surprise him with a whole tuna. The military didn't purchase tuna for the beasts, so I knew it was a treat.

"Thank you!" Our Link was full of gratitude and anticipation. I just didn't have the stomach to watch him rip into it, so I left him to eat it in peace.

While he feasted, I visited Valtora to feed and groom her, much to the caretakers' relief. She pushed her beak into my hand before shooting me a betrayed look. *Where's mine?* she seemed to ask.

"I know Father is bringing you something," I promised.

Everyone ate well on Yule, with the palace throwing open its gates for a feast and bonfire with festivities lasting through the night. I always tried to stay up with my siblings, but inevitably, I'd fall asleep with Nate or Rissa using me as a pillow instead. Maybe this year would be the time we made it to toast the sunrise.

I was disposing of the remains of the tuna carcass when he found me. A thin, pale man dressed in a brightly dyed green wool vest who obviously didn't belong on the Gryphon Yard. He was far too twitchy, and any caretaker knew that erratic motions were the best way to make even the mildest gryphon nervous enough to bite.

"Can I help you, sir?" I asked. I washed my hand from a bucket behind the stable.

He looked me over and gasped, two hands flying up to frame his face. "Could it be you? Sivana Walker?" He had a high voice to match his shorter stature.

I was still in a great mood from the echoes of a satisfied belly coming from my Link to Ari. I smiled and looked down at myself. "Last time I checked, that's who I was."

"My partner and I have been looking *everywhere* for you." He beamed, patting down his pockets before drawing out a pencil and diminutive pad of paper. "It's *such* an honor to be in the presence of Kaiamear's hero."

I squinted at him. "Who are you, exactly?" I had a bad feeling when he paused to stare at my broken arm and started writing on his pad.

He passed his pad from one hand to the other, fumbling when he realized he wanted to extend his left hand to shake. "Miles Glimmerwick, my dear girl." His smile started to fade when I stared at him rather than take his hand.

"*You!*" I practically shouted. "Do you know how much trouble your fake interview caused me?"

Miles winced, having the grace to look sheepish. "So sorry. I didn't have much to work with. Maybe you and I can have a sit down, talk it out…"

"No. No interviews. Don't you dare print my name again." I could feel myself reddening. I'd wanted to strangle this guy since his story had ruined my first room at the Academy.

He put his palms up. "I can explain."

"Do all journalists put words in peoples' mouths? Is the *Kaiamear Gazette* all full of untrue dribble?" I demanded. "What you printed about me *isn't me at all.* But everyone at the Academy thought it was. You misused your power, Glimmerwick."

He stood perfectly still, like my anger would dissipate if he just didn't react. But I charged right on instead. "I don't have an agenda. I didn't even want to attend the Academy! Linking with Ari was an accident. A happy one, but still something that wouldn't have happened if a *rozash* hadn't attacked us at exactly the right time. If you'd actually have talked to me beforehand, you'd have known that! I'm only going to be a gryphon rider because I wanted to save the life of a blind gryphon. Everything that follows is because of that fact."

I turned and stomped away, unaware of him scribbling furiously on his pad of paper behind my back.

Ari's presence probed mine gently. *"I thought today was a happy one,"* he said.

I went to retrieve him, leading him fully saddled back to my family's apartment. "It is. C'mon, we're going to make wishing cones," I said, wanting a distraction as I calmed down. A pre-Academy Sivana would've never shouted at someone like that. Time with Mother and Rissa was showing me just how much I'd veered away from the quiet, ladylike persona I'd tried to emulate.

Mother had bought huge, spiny pinecones this year. Outside the capital, most families would burn a Yule log, but we wrote our wishes to stuff into cones instead to toss them in the great bonfire this evening. I picked out a fat cone for Ari and me, stuffing it with several rolled-up bits of paper holding our wishes for the next year written in my left-handed scribbling.

Rissa came out of our room to write her own wishes out, stopping short when she noticed the gryphon plucking a branch off our tree and chewing on it. She turned her attention to me. "Looks like you need a whole log," she commented, waving to the wishing cone I held. It bristled like a hedgehog with rolls of paper.

"You try making one with just your left hand," I complained.

To my surprise, she did. We compared our ugly cones with a flurry of giggles.

I MADE it to the sunrise this year, resting my weight on Ari's solid flank while my siblings slept nearby on the grass right outside the palace. I lifted a glass of juice to the lightening horizon while around us, a roaring cheer rose from the crowd of others awake to see it. Hundreds of people all on top of each other, toasting with spirits and hugging. We'd all be passed out within the hour.

I smiled to my sleepy gryphon, sharing a deep contentment which lasted through a nap and a change into a set of robes for a visit to Temple Row. Mother insisted the whole family start fresh after Yule by visiting with the gods. I only went out of duty, expecting silence from the gods as always.

Since Temple Row was at its most popular right after Yule, we didn't have much time before each shrine. I visited Lord Orion last with Father and Nate. The air of unwelcoming energy was gone, but nothing happened after I prayed to the god. I took it as continued disapproval.

We walked back to the palace in silence. I was so lost in my thoughts that I jerked in surprise when a stranger called my name. A boy stood on a street corner, shaking a handful of rolled-up copies of the *Kaiamear Gazette*. Ice gathered in my chest as I went over to buy a copy, flattening it out to read the main headline.

"EXCLUSIVE INTERVIEW WITH LADY GRYPHON RIDER"

"What the…" I felt myself flush scarlet as I saw a familiar name underneath as the author.

Mother guided me home with a hand on my shoulder while I read choice bits aloud to my family. "I had the distinct honor of sitting down with the up-and-coming gryphon rider, Sivana Walker, whom you may recall saved our great capital from a rogue rozash attack."

I read the next line over several times before I gave voice to it. "In this journalist's humble estimation, we have made a mistake in the color of her character. She was polite and well-mannered"—I could hardly keep a straight face—"and has returned from the Academy with one arm in a sling. My sources tell me that this was no accident, but an intentional attack meant to cripple her. Who would do such a thing, you might ask…"

Father's mouth dropped open, but Mother elbowed him before he could interrupt.

Miles Glimmerwick proceeded to write a whole article quoting an embellished version of what I'd yelled at him. He finished up by writing, "So you see, my fellow proud Altari-ans, we must pray the gods continue to bless such a generous soul as Cadet Sivana Walker, whose big heart means a blind gryphon gets a second chance at life."

"Gag," Rissa muttered.

I glared at her for ruining the warm feeling I had from such a glowing article. "Hey, I really do have a big heart, okay?"

"Girls, stop," Mother said, holding up an elegant hand. "This is…a surprise." She turned a concerned glance on me, not nearly as happy to hear what was written about me. "I would bet on the Goddess's good name that Glimmerwick was ordered to change how he portrayed you. Someone with great power or influence is striving to be your ally, Sivana."

"That sounds great," I said.

"Not if it puts you in debt to them, sweetie," she sighed. "That never ends well."

CHAPTER 22

THE ALTARE OF TOMORROW

I LEARNED what Mother meant soon after returning to Fortress Aerie. Father had flown me back and disappeared into the Commandant's office. We were a few days early, so I ate dinner in a nearly empty mess hall at the same table as a random assortment of cadets who'd stayed here for Yule.

Father drew me over to a more private table as I mopped up the dregs of my soup with a heel of bread. "Good news. There's a Tulari inspector here."

I picked up on his beaming expression. "Right now?"

"That's right. The Commandant said your last appearance in the *Kaiumear Gazette* seemed to light a fire under the Chief of Staff. It's rare to get a magic-user's attention so quickly unless a lot of money is involved." He clapped me on the shoulder. "We will have justice for you after all."

I flexed my right arm. It'd since been freed, looking and feeling like nothing had ever happened. That was the touch of magic, I thought. The mysterious magestone had ensured I could pick up where I'd left off with the new semester.

Father and Valtora left early the next morning, and I didn't spend much time outside once they disappeared into the horizon, not when the winter chill soaked through my fur-lined leathers to chill my bones. Practicing riding for the next two or so months promised to be *fun*.

I was a step into Kite Flight's common area when I froze in place. No one else from my flight had arrived yet, but a man had made himself right at home on one of the chairs, his feet propped up by two stacked cushions. "Good morning, Sivana. Shut the door, if you would," said the last person I thought I'd see again in person.

I sketched a hasty bow to Crown Prince Isaac and inched closer while eyeing him uncertainly. I saw a bit of the family resemblance between him and Mateo in the heavy set of his brow, but he still reminded me unpleasantly of their royal father with his thick cheeks and sausage-like fingers clasped delicately around a steaming teacup.

Where'd he get tea? There was no tea at the fortress, at least not for the cadets.

"So nice to see you again," he said, and I realized I was staring. He gestured for me to sit across from him, so I did. "I'm saddened that a hero of Kaiamear has been treated so poorly here. Bullying. Paint. A broken arm."

He paused, waiting for me to say something. My tongue felt like it was tied in knots. All I wanted to do was ask why he was here.

"You have so much potential," he said after giving his tea a slow sip. His smile was kindly, like when he'd defended me to his father, but for some reason, this time it made nerves creep up my spine. "The first female gryphon rider. Know what I see when I look at you? A symbol. You represent *change*, Sivana. My mother, Gatekeeper bless her, wanted Altare to sow a new crop of intelligent, talented young people for our next generation. The results have been a little unexpected. Do you know what your generation wants most?"

I shook my head, feeling completely out of my element. Mother would probably run circles around this man, but I just heard him out.

"They want something different. They don't want to labor on their lord's farm or fight in a war they have no stakes in. Your generation looks at the status quo and cries out for one thing. Change. For the first time ever, young Altarians are intelligent enough to know they deserve better. They want to *choose* something better for themselves. Isn't that how you felt, laboring in the gryphon stables, knowing you'd never get a chance to Link with one of the beasts you love so much?"

I opened my mouth to say no, but...he wasn't wrong. I'd never expected to Link with a gryphon, especially not Ari, but I couldn't lie and say I didn't dream of becoming a new gryphon rider with Ironfeather or Mireille before they were snatched away.

"Yeah," I murmured. "It never felt fair. But that's how it is."

"No, my dear. You've already proven that is how it *was*. Long ago, I'm sure a man decided women couldn't ride gryphons, but when he wrote the rule, he forged Lord Orion's signature on it to give it more weight. You sit before me, untouched by the God of Man's wrath." The crown prince looked at me with a kind of awe. "Yet, my father is set in his ways. He would rather see you—living proof that he is wrong—dead than living out your life."

I tensed at the reminder, helpless fear rearing its head again.

"Don't mistake me, though. He doesn't want you to disappear because you broke a godly edict. It's because of what you represent."

"Change," I said from numb lips.

"Yes. Your story is but one of many that gives our people hope for a better future. But my father does not want things to change. You have to understand the target on your back is from an old man's frustration. You are the strongest living symbol that the Altare of today will not be the Altare of tomorrow."

My fists clenched by my side. "Killing me won't change that, though," I pointed out.

"I know. Which is why you should consider me a friend." He shifted, offering me something resting by his seat.

He pressed a cold crowbar into my palms. I glanced from it to him, puzzled.

"I made sure an investigator found that. And this." Next, he handed me a massive bolt, like the kind that'd secured the net in the Flight Training room. This one was bent at a dramatic angle, its head scuffed with pry marks. If a Tulari had found this, they could use magic to trace it back to who'd damaged it.

"Does this mean…?" I asked in a hopeful hush.

"Yes. I took care of a problem for you." Prince Isaac stood, and I hastened to follow suit. He looked me in the eye, all hints of his warm demeanor vanished. "When the time comes, I will require you to take care of a problem for me. Understand?"

I tried to swallow past the sudden lump in my throat. This was exactly what Mother had warned me against, agreeing to an open-ended debt begun from someone else's random act of goodwill.

"You're working with Miles Glimmerwick, aren't you?" I blurted.

His smile was just a baring of teeth. "He's a little dense, but he tries. Poor thing."

I blew out a tense breath. "Well, I-I understand, Your Highness. If the king wants me dead, and you've protected me a-as you say you have…" I tried to sidestep how I felt like he'd actually saved me twice. The less perceived debt, the better. "Then I shall try to repay you someday."

"Very good." His warm smile returned. "You shall never see this Commander Davis person again. I understand the Commandant has found a friendlier face to replace him already."

He bade me goodbye, leaving me to collapse back into a chair. I muttered a quiet curse, sure I was now between a rock and a hard place politically. Mother would scream at me if she could.

Yet I wrote out exactly what happened to her first and hoped that the man who'd failed me constantly, gave me countless demerits, and finally tried to mark me a true heretic of Lord Orion in an attempt on my life was truly gone for good.

By the time the rest of my flight arrived for the next semester, I'd shaken off most of my dread and looked forward to learning flying from someone who wasn't Commander Davis.

We'd agreed to exchange late Yule gifts since we could shop for them over the holiday. I was more surprised than anything that everyone participated, even Weslecker, who'd obviously spent the most money. He'd given me a flight jacket lined with fine, black fur, sure to be cherished through the colder months.

It was cool to see my flight before they had to make a mandatory trip to the barber. Biggs's hair had grown into a cloud of tiny corkscrews around his head. Weslecker's auburn locks were oiled into a side-part, long enough to be forced into an attractive style. And Sharde looked a lot like my brother, with his hair nearly brushing his shoulders. He was practically a walking demerit now. I wondered when Sarge would start chasing him around the Green with a razor.

The other boys were looking a little scruffy by comparison, and I had to hide a laugh when Credell proudly showed off the curls on his upper lip as a mustache he'd been growing all break. Pereyra pointed to the full goatee he had groomed around his mouth and exclaimed, "Me too!"

A maid interrupted with a knock on the door. Sharde jumped up to get it, returning with a box and a confused look. "It's for you," he said, passing it to me.

The bottom of the box was warm. I was confused too as I opened it to reveal a freshly baked cranberry-orange pie. The card underneath wished me a happy Yule…from a friend.

My flight and I certainly enjoyed the pie, but I started to wonder who exactly this generous "friend" was.

CHAPTER 23

HE'S GONE

My second semester schedule was the same until the afternoon....and full of nasty notes like the other cadets discretely slipped into my path to remind me just what they thought of me. The side pocket in my bag was already full. I decided I didn't want to let it get me down.

There was a gap of time where Basic Gryphon Care used to be. My fellow first years were shuffled to an advanced version, but Sharde and I sat around waiting on the Green for our new class instead, Aerial Agility.

"I'm telling you, it won't be Davis. He's gone," I was saying.

"Then why's his name on my schedule?" Sharde asked.

I rolled my eyes. "We could always end this debate early and check in on the first years."

He and I glanced way up at the stables, where our new instructor had to be teaching.

Sharde shrugged and lay out on his back. "Nah. Let's enjoy a warmish day while we have it."

There was no snow on the Green today, but its brown and brittle grass suggested we'd just missed it. Puzzlebox rolled around close by, squeaking happily. Sharde had taken off her saddle and harness for now, while Ari still wore his, preferring to nap.

His mostly white gryphon ended up on her back next to me, cheeping for attention. "Aren't you the sweetest thing?" I cooed, ruffling her belly fluff. "Hey, Sharde? Is she getting bigger?" Now that I looked more closely, her wings were more developed too, with fewer soft feathers in between the primaries.

He smiled up at the sky, hands behind his head. "Yeah. I think she's finally becoming an adult. Slow and steady, right?"

"For sure. Does that mean you're going to try to be a cadet soon?"

"Pfft."

"Okay, just asking. You're actually in regulation for once and all," I said. He'd gotten his hair cropped short, but it was more than that. He hadn't mouthed off to Sergeant Kobarn this morning, so no demerits today that I knew of.

We spent several minutes in companionable silence, save for Puzzlebox's happy twittering. "Your pops told me if I want to be assigned to Final Flight, all I gotta do is ask for it," he said finally. "Apparently no one ever asks because the pay sucks and there's this feeling that it's like...just for old guys. The Commandant wasn't going to tell me because the Academy's goal is to beat me down until I'm a good soldier. Once we're assigned to a real Flight, you can't ask to be put in Final Flight, did you know that? It has to happen right at the end of training."

"You'd be a great gryphon knight," I said.

His brow furrowed. "No, Sivana, I really wouldn't. I hate everything about this place...except for the gryphons. That's why I'm here."

I considered and sighed. "Me too." Except I wanted the end goal, and he wanted...something different. It was just like Prince Isaac had said; people of my generation wanted to choose something better for themselves. Here was living proof right next to me.

"Did you know Cortes could've Linked with Puzzlebox?" he asked.

It took me a moment to realize he was talking about Prince Mateo. I hadn't really let myself forget that my classmate, while a fellow cadet, was still royalty. "He was here last year?"

"Yeah, briefly. The other gryphons refused to Link with him, except for Puzzlebox. He didn't want her."

At this point, his gryphon was draped over both of us for double the attention. I didn't know why anyone wouldn't want her…

But then again, I sort of did. "So, he waited a year to get a youngling born of the First's gryphons," I said slowly. "It makes a lot of sense, actually. He gets to be with his friends and has all the benefits of being a year older than everyone else. I'm glad he did it."

Sharde shot me a startled glance.

"B-because she found you," I added quickly. Gods above, I hoped I wasn't blushing. I was happier still to have a friend here to spend so much time with. Besides, I couldn't imagine Mateo with Puzzlebox, especially with how slow she was developing.

The Commandant's voice called, "Look alive!" We scrambled up so quickly that Puzzlebox squeaked a complaint and cast a petulant look at the smartly dressed officer and his black gryphon striding from the fortress. "Two of my cadets just lying about. Unacceptable."

"Sorry, sir," I said, nervous he'd shove me into another class.

He ignored me and said to Sharde, "Saddle up your gryphon. You'll be flying soon."

I went to nudge Ari awake, feeling my palms start to sweat in my riding gloves. It wasn't because of the Commandant's presence, either. Soon our instructor would descend upon the Green to teach us flying skills, and I'd know for certain if I owed Prince Isaac the favor he held over my head.

A familiar set of second years and their gryphons started joining us. I studiously ignored Callan's presence, instead pretending to check over Ari's harness. I fidgeted with his reins, setting both sets out so they wouldn't tangle. When all the second years were here, there was still no instructor.

In the meantime, I tapped a nervous tune out on Ari's saddle until he moved away from me with an annoyed twitter. *"Quit fidgeting. They're coming,"* he said.

My gaze flashed upward, spotting an adult gryphon take wing from the stables and circle for a landing in front of us. My eyes just about popped out of their sockets. A familiar face looked everyone over sternly. He wasn't Commander Davis.

"Good afternoon, cadets," he said.

"Good afternoon…" We chorused it confidently until we were supposed to say his name. The boys devolved into a mush of murmurs, while I exclaimed, "Commander Rudrick!"

My father's recently promoted second-in-command, here, promoted again to instructor and the rank of Knight-Commander. It was surreal to see someone from the First so far from home.

"That's right. I'm Commander Darion Rudrick, formerly of the First Gryphon Flight. And this is my gryphon, Snowpoint." He gestured to the pure white gryphon next to him, who held her head high. I wondered if Ironfeather and Mireille had held them up, greeting their mother after so long. "I will be your new flight and aerial combat instructor."

I learned pretty quickly why the Commandant was here—to lend us Night. Our first flight class without nets would be supervised by the experienced gryphon, who had a hundred percent track record of catching cadets…so far. She circled the skies without her rider while we practiced old maneuvers in the open sky, letting our gryphons get used to moving with the wind and using it to their advantage.

Class flew by. Once it was done, Ari and I approached our new instructor. Snowpoint closed the distance between us and spared me a quick nuzzle before she put her paw on Ari's shoulder, pushing him over. She sat on him while he squawked in mock complaint.

"Hey, stranger," Rudrick said to me, watching their antics with a grin. This was the man I knew.

"Congratulations on your promotion!"

"...Sir," he whispered behind his hand.

"Sir," I appended.

"Why thank you, Cadet Walker. My wife's not exactly happy about moving to the mountains in winter, but I think she'll find the view of rushing cadets charming after a while," he said.

I should've figured the whole Rudrick family had moved here. He was young for an instructor, with two kids my siblings' ages. He told me they were staying with family to finish their schooling. "I'm not going to lie. My daughter might be your biggest fan. She's going to apply to be a cadet this summer." He had a laugh, but I hoped she would; I hoped a lot of girls applied.

"And Snowpoint loves it here. Most tame gryphons don't get to raise their kids. She's already scolded Cadet Weslecker for missing a tangle in Ironfeather's fur."

I winced. "There go his hopes of passing out of Advanced Gryphon Care early."

He raised a brow. "Why's he trying to do that?"

"Well...Weslecker gives me some extra tutoring with the cavalry saber. He's very good with it, and I'm, uh..."

"Not too great?" he supplied, looking sympathetic. "I might be able to spare him occasionally."

My expression brightened immediately. If Rudrick were anyone else, I doubted the rules would bend for us.

"But, Cadet Walker, I have to warn you," he continued, holding up a hand. "I know your family *and* the gryphon you ride. There's no reason for you two not to earn Best in Class this semester."

"Like that's happening," Ari commented. Snowpoint gave his ear a nip like she'd heard him.

"We're going to do our best," I said. If we could go from barely passing Flight Training to being the best in the follow-up class, that would be a miracle. It'd be exactly what we needed to avoid the king's threats. Rudrick had been there the night Ari and I Linked, so he understood what was at stake much more than anyone else here.

CHAPTER 24

WESLECKER'S BEST FRIEND

The second semester seemed worlds easier than the first, and it was because Commander Davis left. The source of countless demerits and ridicule, gone. I really did owe someone powerful for intervening on my behalf.

Callan wasn't nearly so mouthy in Aerial Agility class, either. It took me a while to realize the second years were enduring a different kind of hell. Most of them bore bruise-like half-moons under their eyes in exhaustion. Two sets of drill sergeants worked them harder than ever during PT, and they choked the air over the Green in the evening, practicing maneuvers in teams of five riders.

"What's going on with the second years?" I asked my flight when we decided not to play talonball while the second years were out in force. We returned to Kite Flight's roost, chitchatting while Ellie scribbled notes from her latest research over in one of the desks.

"They call it the Trial by Fire," Sharde answered. "I wondered the same thing last year. With the third years gone, there are twice the resources to work the second years hard. They go to all their classes and then practice with their gryphons until they drop. Everyone works on lance skills and formations until they could be placed on a battlefield and consider killing rozash easier than being here."

Biggs tossed a ball between his palms, looking to the empty space where Valentic usually sat in the evening. "Well, that sucks. How long does it last?"

"All semester," Sharde said.

Gods above, I thought.

"Don't get too comfortable. Things heat up for us too when our gryphons get big enough to fly," he added, pointing to our gryphons. Echo and Ironfeather, in particular, had grown while I wasn't looking, entering a teenager-like phase that was all big paws and lanky limbs without the bulk to match.

"Won't be long now," I said mostly to myself. They'd be a year old by April, and most riders considered yearlings sky worthy.

I pushed myself harder after that evening upon realizing Ari and I were nowhere near where we needed to be. My dominant arm needed some extra work, and I was dismayed to find my dueling skills were dusty at best.

"Try adjusting your stance," Weslecker said one Friday afternoon, let off the hook for his gryphon care class. His hands were warm against the biting chill of rushing mountain winds as he held my wrist and helped me pose my body properly.

"Better. Now, pretend the dummy is Cadet Cortes."

I rolled my eyes and hit the sack of straw with a few sweeping motions of the wooden practice sword.

"Not angry enough. Try imagining Cadet Callan. Hit it like you want to hurt it."

I gritted my teeth and repeated the motion, feeling the impacts through my muscles.

"Self-defense is noble," I muttered, echoing the wisdom our instructor always shouted. "You have a right to defend your life if someone comes at you with force."

It didn't help much to imagine the practice dummies as real people. As angry as some of the boys here made me, I'd never wanted to kill them, or anyone else. Ari liked to remind me that this was the kind of softness they were trying to beat out of every cadet by the end of the Academy.

Often, Weslecker would tutor me more in the evenings, spending time together like we had in the first semester. At first, I was distracted by the second years, because watching them endure a wall of shouting from various instructors and drill sergeants—and in some cases, each other—was what I'd thought the Academy would be like in the first place.

But as the nights passed and I continued improving and learning all the steps to the dance that was the Triple-R, Rushing River Rapids style, I realized I said yes every time Weslecker offered for different reasons. I...liked spending time with him. He wasn't so bad when he showed me his passion for the skill of dueling rather than talked about his family's vacation homes or other assets that made the rest of the flight see him as snobby and out of touch.

"So, you and Weslecker?" Ellie asked after lights out one night.

"What? No," I protested. No matter how I thought I felt, I couldn't be accused of fraternizing with a fellow cadet.

"You're spending a lot of time together." She said it in an entirely Ellie way, too, like it was a logical conclusion and I was trying to insist on the wrong answer.

"That doesn't mean anything," I said, batting away a sudden rush of nerves that could kill any butterflies trying to flutter in my belly. "That would be fraternization. I'd get us kicked out of the Kite Flight dorms."

"Hmm. I wouldn't tell anyone," she promised.

"It's not like that, I swear."

Silence fell between us long enough that I thought she might've fallen asleep. "Can I tell you a secret?" she asked as I started nodding off.

"Huh?"

"Uh. I kind of, well…I like…" she mumbled the rest.

"What was that?"

"I like Sharde," she whispered.

"That's nice." I barely cracked my eyes open. "Wait… *Sharde*?"

We were too tired to continue that conversation, and the next morning, she pretended she'd never brought it up. I wasn't sure Sharde had noticed her past teasing her for being so smart, but I started brainstorming how to get my brainy friend to say more than two words to him.

I started noticing Weslecker a lot more now that she'd asked about him, too. He cheered for me the loudest at January's monthly competition when I won my first duel against an Osprey Flight boy. He was also the one to peel me off the ground after Prince Mateo flattened me when Kite and Falcon Flights dueled for first place.

The other boy's dark eyes were colder than the snow as he glanced between Weslecker and me. "Are you okay, Walker?" he was asking, helping pat off a layer of ice and crushed grass from my back.

"Yeah. Thanks," I said, flashing him a smile, which he returned warmly.

Weslecker kept a space open next to him in the circle of watching cadets while I shook Prince Mateo's hand to seal his victory. "Be careful. He's my best friend," the prince said in an undertone, his hand like a vice.

Huh? My brows drew in confusion. "What are you imply-ing?" I asked carefully.

"Whatever. Don't worry about it." He released me, and I shook out my hand.

Ironically, the only person who could give me insight was Weslecker himself. "What's going on with Prince Mateo? He seems…angry," I asked.

We waited in the mess hall for the announcement of rankings while the second years flew their gryphons' wings off. The weather had kicked up toward blizzard conditions, and I'd learned that meant it was a perfect time to practice inclement weather flying.

Weslecker considered, passing a mug of heated water between his hands. "Did he say something weird to you?" he asked, his green eyes alight with concern.

Yeah, about you, I thought. But I didn't fancy talking about whether there was something between Weslecker and me. There couldn't be, not with what was at stake for me. "He tried to warn me away from you," I said.

The other boy didn't seem surprised. "Yeah, um. He's feeling a little overlooked. I'm probably not supposed to tell you this, but his father makes him write weekly reports about how you're doing. The king's never taken much interest in Mateo because he's the third son and all..." A bitter chuckle rose from Weslecker. "...I know how that feels."

Every story he shared from his childhood included him being alone for long stretches. It sounded like his duke and duchess parents had little time for him.

"He's been a little weird about how much Mireille likes you. You haven't Linked to a really young gryphon, but their emotions can get overwhelming. They haven't learned to control themselves yet," he added.

I drank some of my hot water to avoid eye contact. I'd already experienced how Ari's stronger emotions flowed into me, especially early in our connection when all I wanted to do was lie around in a depression with my gryphon.

Ironfeather and Mireille loved me, and it occurred to me that their riders had reacted in completely different ways to that. Even now, Weslecker sat a little too close to me, while Prince Mateo's glare was burned into my memory. He'd accused me of trying to take his gryphon before. With his father, his gryphon, and now his best friend taking notice of me...

Well, I may understand him a lot better. I needed to be more careful; a Prince would be the worst enemy to have.

But when Falcon Flight was announced as first place and Kite Flight as second, I caught the newest look Mateo shot across the mess hall at me. Maybe it was already too late to smooth over this particular problem.

CHAPTER 25

SOMETHING OF A CELEBRITY

Altarians have a saying every time something nice turns bad. "A bloom doesn't last forever."

The *Kaiamear Gazette* ran another completely fake article about me, and I received a copy of it alongside a gift from my mysterious "friend."

Here we go again, I thought.

Miles Glimmerwick updated the city about how I was doing at the Academy. He'd toned down the praise that'd made my sister want to gag, but I only saw Prince Isaac's fingers pulling the strings as I read the piece. The gift was more welcome, at least. It was a thick lotion made to heal dry, chapped skin.

I was called to the Commandant's office within the week.

Ari stayed in my room, snipping his beak when I'd asked if he wanted to come too. *"Good luck petting Night,"* he'd muttered.

I'd puzzled over his angry remark until I was sitting across from the Commandant, realizing I'd been pondering ways to convince the older gryphon to trust me. One of the things I'd wondered was if she felt territorial if another gryphon was in the room with us. Well, it didn't work, because Night glowered at me like always from her nest in the Commandant's office.

"Good afternoon, Cadet Walker," he said, a copy of the *Kaiamear Gazette* acting as a screen between us. It was the same version my "friend" had sent me, and I could spot my name from the huge headline on the front.

"Good afternoon, sir," I replied automatically, sitting rigidly across from him.

"Nobody by the name of Miles Glimmerwick has visited you in the past month," he commented.

"No, sir."

"I've checked the mail records, and you haven't corresponded with him, either." Now his cold eyes stared at me over the *Gazette*.

A fat bead of sweat traced the outline of my spine. "I-I-I really haven't, sir," I blurted. But it was interesting to know that there were records of who I *was* sending mail to.

He sighed, placing the newspaper to the side. "I don't think I can keep this from you for much longer, Cadet Walker. You're something of a celebrity now."

My face blanked with confusion when he pulled a sack out of his desk drawer and passed it to me. "Most of these arrived while you were still on break. Exactly a week after the *Gazette* reported on your broken arm, in fact."

I opened the sack and pulled out letters. Dozens of letters. He handed over a second sack, this one piled with boxes. The letters were sealed, but most of the boxes were open and rifled through. My cheeks flushed hot with mortification. Strangers had written me, sending gifts and what I assumed were well-wishes.

"I expect more are coming with the next air courier," the Commandant said.

I put it all aside and clutched my head, genuinely lost for words.

"Your situation is a little too large for you, young lady."

His tone was the gentlest I'd heard from him. "I was tempted to send it all back and tell your fans that military establishments don't accept this kind of mail, but...perhaps it will motivate you."

My gaze moved from the pile of letters to his serious face. "You're not on track to pass this year," he said.

"What?" I asked, feeling like he'd just sucker punched me.

"It's not entirely your fault. Your PT tests are held to the standards we've always had. They were made for young men," he said. "Not to mention your gryphon..."

"He's doing so much better with Commander Rudrick's class," I protested.

"Keep in mind that we have certain expectations of all gryphons and riders. No rozash is going to view a young woman and a blind gryphon on the battlefield as anything but a free lunch."

My heart dropped. I thought we were doing well and overcoming so much already, but it still wasn't enough. "Sir." Trembles wracked my balled-up fists. "If we don't pass, the king will execute Ari."

He stared at me, as unmovable as stone. He already knew.

"What do I have to do? Tell me what I have to do to improve," I said desperately. "I'll work harder than any boy here. I'll—"

The Commandant raised a hand, and I immediately hushed. He purposefully tipped his head to peer at the spot where Ari usually sat when I was called to this office. "You've already proven your work ethic. I don't doubt you will work harder still to improve your physical fitness. Your gryphon, however, appears to have already given up."

I opened my mouth, then closed it again.

"You forget I trained Alamid Maros and Ari when they were young and eager. The gryphon you brought back to the Academy is a sad shade of who he used to be. You have to understand what that looks like from my end. You love him and have given up a lot to bring him here. But he needs to want it as badly as you do, Cadet Walker. I daresay he needs to want it *more* than you."

It felt more final to hear this from someone who'd watched our progress and challenged us rather than the king making an on-the-spot declaration of Ari's execution. I'd continued trying to be the best cadet I could be, assuming along the way that Ari would eventually get up and join me.

Was I too blinded by my Link to see the real Ari? He was tired and old compared to every other gryphon at the Academy, except for Night and Snowpoint.

"What do I really have to do?" I asked, biting into my lip when my eyes threatened to water with traitorous tears.

"If I were you, I'd start by talking to my gryphon. Spend time with him, not other people and definitely not other gryphons. Don't lose sight of the fact that he needs you more than anyone else. You still have time to turn this situation around."

I nodded slowly, feeling like I was maybe an inch tall. I was mortified I hadn't thought more about what Ari would think with how much I fawned over other gryphons. Earlier, I'd hoped today would be the day Night allowed me to pet her glossy feathers and *that* was why he hadn't come with me. Ari could read my thoughts over the Link; he knew.

It stopped right now; Ari would have my undivided attention.

The Commandant interrupted my thoughts as he crumpled up his copy of the *Kaiamear Gazette.* "You're dismissed, Cadet Walker."

I popped obediently to my feet and turned to leave.

"Don't forget your fan mail."

"Fan mail," Ari echoed in disbelief when I returned to Kite Flight's roost and nudged him awake. I sat on the floor beside him and pushed Puzzlebox away, giving her an apologetic look but staying firm to my new resolution as I encouraged Ari to lay his head in my lap.

"That's right. Those articles about us are worth something after all," I said, resting an arm over his shoulders as he got comfortable.

"Well, read me a few," he invited with a sigh.

I started cracking seals, scanning the contents first. As I'd suspected, a few of these letters weren't all that nice. I only shared the ones that had kind words for us both. We'd inspired a few daughters, nieces, and granddaughters who all wanted to be gryphon riders now.

People from all over Kaiamear wished us well, and it woke a warm fuzzy feeling in my chest that, just maybe, I'd earned something with all the hard work that'd gotten us to our point.

But then I turned inward and reached for the Link between Ari and me. On the other side, I could feel his doubt and the thoughts that suggested he didn't feel like he deserved any praise.

"We need to talk," I said privately.

He tensed, and I felt him probing the Link too, wondering what exactly we needed to talk about.

I let him see the whole conversation with the Commandant. He went silent as we relived the hammer the Commandant had dropped about our place at the Academy.

"I do want it. I want to pass," Ari protested, though his voice was weak. *"But…it's not easy to be here, to know everyone around me pities me. Always needing to find a different way to do things that used to come so easily to me.*

"And it bothers me that Commander Davis could've ended my life, had he not messed with the net. If he'd just waited, we would've

failed Flight Training, and that would be it. I've dodged fate twice. For how much longer will I be lucky, Sivana?" he asked.

"A wise instructor says the hardest workers are the luckiest," I said.

"Please. Luck is luck, and fate is fate. One day, I will go to rest alongside Alamid. The only thing I wonder is if I will be the one to put you in the next grave over."

"What?" I asked quietly.

"Take the stars out of your eyes for a minute," he murmured. *"We are one mistake from your untimely death. That's the most important thing Davis taught me."*

I brushed my hand through his feathers. *"That's a risk I'm willing to take."*

"Well, I'm not!" he exclaimed. *"You shouldn't waste your life on a has-been like me. I know how you feel about the younglings. How you wish you could have Mireille instead."* His words were like a knife to my emotions, forged of my own traitorous thoughts.

"I'm sorry. I never really meant that," I rushed to say.

The heavy barrel of his chest rose and fell with a great breath.

"No, I know...I'm not good enough. I couldn't save Alamid when I had eyes, and I hardly deserved him then."

"Ari, what?" I asked, aghast.

"I've been an imposter my whole life. I didn't deserve to be one of the First's beasts, and I don't deserve a second rider." His misery flowed over into a pained keen. *"I wasn't good enough when I had eyes. Why am I even trying now?"*

I hugged his neck as he took another large gulp of air. This was how gryphons cried, with great gusting breaths and keens from deep in their throat. He trembled and wailed, drawing a concerned glance from every other gryphon in the room. I waved the rest of my flight's concerns away, wanting to try and fix this myself.

"Ari, I'm so sorry. I don't want another gryphon. You are

enough, and I know for a fact that you were the fastest gryphon in the First. You earned your place there. The only thing I want to see is you getting up and truly living again. You've said yourself that this is what Alamid would want. And if things were reversed, I know you'd want Alamid to continue on too."

Puzzlebox padded over again, placing her brightly colored toy before Ari and nudging it toward him. She ignored my shooing motions and thumped her weight on top of him for a tight snuggle.

I sniffled from the echo of his emotions, then released a watery laugh. *"And you have other friends to help along the way,"* I added.

Ari rested his talons on the toy, drawing it close enough to nudge with his beak. *"Why does she like this thing so much?"* he muttered. *"It's…a box."*

"I don't really know," I admitted. Puzzle boxes were meant to be played with, and gryphons didn't have the dexterity to slide the moving parts.

He rested silently for a few minutes. *"Whatever brings her joy,"* he said, finally tucking it into his neck and nuzzling Puzzlebox with a low murr to reassure her. *"You know what'd make me happier? I want to play hoops. Alamid and I were the best at it."*

This wasn't the first time he'd mentioned it, but this time, I swore I'd find a group of gryphon riders willing to play the aerial sport with us. The first problem I considered was that the only candidates for a pickup game were the already over-worked second years.

CHAPTER 26

NO PROMISES

First, I needed to learn how to play hoops on gryphon back. I'd watched the game from the ground, seeing only chaos at first. The game was played with five gryphon riders per team and two differently sized balls, each with different rules for scoring. The larger ball was supposed to be thrown through one of the hoops and caught by a teammate on the other side. This was worth more points than the second ball, which was used for scoring when a rider dove through the largest hoop while holding it.

"It's meant to be a little messy," Ari explained while we observed two teams of second years playing. The ebon gryphon Night flew around the field like a shadow, a large brass ring clasped in her beak.

"Because battlefields are messy, right?" I guessed. An ideal hoops player could keep an eye on three targets at once and respond in a split second when Night decided to drop the ring. If it hit the ground, that was it, they couldn't pick it back up. But catching and scoring with the ring was worth a lot of bonus points.

"It's harder than it looks." But Ari yearned to play; I could feel it now. The gryphons were meant to ram each other so

their riders could steal the ball, but there were no flying feathers or screeches of pain. If anything, it looked like they were having a good time, frolicking midair while the humans shouted and made a big deal of scoring.

We started off easy enough, with Sharde and occasionally Valentic as our opponents. Throwing a ball midair with any accuracy was *really* difficult, and I could only blame the wind itself. But like anything else, we practiced. And Puzzlebox basically climbed me in eagerness any time I started saying, "Do you want to play…?"

We weren't amazing, but Ari was having fun. That's all I really cared about, and I reminded myself of that weeks later when I finally wrestled up the nerve to challenge a team of second years to a pickup game before Aerial Agility class.

"Sure, baby," one of them said, a grin splitting his face. A pack of boys watched my expression, eager to see a crack of annoyance or worse, flirting back.

I rolled my eyes. "Let's see what you say when we kick your rears. C'mon now, I call dibs to Sharde and Valentic. We need seven more."

Callan eagerly piled into the opposing team and…yeah, we got annihilated. I didn't know what I was expecting. Ari enjoyed the game, but I could tell my stress was bleeding into his headspace. *"We don't have to win,"* he reminded.

"But…it's Callan," I muttered. It was the principle of the thing; now that I'd noticed it, I couldn't stop seeing how his touch turned every competition into a victory for him. It was like his Endoline parents had blessed him to win everything at the cost of his name. I couldn't stand it. The fact that everything at the Academy was a competition grated when we weren't winning.

The space between my afternoon classes became hoops time, and I was in every game. Instead of helping with my fighting skills, Weslecker spent the days he got off watching us struggle instead. He saw me lose, mostly. The second years shuffled teams to avoid being placed with Sharde and me.

One late winter afternoon, the wind changed. I noticed the flash of metal as Night dropped the brass ring toward the end of our game. *"The ring!"* I shouted to Ari, aiming his head toward its falling form.

A dark blur was already diving toward it as Ari stretched his body out, reaching top speed. We sliced through the sky, cold wind streaking my cheeks until they numbed. We flashed past Callan and Sunset, grabbing the ring mere yards from the Green.

Ari sensed my triumph and wheeled around, crowing victoriously as we swung upward in a smooth arc. I guided us toward the biggest hoop, my face split with a huge smile. With these points, we'd finally win a game of hoops against Callan…

But then a force rammed Ari, shooting us sideways. His cry became a call of alarm as we pinwheeled, the ring going flying when I grabbed the reins with both hands, trying to wrest control before we crashed. Cloudy sky and earth spun in a dizzying array; with each rotation, the ground loomed larger.

I realized no force could stop us from crashing and clenched my eyes. Our momentum came to an abrupt stop, but pain didn't follow. A fall from that height should've broken bones, or worse.

Slowly, I peeled one eyelid open, then the other. Black feathers filled the field of my goggles. Night's wings jolted Ari and me with each flap, her talons drawing the saddle into a painful pinch where she'd caught my gryphon's harness.

She lowered us to the ground, growling low as her beak swung toward the hoops, eyes narrowing on the group of second years cheering while Callan pumped the brass ring in the air.

He'd won again, but this time, I'd nearly kissed the dirt

for it. My shaking fingers hit the buckles around my waist, fumbling while trying to untie myself from Ari. My vision swam, potent fury kindling off the embers of fear left from that near miss. I could barely stand, but my hands formed two quivering fists.

"That bastard," I breathed. Night turned toward me, the foreign feeling of her mind touching mine. She spoke to me like Valtora did, and I understood her nearly as well.

My rider will not discipline him because tackling you is within what's allowed in hoops. You should not have lost control so easily.

I stayed still as stone, sensing there was a "but" to the medley of feelings and images she expressed herself in.

I do not like his behavior. Snotty hatchling.

"I don't like it either," I breathed. For a moment, my fingers had loosened; I was too awed to have Night's direct attention. But now I refocused on what mattered most… getting back at Callan.

What are you planning, little female? Night's yellow gaze pierced right through me.

"Nothing," I said quickly. What she knew, the Commandant would know.

She nudged Ari with her beak. A warm feeling passed between them, and I caught the edges of pure approval and encouragement rolling off the older gryphon as she nuzzled Ari.

Then she glanced back to me and nodded curtly, her mental presence withdrawing. My lip twisted in disappointment until she padded closer, flicking her ears in a gesture I recognized immediately.

I held in a gasp and rubbed her head, taking in how soft her glossy feathers were. Her fur was thinner than I expected, a sign of age. If she'd let me draw my hand down her spine, I'd probably feel each individual bump from time taking its toll.

Ari twittered a laugh. "What?" I asked.

"*Nothing,*" he replied.

I glanced between the two gryphons. Night was laughing too, and it felt like some inside joke was happening between them. She glanced up a moment later and pulled away from my fingers. Following her gaze, I spotted where Commander Rudrick had descended from the stables and was about to start class.

As we lined up, I realized the elder gryphon had distracted me so I didn't have time to walk up to Callan and slug him for that dirty midair tackle. There were too many witnesses now.

"WE'VE GOTTA DO something about Callan," Sharde said as we ate a late dinner that evening with the rest of our flight. There were no second years here yet, but we'd seen them finishing up a late training session on the way to the mess hall.

"What'd he do this time?" Biggs asked.

Sharde and I regaled the table about how I'd finally caught the brass ring in a hoops game, just to have Callan and his gryphon tackle Ari viciously and steal away the game victory. "Technically, he didn't do anything wrong," I said.

Weslecker's brows traveled to his hairline. "Like hell he didn't," he blurted.

"Aren't you tired of giving him the benefit of the doubt?" Sharde asked me. "As competitive as the second years can get over hoops, none of them have tackled Ari *that* hard. Callan wanted you to crash."

I glanced to Ari, who projected a feeling of agreement with my friend. "Well, what else do you want me to do?" I asked with a sigh.

"*We*"—Sharde indicated the rest of the table—"are stronger as a group. I suggest a show of force."

"A fight," I said flatly. I didn't see how that would solve any of my problems except remove the last thin veneer of civility between myself and Callan.

He shook his head. "I'm not saying we punch the guy, even if he deserves it. We just intimidate him a bit, knock him off his high horse."

I had a bad feeling in my gut as he laid out his plan, but the other boys jumped on it with enthusiasm. It felt good to have everyone else want to work toward a goal on my behalf, even if it was because we were all tired of Callan's insufferable personality. When Sharde asked who was in, I volunteered alongside everyone else.

All we had to do was wait. The second years were going long on their training tonight, so it was likely Callan would return Sunset to the stables after dinner. It would be less hazardous to our health to have a "discussion" with him when we didn't fear the bite of his vicious beast. I went to bed down Ari, waiting there while Sharde and the others got into their own positions at my friend's direction.

As I brushed out my gryphon's pelt, I wondered if Sharde had had to do this before. My gryphon was at ease tonight, tired in the right way after an afternoon of hoops and flight training. *Try not to get into too much trouble,* he said, relaxing on his bed of straw in a lazy sprawl.

"No promises."

I stepped into a shadowy corner of his stall when I heard the tired voices of several second years leading their gryphons to bed. Callan was the type to take care of Sunset personally, when she was prone to snapping at caretakers. Other second years passed their gryphons off to the waiting caretakers and left, which was part of the plan.

Callan would be a part of a much smaller group of boys when he emerged from his gryphon's stall. I snuck out of Ari's and waited, my heart leaping when I recognized Callan walking toward me a minute later, accompanied by a couple of his friends. By lamplight, I didn't see any of their features closely, but I heard them.

"You sure were lucky today, heretic," Callan called to me. Masculine laughter followed, like he was some sort of comedian. I shot a glare over my shoulder and started leading them out of the stables.

As soon as I cleared the stairs, I turned to walk backward through the hallway that led to all the first-year roosts. "You tackled me too hard," I said.

He scoffed, and his friends cackled like a pack of hyenas. Among them, I noticed, was Prince Mateo, smiling cruelly while the rest jeered. "There's no rozash out there that'll hit you softer because your beast is defective," Callan said.

My blood churned hotter in my ears. Game on. I was no longer pretending to argue with him so he'd follow me to get the last word in. "Ari survived having his soul torn nearly in half from his first rider's death. He's a prized beast that flew for the First."

"Was. He *was* a prized beast," he shot back.

"I'd love to see you survive half of what Ari has and still have the strength to come back for more," I sniffed.

I reached the end of the hallway and loosed a nervous chuckle. The prince hadn't gone back to the Falcon Flight roost, and most of my flight members waited behind the door to my left, which was a large storage room. Callan smiled like a predator with his chosen prey already cornered.

"Excuse me! Can you help me?" shouted my flight's most mousy boy, Credell, who drew off one of Callan's friends with some make-believe emergency. I took a deep breath when Callan caught his other friend and the prince by the arm, indicating that they should stay.

For a moment, I wondered what they'd do if I hadn't intended to walk past my flight's rooms and let myself get pressed against this wall. There was nothing friendly in

Callan's face now that he had the superior numbers and no gryphon could come to my rescue.

He cracked his knuckles. "Let's talk about it, Walker. Tell me how your gryphon is so much stronger than me after I'm done with you."

I swallowed my nerve and darted to the side when he came at me. I shoved the door open, making a show of tripping on a small box conveniently placed just a pace away. "No, please," I said, hoping they didn't hear my utter lack of fear as they closed the door, shutting out the light from the hallway.

"Soon as you fail this year, your name will explain how you travel, Walker," Prince Mateo said somewhere close by. I'd crab walked backward from where I'd landed, and the three boys rooted around blindly for me, bumping into boxes and rattling what sounded like glassware in the process.

Callan's friend laughed. "Walk on home!"

I ground my teeth, making sure I was wedged as far back into this room as I could go before my response gave away where I was. "Only you lot would joke about my gryphon dying and think you're not monsters for it."

"Quit hiding. If you want to pretend to be a man, heretic, fight like one," Callan said. He sounded close. My flight was here too, and in the moments I had before springing the trap, I couldn't just let it go and end this peacefully. If Callan wanted a fight, he'd have one.

I rolled to my feet as someone lit a lantern, blinding us all. Callan stood only a couple feet away, and I used this opportunity to punch him right in the face. "That's for the dirty tackle!" I shouted.

Raised voices sounded all through the room as our plan devolved immediately into a melee. I'd struck first, but the boy stumbling away from me and shielding his eye was Prince Mateo, not my intended target. We had the numbers—

the three of them verses myself and all the first years in my flight, sans Credell.

"What have you done?" the prince said in a low voice. He shoved me backward, and the back of my head smacked against one of the metal shelves lining the wall. Stars danced across my vision.

I held my palms up. "I'm sorry. I didn't mean to hit you," I said quickly. Everyone knew striking a royal was a death sentence, even one that needed a little smacking around. He had me up against this shelf, at his mercy as my friends brawled with the only person I'd wanted to punch.

Mateo opened his mouth to respond when a shrill whistle pierced the air. I winced, holding my throbbing forehead.

"What in the fresh hell is this?" screamed a drill sergeant. Most of us had frozen when the door banged open, giving him a great view of Callan standing over Sharde, holding his head steady while lifting a fist poised to strike.

Standing behind the drill sergeant was Callan's other second-year friend, mouth hanging open in shock. Credell looked over his shoulder and flashed us an apologetic grimace.

CHAPTER 27

A BONDING EXPERIENCE

We lined up against the wall and waited to speak with the Commandant one by one. I was toward the back of the group, sandwiched between Prince Mateo and Biggs. The former studiously ignored me, turning his head away so I couldn't see the developing bruise on his face.

Biggs was supposed to be last. He and I had the smallest injuries, but my hand was aching to the same steady throb as the back of my skull.

My dread increased with each shuffle forward. The Commandant was holding everyone for a good five minutes each, or longer in the case of Sharde and Callan. It was at least an hour before another boy tentatively joined the back of the line.

I glanced to the pair of scowling sergeants making sure we stayed civil and hissed toward Credell, "You shouldn't be here."

"I didn't want to be the only one not punished," he whispered back.

A short bark from one of the sergeants silenced us. They probably noticed Credell wasn't with the original group, but they didn't chase him away. I thought it wasn't fair to punish the quiet boy, as he hadn't gotten into the fight with us...but I still understood why he'd come.

It was nearly a punishment *not* to be disciplined when everyone around you was. I'd prefer extra duties to having my flight-mates hate me. They were all I had here.

When I was finally called into the Commandant's office, I breathed a tense sigh. He had his magelight tuned extra bright, spotlighting one of the uncomfortable seats he gestured me into. Night rested in her usual spot. She didn't connect mentally with me again, only sparing a short shake of her head.

The Commandant himself was as polished and disapproving as ever. "Good evening, Cadet Walker."

"Good evening, sir."

"I've heard many an interesting thing about the fight tonight." He steepled his hands over his desk, pinning me with a cool glare. "It sounds like *you* started it, in fact."

I was definitely sweating under my uniform. There was a good chance he'd heard all the details he needed to verify that I was the first to throw a punch. This was just a test of honesty, because whatever punishment awaited me could be a lot worse if I lied on top of it.

"Yes, sir, I did," I mumbled.

His brows raised fractionally. "Striking a prince, no less. Cadet Walker, do I need to stress to you the severity of that action?"

"No, sir. It was an accident," I said.

"The king already demands weekly reports about you." The Commandant pinched the bridge of his nose while I held in a gasp. The king already received reports about me from his son, but it made sense he'd get information from more than one source.

My gaze dropped to the whorls of his desk as I considered what came next. I'd struck a prince and practically shoved my execution warrant into King Cortes's hand. I'd just given him exactly what he wanted for a moment of satisfaction.

"Of course, Cadet Cortes was unable to identify the person who struck him. The ambush by Kite Flight began in the dark," the Commandant continued. "So, the king need not know that anything happened except his son had a brief trip to see a healer for a bruise."

My jaw dropped open, at first in confusion, before I saw the look of stark warning on his face. "We do not condone fights at the Academy, Cadet Walker, and he will be the only one to receive healing magic for this incident. You, most of your flight, and your three new bonus friends will be serving extra duty together every day for a month."

I quickly schooled my expression. "Yes, sir."

"There will come a time when you all will fight against the same enemy. Academy rivalries and training flights won't matter. The only thing that will in those crucial moments is your mutual survival. I hope you learn to value each other during this time."

I held in a disbelieving laugh that Callan and I would ever "value each other" again.

"Sir, it will be my whole flight," I said. "Cadet Credell fought as well."

He raised a brow. "Did he now?"

I didn't answer, following the careful line between truth and integrity for my flight-mate.

After a long pause, he grunted and scribbled something on a page before him. "Well, I didn't know he had it in him. He will be joining your flight in punishment duties. Your entire flight now except for your Cadet-Commander. It'll be a bonding experience."

THERE WAS nothing like laboring alongside Callan; we sure bonded over our mutual hatred of each other. I learned a new respect for Sharde, who served extra duties on weekdays all the time. It was exhausting.

We were placed wherever the fortress needed us most. Usually, it was working in the garden. I'd only heard rumors of it earlier, but we had a few basement levels lit exclusively by magelights attuned to mimic natural sunlight. There was weeding, picking, washing to do…you name it, we did it.

The only benefit I saw was that Callan and his second-year friend ended up skipping a lot of their evening trainings to labor in the garden. They lost significant rank, and I viewed it a lot like Callan finally losing at something.

Sure, it just made him hate me more. Some nasty rumors were started about what I was really doing with my flight-mates, but I tried to ignore it. I had no energy for the gossip and fell immediately into dreamland every night just to wake blearily and do it all again.

A monthly competition came and went. Kite Flight came in last…because why bother? We would be laboring that Saturday anyway.

Things didn't look up until late March, when a heavy box arrived from the Tulari Academy along with a note in my brother's terrible handwriting.

My flight-mates shared dispassionate looks when I brightened and placed the sealed box between us. I was worried they blamed me for the punishment, even if we all agreed that Callan deserved it. Conversations were certainly clipped in our common area. But maybe an offering of something fun would help smooth things over.

"Gods above, doesn't every Tulari learn how to spell?" I grumbled first, trying to decipher my brother's note.

"Spellbooks would be really dangerous if they didn't," Ellie commented, and there were a few tired chuckles.

From what I could tell, Nate was apologizing for the delay

and saying it was hard to mess up a spell in a specific way. But he'd sent us faulty magelights just like I'd asked during the holiday break.

I explained to the group how he'd made them work, seeing modest interest. Korvic frowned at me, though. "Wasn't our last prank enough? I don't want to get in even more trouble if those things explode."

"I agree," Feyring said. For once, Korvic didn't roll his eyes at him.

"They won't *explode*," I protested. "They're just going to make an annoying noise."

Sharde, who'd seemed excited at the prospect of pranking Falcon Flight again, let his face fall. "Yeah, you're probably right. We've gotta keep our heads down for a bit."

I sat back, a queasy feeling in my belly. "That's okay. I won't open the box. We can save it for later."

I propped that box in a corner of my room and figured maybe we'd open it when the extra punishment duties were complete. Until then, we didn't do anything else as a flight until the subject of heraldry came up in class.

We had to decide a few things that would follow us into knighthood. A personal symbol, which would be incorporated into any flight coat of arms we otherwise wore. Whatever was decided as a flight would be permanent through the rest of the Academy.

The only thing assigned to us was a primary color, dark blue. We sat around a plain triangular kite shield like the ones we'd carry into battle, this one already painted the right color.

"There are clear rules for this," Ellie said after we had a good stare at the blank canvas that would become something so important. She held a piece of paper and rattled it all off.

The design should be unique and distinctive at a distance. The primary color will be blue but contain a metallic color plus a main design in another primary color that covers three-fourths of the shield. The last fourth should represent the individual knight.

We couldn't use the color purple or Altare's flag, which was a white background with a golden gryphon rampant. Both the color and the symbol of a rearing beast were property of the royal family, and chances were high that Prince Mateo would carry a shield distinctive from everyone else with this iconography, as befitted his status.

"I think our primary design should be a box," Sharde said. I knew for a fact he used a box as his personal symbol, for his gryphon.

"No, that's boring!" Biggs exclaimed. "We should use a kite bird."

Korvic scoffed. "The same thing every Kite Flight before us has used?"

"How about a dunce cap, then?" Sharde sighed. "That's how everyone else sees us."

We all shouted at once. Sharde stopped making suggestions.

Ellie noted down a few possibilities while we argued about it. "Guys," she said slowly. "Why don't you just use a toy kite? Like the one you fly?"

"That's *so* girly," Biggs complained immediately.

"No, just think about it. Everything you put on this shield is symbolic. You don't have to put bows on it, just a diamond-shaped kite and maybe a little string," she said.

I saw what she was going for, relating to it all too well. "It could be a symbol of us succeeding even though we're one thing and should be another," I said. More than anyone here, I could relate to that. A girl trying to play a boy's game here at the Academy.

In the end, that's what we went with. Blue shield, black diamond-shaped toy kite with a cross pattern on top of the kite to clarify what the diamond was. The cross and string coming off the kite were painted in silver, and we agreed on a thick diagonal band of silver to section off a fourth of the shield for our personal symbols.

There was only one symbol I felt could accurately represent Ari and me. I turned in a yellow design that looked like the curve of a closed gryphon eye.

I was pretty sure the trainers were going to tell us to pick a different design than a giant toy kite. But maybe we made the Commandant laugh, because it was sent to the capital so we could have our individual shields made instead.

CHAPTER 28
REVNA

I started my classes with a scowl, a crumpled-up note in my fist. It suggested that I was a harlot in a girl's neat script. I'd found it in my locker, waiting on top of my uniform for the day. Maybe I'd gotten complacent, but I'd thought we were past this.

During the first semester, I'd gotten an avalanche of these little notes. They'd tapered out…just to return now, during the depths of my punishment-duty-fueled exhaustion. It was like Clara sensed weakness, first picking on Ellie as an easy target and now turning her attention to me while I was slammed with extra work.

I disposed of the note as I entered my first class, sitting with Credell. He looked about as good as I felt, with dark half-moons marking the skin under his eyes. Biggs flanked the quietest boy in our flight, because we all knew who the best in Anatomy and Physiology was.

Credell set his spine as Lord Gadric walked in alongside Ellie. "Good morning, students," he said with a warm expression.

"Good morning, sir," we chorused back.

Ellie headed to the chalkboard to start writing as our

instructor talked. "I'm still grading your essays on gryphon digestion, but they're looking excellent so far."

A tired smile crossed my face. I'd needed Ellie and Credell to explain to me a few times what a gizzard was and how it worked. Gryphons ground up their food with one like birds did since neither species had teeth to reduce what they ate to digestible bits.

It involved swallowing stones to use in the gizzard…and it blew my mind. I'd never seen a gryphon select rocks to gulp down, but apparently, they all do this starting at a young age.

My gaze drifted to the chalkboard, caught by the word "dragon." "Our next unit involves a research project. We'll be looking into the evolution of the rozash species and how they've come to overrun the deserts of Lithos."

I shifted forward in my seat while Biggs groaned. "Another essay," he muttered.

"But we have a reason to learn about *dragons*," I whispered.

One of my favorite paintings back in the palace depicted the early days of Altare, with the first king himself on gryphon back, his legendary magic-infused sword poised toward a full-sized dragon belching curls of flame. It was a monster of a creature, larger than any rozash would ever be, with lava-lined eyes and sword-like claws made for cleaving knights in half.

"Don't worry," my father had said the first time he'd found a young me staring up at the painted scene. "That's a dragon. Nothing like them exists anymore."

I'd turned a heartbroken expression back to him. "Why not? It's so cool!"

My father had explained the same things Lord Gadric was saying now. "…We believe dragons bred themselves out of existence with a weaker species of desert snake. The resulting cross became rozash, some capable of breathing dragon fire or spitting snake acid. The goal of this unit is for you all to assemble research teams and assemble information on a piece of the pie that is rozash evolution."

I immediately glanced toward my two flight-mates, creating my research team with just a mutual look. Hopefully Ellie would help us too, because this project sounded difficult and like it would require a lot of research outside of class. When did I have time? The punishment duties took up nearly all my free moments.

I simmered on the problem through my next class and came to World Cultures with a scowl. Why'd I have to punch Prince Mateo? Why'd I even agree to "intimidate" Callan? I'd known it would become a fight the moment he'd taken my bait so easily.

"A warrior does not slouch," Instructor Signe said when I passed her. I snapped upright immediately under her unusual violet stare. I slipped into my seat front and center, a place I'd had to trade a full bag of mallows for with one of the Harrier Flight boys.

World Cultures was easily my favorite class. Some of the boys found it too easy to zone out under Signe's even voice and fail the constant quizzes and mid-story questions she used to assign us grades.

I had a perfect score by comparison. She weaved the sagas of her people into a story I couldn't get enough of. Tall tales, larger-than-life heroes, and huge, epic battles all flowed from her mouth with the skill of someone who'd told them count-less times.

Most of it wasn't written down. But today, like many days, an unfamiliar man sat in the back with a quill and inkwell at the ready. I didn't know why Signe's stories were sometimes recorded. She never acknowledged the scribes that would come and go.

When the last cadet entered, she shifted on her stool. Instead of a greeting, she began in a quiet voice, "One spring morning, a young woman rode the skies in search of a storm. She was an eldrafn rider, blessed by the Goddess of Thunder, Idunn. Her village was strong because of her beast. Tell me why." She jerked her chin my way.

I smiled eagerly. "Because eldrafn are more than a symbol. Most Rathi villages don't have their protection and tend to fall to raids from villages and towns that do."

Eldrafn were, thankfully, quite rare. They were predators of gryphons and nearly impossible to kill, as they were living storms that could take on a solid bird shape. I'd heard that proper techniques to fight them were taught to third years.

Signe nodded. "That's right. This girl was one in a generation for her village, to be chosen by her eldrafn, Revna. She sought to make her people proud this day, because Revna had taught her one of the eldrafn's many secrets. They do not reproduce of males and females, but instead of the elements themselves.

"The girl wanted to bring back an eldrafn egg to further her personal legend and turn her village into a regional power. They needed to find the biggest, meanest thunderstorm and travel to its eye. Within it, formed of the elements and suspended by a cocoon of air, would be a forming egg," Signe explained. She cupped her hands as she spoke.

"The eggs only hatch naturally when they're a part of the worst kind of storms, the ones that hit hard and devastate everything in their path. Smaller storms release their eldrafn eggs, which get dashed to pieces by the unforgiving ground.

"Any human-harvested eggs need to be energized directly with electricity from another eldrafn or several storms. This is how the Rathi gain more of their beasts. However, it is dangerous even for experienced riders. The girl only understood why in theory. Students, give me a few reasons why harvesting an eldrafn egg would be dangerous."

Several hands went up, including my own. She ignored me, pointing to Sharde hiding in the back, who certainly wasn't advertising his eagerness to answer. He sighed and asked, "Didn't you say last year that strong winds start tearing apart the rider's adult eldrafn?"

"That is true," she confirmed, calling on another person.

"They could get struck by lightning," the other cadet said.

"That would kill most people," Signe agreed. "However, eldrafn absorb electricity of all sorts, shielding their riders."

Finally, she called on me again. "What if they go all that way and there's no egg?"

"That happens often," she said, nodding in approval. "In this particular case, the girl and her eldrafn were chasing a particularly promising thunderstorm. They approached it as it released its rain from dark, flat-bottomed clouds. Strong winds battered them from all directions."

I imagined what that'd be like. Ari and I hadn't flown together through weather that bad, let alone sought it out on purpose. My gryphon stirred where he rested on a cushion next to me. *I wouldn't usually fly in a downpour anyway,* he grumbled.

"Revna screeched in pain as the wind began tearing at her body, but her rider was determined. There had to be an eldrafn egg in the heart of this storm. They'd traveled so far. She saw the challenge ahead and thought only of her personal legend. She and Revna had been bonded for a few years, long enough for Revna to reach adulthood as a massive raven-shaped storm three times the largest female gryphon. It was just enough time for the girl to consider them ready to harvest new eldrafn eggs."

I glanced down to Ari, a nervous squirm starting in my gut. *Have you heard this one before?* I asked him.

I think so. And I think what you're thinking is right.

The grim set of Signe's trembling mouth seemed to confirm my thoughts, but I listened to her with the hope I was wrong.

"The girl guided Revna through the clouds, in search of a

patch of peace as the wind snatched at her and her mount. It fought them bitterly, whirling static-filled moisture into their faces.

"Revna's pained cries grew in pitch as they continued into the center of the storm. You see, eldrafn don't have the luxury of magic able to translate their meaning to humans. The girl understood her mount was struggling, though, and asked her to hold on a little longer. The hardship would be worth it."

I shook my head in disagreement. The decision to keep going seemed foolish.

"And so they did, finding a glimmering gem suspended in a patch of calm air. The girl stood in her stirrups and reached —" Signe leaned up on her stool and mimicked the motion, before closing her hand around air. "—She grabbed the egg and cheered, looking down to share the moment with Revna. But her eldrafn was barely there, just an outline of lightning-laced purple clouds below her. Their eyes met, and the girl realized they were falling."

"No," I gasped.

"Revna curled what was left of her body around the girl, and they fell out of the sky together. They screamed all the way down."

Signe paused, and we could've heard a pin drop in the utter silence of the room. Even the least engaged boys were leaning in, waiting to hear how this story ended.

"They landed in the mud together. Revna shielded her rider from the worst of it, but the girl's leg was shattered beyond repair from the impact. In a haze of agony and heartbreak, she held the last shreds of her beloved eldrafn before the wind blew them away. She was left there with an egg the size of her fist.

"By some act of will, the girl dragged herself back to her village. It took weeks of leaning on the brink of death before she arrived. And do you know what her village elders said to her when they learned her actions had gotten her eldrafn killed?"

Ari sat up, ruffling his feathers. I started raising my hand before realizing it was a rhetorical question.

"They took the egg, which would need many storms' worth of electricity to hatch. And then they told her..." She pointed to the door and said with quiet venom, "Get out."

We glanced around when she held the pose, nodding and pointing again from a few questioning glances. This was the end of class.

"But what about the girl?" I asked as I stood. Signe shook her head and flexed her hand.

I left and spent the rest of the day quiet in contemplation, considering the fate of the girl from Signe's story. Without the fellowship of her people, her life couldn't have had a happy ending.

I was due for my daily punishment duty, this time in the kitchen, when an idea occurred to me. Instead of heading for the sweltering heat and demands of pot scrubbing in a busy kitchen, my feet turned down a different path. Instructors and other important adults lived on the fourth floor, but I had no idea which room was Signe's.

Ari nudged me out of the way and leaned his beak toward the ground. He rooted around and led the way, stopping at the second door from the stairs. *"This one."*

I glanced over my shoulder, fairly certain I was about to get demerits for bothering an instructor after hours. Still, I knocked and waited.

Something banged on the other side of the door, plus muffled curses. Instructor Signe opened it, leaning heavily on her cane.

A girl banished from her village after suffering a terrible wound to her leg. Someone with no place to go after accidentally killing a precious magical beast. How hadn't I figured it out immediately? "Was she you?" I blurted.

Signe blinked once before stepping aside. "Come in," she sighed.

She limped her way further inside as I glanced around. Ari carefully stuck to my shadow in the unfamiliar room. It was double the size of the room I shared with Ellie, with a thin covering of rugs underfoot, plus the pelt of some thick-furred animal placed at the base of a cushioned chair that looked well-loved. A meal rested on a table within arm's reach of the chair, and fragrant steam still rose from it.

"Stay there," she ordered, limping her way into a conjoined room that had to be her bedroom. She returned with a wooden box wedged under one elbow.

Signe sat in her padded throne and indicated I should drag over one of the chairs resting against the wall. She placed the box between us on the table, and I trembled, feeling like I was about to be let into some huge Rathi secret.

"I hid this from my village elders, implying that it'd been destroyed when we hit the ground," Signe said, lifting the lid and tilting the box. Within was…a flat rock about the size of my head.

It was a matte purple color, with small black veins shot through it, branching like lightning strikes. "I've never shown this to a cadet before. Do you know what it is?" She asked.

I shook my head.

"The missing part of my story, young woman. Revna's heart." She placed wrinkled fingers over it. "When an eldrafn dies, its heart remains, solid like stone. It transforms into their new egg. With enough power infused into it, the eldrafn rises again. I made sure my village didn't get this part of me back. Call it selfish, but I knew they'd hatch her alongside the other egg I returned with but give her to another rider who was both whole and free of the weight of failure."

I felt my eyes sting. "I'm so sorry," I murmured. "I would hide her heart too. But…it's still an egg?"

She lifted the heart from its box and handed it to me. I

took it with both hands, my hold on it dipping. It was far heavier than it looked. "It's null," she said. "An egg about to hatch would be charged with electricity. You, absent of my goddess's blessing, would not be able to hold it. I...I have failed for ages to hatch it. Revna needs the power of a living eldrafn. Nothing else will do."

She took the egg back and rested it carefully in the box. "That is what happened to the girl," she said. "Does the ending of her legend satisfy you?"

"No," I said immediately.

"Then you have learned a valuable lesson today. Not every personal legend is as successful and heroic as the ones I've shared with you," she said. "I know you are not Rathi, but do be careful with your own legend, young woman."

I shook my head. "But Instructor...your story isn't finished," I said.

"Sure. It is in its last chapter, though." Her gaze fell to the box again. "One way or another, I will see my beloved Revna again one day."

CHAPTER 29

TOESIES

TIME MARCHED ON, slipping through my fingertips and circling back to nip my heels with exhaustion. It felt like I got up one day and realized the youngling gryphons of my flight weren't babies anymore.

They were yearlings. And while I had a gap in my schedule, they were learning to fly without their riders. I looked up from a pickup game of hoops one afternoon, suddenly face to face with a happily trilling Mireille.

Ari squawked a warning, causing the yearling to peel away from us before we could collide. *"Silly young thing,"* he groused.

I patted his neck, grinning when I turned to see Ironfeather lurching through the sky, his beak parted in joy. He arrowed straight for his sister while Snowpoint circled below, keeping a watchful eye on them testing their wings. "C'mon," I called to Ari, turning us so we could frolic with the younger gryphons.

He grumped for less than a minute before nudging and nipping them, playing like a yearling himself. When Puzzlebox and Sharde joined us, our hoops game disbanded, becoming a flurry of feathers. The Green filled with the rest of the yearlings flying for the first time, spurred on by the promise of fun.

I described it for Ari over our Link, feeling how he radiated a sense of pride for the newest generation. The other gryphons came to him, circling in for a telegraphed nip or chirping to make them easier to chase.

I wished we could have more carefree afternoons like this. The Green was starting to resemble its namesake again as spring came in late this far into the mountains. We'd trampled fresh flowers during April's monthly competition. Falcon Flight's flag waved from its pedestal, looking a little worn from being out in the elements for so long.

In the few still moments I had, I wondered if we would ever see Kite Flight's flag there instead. We were a steady third-place showing now that we'd learned to work together. With few exceptions, the rankings went Falcon, Osprey, Kite, Harrier. We had one more chance coming up next month, right before the official Pass in Review with the king and generals.

I'd heard there would be special rules to keep us on our toes. The one thing I seriously hoped for was a chance to finally see Kite ranked above Falcon.

The opportunity came in an envelope one evening to the roost. Biggs called everyone over to look at a letter slipped under the door.

It was addressed to me... My cynical side said, "Of course it is." But it was from my "friend" with a warning not to sleep too deeply tonight.

I exchanged a glance with Ellie. "Maybe you should give your father a visit," I suggested. "It'd be a shame if someone were to try to sneak into our rooms or something."

Sergeant Kobarn just so happened to be in the area when a team of boys from Osprey Flight tried to place lit poppers all throughout our dorm. Poppers were illegal in closed spaces; once they got going, they made a ton of noise and showered colorful, *real* sparks all around them every few seconds.

"Thanks, friend," I said to myself after hearing they'd gotten a bunch of punishment duties.

Sharde brought up what I was thinking the next day as we lounged together in our roost after a grueling day of physical training. "You know, Osprey Flight made a rookie mistake," he said. "They must've told the wrong someone what they'd planned on doing, and word got out. Why don't we show 'em how it's done?"

"I thought we were out of the pranking business," Weslecker drawled.

"Well, I keep thinking about what a missed opportunity we had about a month ago." Sharde glanced to me, and I shot to my feet in excitement. My brother's artfully broken magelights were gathering dust in a box.

Without prompting, I got the tightly sealed box and placed it before the group. A few of the boys looked uncomfortable, notably Feyring and Korvic, but no one shot down the idea of using them quite yet.

"They'd be good for one night," I said. "So, if we're doing this, we'd need to plant them right before a big event." Like the monthly competition.

"Run through what these things are supposed to do again," Weslecker prompted while reaching for the box.

I pushed his hand away. "Once activated, they emit a faint but annoying buzzing," I said. The kind of sound that would make it hard to sleep if it were a few feet away. "If you clap your hands to turn it off, it bounces around instead, and the noise becomes louder. Did you guys know most magelights are enchanted to resist going through a doorway once activated in a room? It takes a Tulari if someone wants to move it. So, it'll take a Tulari coming to their room to remove them."

Falcon Flight was the only group wealthy enough to have magelights in their dorm. There were Tulari in the fortress, but the process of getting one to come to them in the middle of the night would make quite the stir.

"My only concern is…well, I guess you guys haven't seen this happen." Weslecker glanced around and sighed. "Mage-lights tend to explode if they're made incorrectly. I think it could be a funny prank, but we'd get in serious trouble if that happened and someone got hurt."

Sharde scoffed. "Please. If we do this right before the monthly competition, what are they going to do? Not promote us to second years?"

My guts knotted instantly at the thought, and I wasn't the only one. Ari nipped my thigh. *This is a bad idea. All your pranks have been,"* he muttered.

I hesitated. There was a thrill in fulfilling a good prank, and the magelights were mostly harmless. But was I really willing to risk throwing everything away for a laugh at Falcon Flight's expense?

"Says the guy who had to repeat his first year," Weslecker was saying, his eyes rolling.

I took the box back into my lap, shaking my head. "Guys, let's not do this. It's too much like cheating," I said, drawing surprised looks. "If we want to prank Falcon Flight, we can do something less risky. I don't want to know what happens if one of these orbs explodes and hurts someone."

Weslecker jumped to my side immediately, while Biggs and Sharde cast longing looks at the sealed box of magelights.

"All right. We'll figure out a different prank." Sharde flashed a big, bright smile.

As soon as the yearlings learned to fly, I realized we sometimes had a guest for Aerial Agility class. Commander Rudrick would have the cadets construct our own obstacle courses by having us roll out weighted carts with extendable hoops or slalom poles that could be lifted several yards into the sky.

I always tried to space out the obstacles, but others liked to make the sharpest turns possible. To my left, a second hoop was erected only feet from mine. I turned to give the other cadet a piece of my mind for putting a nearly impossible turn into today's course.

Prince Mateo was looking up at his hoop, before starting to secure the pole that attached it to its cart with a band of metal. He smirked my way. "Think your beast can handle it?" he asked.

"With his eyes literally closed," I scoffed. I just needed to warn him mentally about what obstacles were in our way in the air. The former fastest gryphon in the First could turn with pinpoint accuracy, but only if he knew what moves to make. We only missed turns because my reaction time was far slower than his. "What are you doing here?"

If anything, the prince looked smugger. "I'm joining the Aerial Agility class."

"You and Mireille haven't been through Flight Training," I pointed out.

He lifted a shoulder. "The Commandant approved it. Mireille's already strong enough to carry me and eager to learn," he said.

I turned that over in my mind, in an extra sour mood when the course was assembled and the cadets lined up to try it alongside their gryphons. Mireille flanked my other side since Prince Mateo was going last, right after Ari and me. She'd clearly grown like a weed. Her head was at my elbow, and her figure was quickly filling into the thick and strong female gryphon build.

What if Prince Mateo fell off her, though? One of the most important things a gryphon learned in Flight Training was how to catch their rider should they become unseated. Yet I glanced to Ari, wondering if we'd really mastered that technique with his blindness.

He answered my thoughts. *"I doubt it matters. What the princeling wants, he gets. Do you see any other first years in this class?"*

"No," I answered.

"That's because he'll be the only one added. Royal privilege, learning how to fly and fight early."

I knew in my gut that he was right.

ONE SATURDAY, I was heading off with Ari for some extra flight training when Ellie stood before the door out into the hall. "You're taking a break," she told me.

I blinked. "I am?"

She smiled wide as she showed me a couple small bottles she'd been hiding behind her back, plus a set of tiny brushes. "You are. You've been working super hard, and I barely see you unless you're passed out. Want to do something girly?"

Ari nudged my side in encouragement. I got the feeling he didn't want to do more training, and that feeling bled along our Link, making her offer extra tempting. "Is that nail polish?" I asked.

Ellie brightened further. "Yeah! I made it myself. I've got a good clear and pink. The red didn't come out the way I expected, though." She held up the bottle, which was a screamingly bright shade that looked like it belonged in a fire. "C'mon!"

We turned the roost into a mini spa after I took a brief trip to get grooming tools for gryphons since Ari insisted on getting his paws done too, plus a couple buckets and cotton balls. There was nothing stopping me from getting my toenails painted; besides, they'd be hidden in my boots. I had Ellie paint them bright, flaming red.

Ari murred happily when we both massaged his feet. She'd made the clear polish so we could paint his talons after a little pampering.

Soon, Puzzlebox found us, wandering out of Sharde's room alone since he was off fulfilling yet another extra duty. She lay out next to Ellie, peering over the girl's lap at what we were doing, before pawing at the other girl for attention. "Aww, do you want to get your toesies done too?" Ellie cooed.

I think Puzzlebox was Ellie's favorite. She'd been spoiled by the sweet personalities of our flight's gryphons, and Puzzlebox was by far the most affectionate. The gryphon twittered back, bobbing her head excitedly.

When Ellie and I had her toes spread and the clear polish out, Puzzlebox cawed and pulled her paw back. She leaned over and gently clasped the pink bottle in her beak, handing it to Ellie. I exchanged a glance with her.

Ellie shrugged. "There's no regulation that says she can't have painted talons."

To the gryphon's delight, we painted them pink. Sharde had a laughing fit that evening when Puzzlebox proudly lifted and curled her paw so he could see it for himself.

"You did this? It's brilliant," he said to Ellie, drawing a bright blush from her.

Within the week, Sergeant Kobarn was stopping us before PT to announce a new regulation: gryphons couldn't have colored talons. Puzzlebox made a soft chirp of dismay.

"Don't worry, girl," Sharde whispered. "Soon as we're delivering mail, I'll paint your toesies whatever color you want."

I FORGOT I'd ever shown my flight the box with my brother's magelights as the end of the academic year swiftly approached. We trained for weeks on a grueling schedule designed to shape both gryphon and rider into their most fit selves.

Sharde joked that this was to make sure we still had muscle tone after the two-month-long summer break, even though we only received that time off for solstice celebrations and to give yearlings a chance to grow large enough to carry the weight of a rider. The boys a year ahead of us only received a month off by comparison, to rest up before they learned the last secrets of gryphon riding.

I hadn't spoken with the Commandant in his office since the fight, and my grades were all passing. Though I didn't want to say it aloud yet, I was certain Ari and I had done it— we were going on to the second year. Ari would live to thrive in courses dedicated to aerial prowess and jousting, two things he had already excelled at in the past.

So, the day before the last monthly competition, I was on my best behavior. I didn't notice the magelight box was gone when I stumbled into bed right before lights out.

I fell into a dreamless sleep until a deep *BOOM* shook the room.

CHAPTER 30

OWN IT

Every first-year cadet lined up in the hallway while a Tulari inspected Falcon Flight's rooms. My heart thudded at double time, knowing exactly what exploded but not how it got in there. It had to be someone from my flight, and I cast a sideways glance at Sharde, who had the grace to look sheepish.

"What did you do?" I hissed.

"Later," he replied under his breath. Both of us whipped back to attention when a wizened form emerged from Falcon Flight's roost and held up two jagged pieces of what looked like glass.

The Tulari they'd called in was none other than the best, the elderly Lord Gadric. He cleared his throat, and it was quieter than the Anatomy and Physiology classroom in that drafty hall. "No need to worry, young men…and ladies." He glanced briefly toward where Ellie and I stood. "Sometimes magelights malfunction, and they make a lot of noise doing it. You can go back to sleep."

One of the drill sergeants called a dismissal, and we shuffled off in a murmur of tired voices. The moment we were all safely behind Kite Flight's door, I rounded on Sharde, hands on my hips. "You went into my room," I accused.

Ellie raised a fluttering hand. "Actually," she said, her voice a nervous squeak, "I, uh, gave them to him."

I threw my hands up and leaned in with a glare. "Why? I thought we agreed, as a flight, that it was a bad idea!"

Ellie drew herself up. "I know you thought using them was cheating, but you guys deserve to win!" A solid blush stole over her cheeks, but she turned to me and dropped her tone. "Sivana, you've worked so hard. I just wanted to help you win for once."

"You know bad ideas have never stopped me," Sharde interrupted. "Look, I'm sorry we stole them from you, Sivana, but no one suspects anything except a faulty magelight. We're fine." He casually slung his arm around Ellie's shoulders, and her flustered face lit up.

My nostrils flared. "Fine? W-we're fine?" I felt the words slip away from my tongue as my ire rose. "There were *two* magelights. What happens if the second explodes too and actually hurts someone?"

Sharde scratched behind his head, not meeting my eyes.

"Since we're moving out in a couple days, another Tulari's going to come along and disenchant all the magelights so they can be stored," Weslecker pitched in. He put a hand on my shoulder, giving it a squeeze. Our gazes met, and I couldn't help but echo his little smile.

"Wait. If they're not Lord Gadric, they'll probably hear the bad one buzz," I said, realization hitting. I slunk out of Weslecker's hold, pacing a circle around the roost. "And they'll do a final count and realize there's one extra. Anyone with any brains will put together that it's the messed-up one, and they'll realize the explosion tonight could be related."

"Oh, shoot," Ellie murmured.

"We're not fine at all," I said, tugging on my hair in sudden despair. If they started questioning cadets, someone could accidentally let it slip that I'd had the faulty magelights for some time. Or worse, they could pull my records and see that I have a brother in the Tulari Academy right now.

"Walker," Weslecker was saying as I paced.

They were going to expel me at the last possible moment.

"Sivana!"

I was such a failure. I'd messed up Ari's second chance just for a stupid—

I walked into Weslecker's chest, and he pulled me into a hug. A yelp escaped my lips. I hadn't been hugged since… Yule. I was slow to put my arms around him in return, and so he was already grabbing my shoulders to give me a sound shake. "It's going to be all right. I have an idea," he said.

"Do you have a Tulari friend here?" I asked. Maybe we could deactivate it first and smash it later.

He shook his head. "One summer at my parent's…" He was about to say summer home or second estate, I think, but cleared his throat. "I found a room with three old magelights that no one ever visited. Even the lights were covered in dust. Get this, I figured out how to break 'em. No one noticed me hauling in sticks and rocks and other things to throw at them, but eventually, I figured out what does it."

"Yeah?" I pushed aside the wonder that a family could be so rich they could have not one but three magelights gathering dust.

"Yeah." He grinned. "The secret is they can't get wet. Let's go in there while everyone's distracted by the monthly competition and dunk it in a bucket of water. No one will ever know."

MY HEART SANK the next day when the instructors announced the special rules for the last round of competitions for this academic year.

We had to choose five people from our flight for each of the events. Our performances would not only be tied to our overall flight ranking, but sportsmanship, and the number of events each cadet was picked for would also affect our individual rank.

The individual rank was an invisible number so far, but it was about to be unveiled during the graduation ceremony tomorrow after Pass in Review. I had a plan to disappear, douse the magelight, and come back, but that was a long time to go missing, and it would probably hurt my ranking. Plus, I needed another person to pull off the plan.

Sharde was our star player in talonball, and Weslecker always came on top in duels. I could miss those events... except Eagle Flight, one of the second-year flights, were trying to get me and Ari to plug a hole in their hoops game, which would overlap those two events on the ground.

Ari yearned to join them. *"Let Sharde fix his own mistake,"* he growled.

"We have to make sure it happens," I said.

Kite Flight gathered in a circle to discuss who would be doing what. "Sharde and I are going to sit out dueling," I said. My brows raised in his direction, and he nodded. "We're going to take care of the...problem."

"You're probably going to miss the agility course, then," Biggs said. I might never come out on top in dueling, but at least I usually did well in the agility event. I raised my hands in a shrug. "But I want to *win*. We have to put our best people in every event."

"And I can't get sent home over a stupid prank," I snapped.

Biggs cast his gaze downward with a sigh.

I softened my voice. "Look, I want to win too. We're still going to do great. Let's get it done." I put my hand forward, and the boys stacked theirs atop it.

We hollered the Kite Flight battle cry. After months of

arguing, we'd come up with "Kite Flight, *whoosh!*" while pumping our fists to the sky. At least we weren't Harrier Flight, who screeched like birds.

I took to the sky shortly after to play some hoops. Ari was flattered to be invited, even if the second years had spread themselves too thin to attend two events at the same time. We were scoring when shouts broke out from the Green beneath us, followed by shrill whistles.

"What do you see?" Ari asked, wheeling around so I could peer over his wing.

The small human forms below us were converging on one point. *"Looks like our plan's a go. Take us lower,"* I suggested, seeing how our other competitors were distracted and peering downward too.

A figure with a head of blond hair lay on the ground, the face red with blood even when seen from above. *"Oof. Sharde got hit hard,"* I remarked, holding my arms up for a time out in the hoops game. I circled Ari around until the other players could hear me. "That's my flight-mate down there. I'm going to help him get to the infirmary."

"But we need you too!" one of my teammates protested.

"Let her go. She's probably got a thing for him," another muttered.

My fingers formed fists around Ari's reins. *"Don't dignify them with a response,"* Ari said, interrupting my furious thoughts. We turned away from the boys with a last glare and circled for a landing.

"Sharde!" I exclaimed like we hadn't planned this. I thought it'd be hard to feign concern until I saw his nose leaking twin trails of blood. My heart leapt to double time as I shouldered into the circle of boys crowding around his prone form.

We got him to his feet, and I insisted on taking him inside to head to the infirmary. "But there's a nurse here," a Harrier

Flight boy suggested as I looped one of Sharde's arms over my shoulders and started for the fortress.

Right. Minor bumps and scrapes were expected on field days like these. I thanked him and changed direction until we were off the Green, then started for the fortress again as whistles sounded behind us and the game continued.

"I actually might need to see someone," Sharde said slowly. Puzzlebox whined from where she flanked him.

My steps slowed. "Of course. The nurse back there could just take care of you…"

He shook his head. "After we get rid of the magelight problem." But his bumped head made climbing the stairs a laborious task. I listened to the distant shrills of whistles and hoped we wouldn't miss too much. I could practically feel my rank fall and cursed our stupid plan, which hinged on one of us getting hurt.

Still, we made it to the dorms with no drill sergeants coming to look for us. Ari and Puzzlebox followed us the whole time, even sneaking into the Falcon Flight dorm with us.

"Nice digs," I murmured, looking around. It was a mirror of the dorm I lived in, but everything was nicer. New cushions, plush chairs, finer desks, and magelights. Everything was cheerfully lit by dozens of magelights.

Sharde shrugged me off and held his head. "I put one out here and another in one of the rooms," he mumbled. "Sir Gadric didn't say which one exploded."

"Should be easy enough to find…" I looked to Ari, who had his ears pinned to his skull. *"Where's the bad one?"* I asked him privately.

He led me to one hovering over the single slatted window the boys had left open. I peered out of it anxiously to see two different groups playing hoops and a team of men setting up what looked like the obstacle course. It was obvious immediately that Ari had taken me to the faulty magelight, as a faint but high-pitched squeal invaded my ears.

"Thank you," I said to my gryphon, petting him once before he retreated from it. With Sharde in bad shape, I took a few minutes to sneak over to our own dorm, retrieve a bucket of water we already had prepared, and return to grab the magelight out of the air and wrestle it into the bucket.

It was slippery and wiggly like jelly, resistant until it was fully submerged. Water hissed as sparks rose from it before it cracked into dozens of glass pieces with a smell like burning hair.

I breathed out a tense sigh of relief. We'd done it. We'd made sure no one would know the prank came from us. With the window open, the odor would filter out shortly.

I turned to Sharde, bucket in hand, ready to take him to the infirmary. The door opened behind him, and in walked Prince Mateo, who stopped short to stare at us both. I hid the bucket behind my back with a slosh.

"What—" The prince shook his head. "Never mind. I don't want to know. This is fortunate timing, actually, because my father just arrived."

I felt my whole body ice over, predicting what he was about to say.

"He wants to talk to you, Walker. Now."

CHAPTER 31

MURDEROUS PIG

Despite his protests, I took Sharde to the infirmary first before facing the Commandant's door. Prince Mateo had said this was where the king wished to see me, and it felt fitting that he'd settled in the one place I dreaded being called to the most.

I knocked, and it wasn't the Commandant's voice that hollered for me to enter. Sitting behind his desk, a file in hand, was King Cortes himself, his thick lips pressed in displeasure the moment he laid eyes on me. "Your gryphon stays outside," he demanded right after I showed the proper respect.

I glanced over to Ari in dismay, but the gryphon tossed his head and took a pace back. *I will be close if you need me,* he said, sitting just beyond the threshold.

Part of me recognized this was the first time I'd ever spoken with the king one on one, because the Commandant and Night were also gone. But the king had claimed the position of power and was undoubtedly leafing through the Academy's records of my progress. I sat across from him, the room silent save for the scratching of a flipped page.

Eventually, he set the whole thing down, his jowls quivering as he beheld me. I wished I knew what I'd done to inspire such hatred, but in the same breath, I thought, *What haven't I done?* From saving Ari up until this moment, he'd gotten reports of my progress and my refusal to lie down and let Ari die. He'd read the same articles from the *Kaiamear Gazette* where Miles Glimmerwick laid my accomplishments on extra thick.

I was the living symbol of change, just as his son had called me. The enemy of an older man in power. I swallowed my nerve as I bowed my head to break our stare-off.

"You came quickly, good. We can get this unpleasantness out of the way," he said. His tone held a sneer. "I've received several updates on your progress, and many have pointed to an obvious conclusion: that training you and your gryphon has been an egregious waste of resources."

My heart pattered at double time, my palms sweating against my thighs. "The Commandant himself says that you both are not prepared to be second years. You know what that means," he continued.

I've failed, that's what it means, I thought, my lips twisting. If I wasn't promoted, the king would have Ari executed. I'd known that all along, but I'd been so sure we'd improved since that heartbreaking conversation with the Commandant. Ari and I had both strived to be our best selves.

Was it really not enough? I took one look into the king's bloodshot eyes and had my answer. That wasn't the face of someone I could please.

"After the graduation ceremony, you and your gryphon will report to Kaiamear for his execution. You will be flown back under armed guard," he informed me. "If you resist, your gryphon will be butchered on the spot. But if you follow your orders, he will be given an honored military burial alongside his true rider. Don't take this from him, young lady. Your attempt to beguile him is at an end."

"With all due respect, Your Majesty—"

"I don't want to hear it," he snapped.

My nostrils flared. I only realized I was making fists when my fingernails bit into the skin of my palms. "You'd kill my best friend without hearing what I have to say?" I said heatedly. "Then you—you're a-an"—I could feel myself trembling as his face and neck shaded toward tomato red—"an unreasonable, murderous pig!"

I regretted it the moment the words hung in the air. For a moment, he stared at me, slack-jawed at my daring. He could do anything he wanted in return for my disrespect. My nation's crown sat on his head at every ceremony. But King Cortes finished weighing his options and simply swung a finger toward the door. "Get out of my sight!" he roared.

I left with haste, finding Ari already on his paws, hackles raised. *"I heard everything,"* he told me as I rushed to the stairs. I plowed ahead, in a hurry to return to the monthly games and the sense of normalcy they'd bring.

Impatiently, I swept at the moisture gathering in my eyes. It was only when we were within a few yards of the Green that I stopped and knelt, wrapping my arms around his solid shoulders. I wept into his fur. *"He cannot take you. We're going to prove it to the Commandant and anyone else watching,"* I said fiercely. *"We're graduating to second year tomorrow."*

"You have a plan?" he asked. Over our Link, he'd returned to a calm and steady state. Nothing the king had said seemed to linger over him.

"I do."

"Is it a good plan?" he teased. I could feel him tugging gently on my braid.

"The competitions affect our rank, and they're still setting up the agility course. I'm going to be first at that event. Not just first in the flight...first total." I released my tight hold on him and cleared my cheeks. The cheers coming from the Green suggested there were duels happening, which meant we'd missed at least half of the competitions already.

If I was first at the only competition I'd had a chance to compete in, surely it would still boost my rank and give the Commandant another reason to second-guess his decision not to pass us. I glanced to Ari, realization setting in.

"You're not worried," I said.

His emotions were a placid lake. He tilted his beak and said, *"I will not fear for my life until the Commandant himself says we are not worthy."*

"The king was reading our file, Ari. Everything the Commandant has written about us."

"So?" He lifted his wings in a gryphon shrug. *"Humans lie."*

Another, louder cheer sounded across the Green. I hesitated, torn between debating my gryphon and seeing what's happening over there. Ari nudged me, and I started moving toward the dueling rings painted in the center of the Green, surrounded by temporary fences and a horde of screaming cadets.

I shouldered toward the front of the group, finding a place between Biggs and Pereyra. The former jumped up and down as he watched the fight while the latter hollered encouragement. I realized why as I recognized Weslecker's outline in padded armor, fencing with a Falcon Flight boy. Soon I was yelling too, pumping my fist when Weslecker scored a hit.

His eyes met mine from within his helmet, and he flashed his teeth before attacking his opponent with a new flurry of blows, securing his victory. The crowd screamed as Weslecker held his weapon aloft. He remained in the ring, accepting a water skin from one of the soldiers.

"So, how we looking?" I asked my flight-mates.

Biggs turned a grin my way. "Every flight had to pick five people for the duels, right? Only Weslecker got to round two from our flight, and that was his third match. We're waiting on the instructors to eliminate one of the remaining guys, so there are four cadets left."

We were used to the instructors pruning a competitor if there ended up an uneven number. It'd happened to me once, but it sucked each time if the cadet wasn't wounded or had fought well. Usually, one person was obviously the weakest choice and thus out.

But Weslecker, he was never pruned. I wasn't even surprised when they ushered in a new cadet for him to duel. My friend was obviously winded at this point, but so was the other boy, their duel slower as they circled and taunted. The crowd was even louder for this fight, as individuals converged on either this duel or the other happening close by.

Weslecker won and took a bow, flashing a cheeky wink toward the crowd. For a moment, I thought maybe...he was looking at me when he did it. I gave myself a little shake. No, he was just adding a flourish to his victory. By the sounds of things, the other duel was still going, so Weslecker took his water skin and leaned on the fence close to us for a breather.

"You're doing great, man. Just one more fight," Biggs said. He, Pereyra, and a few other boys clapped the back of his armor enthusiastically.

"We're in good shape," Weslecker told me. "How's Sharde? We got second place at talonball while you two were in the infirmary."

"He'll be okay," I said. "Did we win the mile?"

"Yeah! I did!" Biggs said proudly. I grinned. The mile run was reliably Kite Flight's due to our fastest runner.

"Wow. Really good shape." I didn't want to say it aloud just in case I jinxed us, but if Weslecker won the last duel and I grabbed success by the throat during the agility course, we could see Kite Flight's flag flying over the Green at last.

Of course, even thinking that brought the specter of bad luck in the form of Prince Mateo, Weslecker's last opponent. I swallowed heavily as the two boys squared up. The prince was nearly undefeated, and I'd felt the sting of his blunted weapon nearly every month when we all had to duel.

I knew that the prince and Weslecker were taught to fight by the same Endolian tutor. They were best friends only separated by the flimsy ties of different flights. That didn't mean either of them held back the moment the whistle blew. The prince attacked aggressively in a sweeping blow I recognized from the aggressive Rushing River Rapids style, a sneer half-hidden under his helmet. Sparks flew from blunted steel when Weslecker deflected the blow and threw out a quick riposte.

"Let's go, Weslecker!" I screamed over the cheering crowd.

To my dismay, Weslecker struggled to match the speed of the prince's blows. One slipped through his guard and struck his shoulder. I winced. I'd dropped my weapon from a similar strike in the past.

Weslecker disengaged and flipped his weapon into his opposite hand. He cracked his neck and murmured something under the noise of the crowd. The prince grunted and lifted his weapon. This time, he took a hit during the exchange, evening out their score. They were going until three strikes, but my heart was in my throat as they disengaged and circled again. Weslecker was still holding his sword in his left hand, wincing as he rotated his right shoulder.

He rushed the prince and swept his legs out from under him, taking another strike in the process. It didn't matter, not with the tip of his blunted weapon at the prince's throat the next second. The crowd's roar was deafening. Cadets pounded on the fence, while I whooped and hollered alongside the rest of my flight.

"We won! We won! We're going to be first!" Biggs screamed.

Some of my cheer faded as I watched Weslecker offer the prince a hand up, just for Prince Mateo to smack it away and struggle to his feet alone. He tossed some of his armor aside as he stalked from the ring.

Weslecker wiggled his helmet off, shock etched in his expression as he watched his friend leave. I reported what'd happened to Ari. *"What a bad sport,"* I muttered.

Ari grunted, his ears folded back until the noise started to die down. In the duel's place was the Commandant, his hand raised for silence. "Cadets. The agility course is still being set up. Go take an hour for lunch before reporting back with your top five picks to win the final event."

Another cheer rose as several cadets started heading back to the fortress. I looked forward to sitting for a bit. But eating before an agility course? Out of the question.

Especially when my whole flight turned hopeful looks toward me. If I won as I intended, so would Kite Flight overall.

CHAPTER 32

KITE FLIGHT, WHOOSH!

Within the hour, I lined up with nineteen other cadets facing a massive structure that would serve as our agility course. From where I stood, I could only see a ten-foot-tall wooden wall with knotted ropes hanging over the side to serve as our first obstacle. While the Commandant explained the rules, I counted the ropes. Twelve.

"You may be wondering why there are hoops on the other side of this structure," the Commandant was saying. I craned my neck to catch a glimpse of the poles with gryphon-sized hoops swaying in the breeze. "That is because your gryphons will also be participating in an agility course alongside you."

I exchanged a glance with Biggs, sharing in dismay. Ari loved obstacle and agility courses, but he could only participate in them with me on his back.

The Commandant paused for us to call our gryphons over. Ari leaned on Ironfeather, who guided him straight to me, while Weslecker followed a pace behind. Black and yellow bruises peeked out of his cadet uniform, yet he still went over to Credell and had a hushed conversation with him. Their attention flashed to me briefly.

Instructions continued as I barely listened, instead intent

on Ari. *"We don't have to do this. If you miss an obstacle, we're out,"* I said. That applied to human and gryphon. One failed obstacle, and we both had to stop where we failed.

"Then I won't miss an obstacle."

"Ari..."

He clicked his beak at me. *"No, I can do this. Don't count me out."*

Ironfeather twittered and mirrored Ari's confident stance. He came up to the older gryphon's shoulder at this point, his gray fluff making way for a beautifully formed set of flight feathers.

I glanced between them and laughed, ruffling Ironfeather. He peeped indignantly. "You're growing up too fast, you know that? I see what you two are planning." Ari would be okay with a seeing-eye gryphon, and Ironfeather was perfect for the job.

Weslecker replaced Credell in line and sank into a ready stance. I wanted to ask if he was sure he wanted to do this, but his face was set, and I knew nothing would stop him now. The only thing I could do was work together with him so we could both stay in the course.

The Commandant stood aside and drew out a whistle. The rest of us prepared to sprint while the gryphons also lined up. As the whistle blew, I took off, scrambling for one of the ropes as boys pushed and elbowed. I started scaling next to Weslecker, the two of us sparing a quick nod before focusing on the task ahead.

At the apex of the wall, I saw gryphons streaking by, blowing through the first hoop at top speed. One missed the next hoop, which was set at nearly a right angle from the first. Whistles blew, and the gryphon's rider was called off the course.

Ironfeather and Ari flew at the back, taking it slow, with the former chattering and telegraphing his turns for the latter to follow. I realized their strategy when three more boys were out because of their gryphons before we hit the second obstacle, a set of thick wooden bars to climb over. They went tallest to shortest, and I lost some ground to the other cadets here.

My arm muscles were already growing tired as the next challenge came. A straight jump to a metal pole, which required a pull-up to swing our legs up and over. Frustrated gryphon squawks sounded from the other side after two cadets fell in front of me.

I rubbed my palms together and jumped, breathing out before pulling myself up with core strength and swinging my legs up and over with a huff.

I continued through the obstacle course, favoring technique over speed as I realized doing this too swiftly would result in mistakes like the other cadets were making. There was no crawling; every obstacle required climbing over walls and poles of various sizes. "Yeah! Go Sivana!" Biggs called from the sidelines, and I realized I was one of the last cadets going and a swelling crowd was watching from the right side.

I approached a structure with several hanging ropes and groaned. There was a drill sergeant shouting orders from the side. Climb to the top and hold position for my gryphon to swoop in and carry me through the last course. "Fly low to the ground!" they screamed.

All the gryphons were saddled, but this would be the first time yearlings needed to carry their riders. We had to be nearly done. I huffed and puffed at the base of a rope while several voices yelled at me, threatening to knock me out of the competition if I didn't move. I was just seizing the rope when Weslecker fell and hit the ground with a groan.

Ironfeather was called out on the other side of the course.

I climbed and cursed breathlessly, pretty sure this was where I stopped too. Other cadets were still going around me, signaling to their gryphons as they cleared this obstacle. My trembling hands seized the wooden pole at the top of the structure as my feet found shaky holds in a knot in the rope.

"Ari!" I called, spotting my gryphon circling several yards away.

He started flying my way, only rebuffed when a gryphon flew too close to him. He sent a pulse of disorientation across our Link until I called his name again between panting breaths. My arm muscles burned to keep a hold on the pole.

"Fly up a few feet. You're going to hit the pole," I told him, guiding him up and around as my muscles screamed at me. By the time he held himself steady by my side, I nearly fell onto his saddle, flopping my upper body over it. With effort, I climbed on and secured my legs in the stirrups, untying his reins from the saddle horn and straightening them out.

We had the advantage for the last leg of the course, taking one last set of hoops and slalom poles together. We'd done this before in Aerial Agility, nearly daily, and the few cadets remaining all had yearling gryphons. Yet there was a confident blur way ahead of us, clearing the obstacles with ease. Prince Mateo and Mireille, I realized.

"Want to see how fast we can do this?" Ari asked eagerly.

"As fast as possible. It looks like this ends with a sky sprint," I said, sharing in his excitement. Ari sprang into motion, picking up speed as I lowered my goggles and leaned heavily into each motion to guide him through the hoops and poles.

We passed two cadets, and one cursed at us while his tired gryphon was forced to land. We were gaining on the three riders in front of us, and I could see Mireille's light gray feathers in the lead. Her wings pumped her forward at top speed, her beak stretched toward the finish line.

No! We have to win, I protested inwardly.

"Sprint coming," I warned Ari. There was one last stretch of air ending with goal flags. A mass of dots below showed that the other cadets were watching and pointing as we passed the last set of poles, and Ari eagerly narrowed his body and sped forward. I leaned over him to reduce our drag, seeing the blurs of two surprised riders flash by. We gained

on Mireille and Prince Mateo like an arrow released from its bow.

In a blink's time, we were passing the goal flags. Ari slowed, his chest heaving while his heart thumped the great barrel of his chest. Close by, Prince Mateo was patting his beast's neck. Our gazes met across the distance.

The watching cadets formed a writhing, roaring mass beneath us as we circled around. I pumped one fist in the air, laughing, exhilarated, and exhausted in the same breath. From gryphon back, there was no way of knowing who'd won between Ari and Mireille. It'd felt like we'd closed the distance, but the two gryphons had crossed the line at nearly the same time.

A pair of instructors were in heated debate below with the Commandant before he called for a lull by raising both arms. "First place in the agility event goes to…Cadet Walker and Arimus!"

"We did it! We won!" I exclaimed.

The crowd went nuts a split second after the announcement. I just hoped the king was watching.

My flight-mates surrounded us as soon as we landed. They were excited enough to nearly carry me off my feet as we bounced and celebrated together.

"Kite Flight! *Whoosh!*"

We whooshed our way to the stage on the Green, where our instructors and the Commandant waited. The three flags that flew over the Green were being reeled in; Falcon Flight's tattered symbol being folded as we waited. I stopped short in surprise to see my father on stage as well, laughing and clapping Commander Rudrick on the shoulder.

Well, of course. If the king was here, so was the First, his honor guard for flying travel. Rudrick noticed me before Father did and pointed. My father turned and tapped a fist to his heart in pride, a smile splitting his face. *"He saw us win too,"* I told Ari, excitedly explaining everything that was happening as he rested against my side, radiating his own pride over our Link.

The Commandant raised his hand for silence, and the crowd of first years calmed quickly. He turned his gaze straight at me, and my joy pirouetted straight to fear at what I saw there. Pity. After all that, the Commandant expressed in a look everything I would expect when looking at a condemned gryphon and his hopeful rider.

"What? What happened?" Ari asked of my sudden turn in mood.

"Good afternoon, cadets," the Commandant said.

"Good afternoon, sir," we chorused.

As he spoke, announcing Harrier Flight as fourth place, I turned to hug my gryphon again. *"Nothing's changed. We have to get out of here before tomorrow,"* I told him. I'd let the Gate-keeper take me before I waited around for us to be taken to Ari's execution.

He nudged me with his beak. *"Stop it. We're about to win this silly competition for once. Enjoy it."*

Murmurs of excitement grew amidst the boys around me as Osprey Flight claimed third place.

"The king can't have you," I insisted, glancing to the sky to clear my eyes of traitorous tears.

I felt hot attention at my side as Falcon Flight was declared second place. Prince Mateo stood several yards away, his dark brow lowered over a furious stare. Another thing I took from him, I supposed.

"And for the first time…Kite Flight will fly in first place honors during our summer break," the Commandant announced.

We were supposed to conduct ourselves with decorum and cheer politely. Biggs cupped his hands over his mouth and called, "Kite Flight!"

I wasn't the only one bouncing up and down as we shouted, "Whoosh!" back and whooped. But my breath caught when the flag was raised. Not the generic training flag of a kite with its wings spread, but one with a dark blue background and the black symbol of a toy kite. I pointed at it and screamed. My flight-mates and I lost our minds for a good ten seconds before being pinned by the Commandant's icy glare.

He dismissed us soon after for free time for the rest of the day. I grabbed Ari and disappeared into the crowd, bringing him back to the Kite Flight dorm without making eye contact with my father. He could be proud of me now, without knowing I was pulling Ari's dusty saddlebags out from under my bed and stuffing them full.

"We'll head out under the cover of darkness. By the time anyone realizes we're missing, it'll be tomorrow," I told him as I packed in a frenzy.

"This is not necessary," Ari griped, his tail thumping the ground as he lounged on a cushion I'd dragged into the room.

"They're going to kill *you!"* I nearly shouted at him. *"It's completely necessary! I should've known all along that they wouldn't ever let us get promoted to second years. The king doesn't care. He'll never entertain the idea of a female gryphon rider."*

"You do realize that by leaving, we'll be considered deserters. No matter what would've happened tomorrow, we'll both be put to death if we're caught after deserting," he pointed out.

"Then we won't get caught."

He loosed a frustrated caw. *"The king could still be lying and expecting you to overreact. You're falling for his trap right now."*

Someone knocked on the door, which was ajar. "Sivana?" Sharde asked, poking his head in the room.

He caught me deliberating with a coat in one hand and a wooden training sword in the other.

"What are you doing? We're not leaving yet," he said.

Ari flipped his tail in extra agitation, drawing his attention. "I'm just getting a jump on things," I said, trying to mask a nervous laugh. "How's your head?"

Puzzlebox wiggled her way into the room and laid herself

out in front of Ari with a concerned twitter. Sharde didn't answer, his gaze narrowed on them. There was a bandage over his nose and a second on his forehead, but he appeared to be fine otherwise.

He raised a brow. "Why is Ari telling Puzzlebox that you have something to share with us?"

I cast a glare toward my gryphon, who was too busy grooming behind Puzzlebox's ears to notice. "I'm, uh, leaving," I said.

"Right now?"

"Yeah." I realized Ellie was standing behind him, peering around his arm and waving to me with an excited smile. "I guess I should tell you why, but the fewer people know, the better."

"Tell us what?" This came from Biggs, who must've been behind Sharde too. "C'mon, Walker, you're the one who won it for us! Why are you hiding in here?"

Something told me I wasn't getting away easily at all. Reluctantly, I put down the saddle bags and followed them into the common area, spotting Birch before Valentic, who flashed a big smile. "Hey, congratulations! We're the talk of the Academy. Couldn't celebrate without you, Walker."

"I might've gotten the kitchen staff to agree to a little something." Sharde picked up a glass and a plate and handed them to me. I sipped fresh lemonade and almost smiled at the sight of a brownie dusted with powdered sugar. Chocolate… so rare around here.

Valentic's expression dimmed. "What's wrong?"

"I, um, have something to tell you guys," I admitted, sitting heavily on a cushion and putting the treats aside. My flight-mates gathered around as I told them for the first time about the king's threat upon coming here. How Ari's life was tied to our performance at the Academy as a forced concession.

"I think Commander Davis was the king's man, too. He

tried to get me out of the Academy and nearly succeeded," I said.

Weslecker nodded, scowling. "Makes sense."

"He's gone anyway. I've done my best, but the king drew me aside today to tell me that I was about to fail and what would happen next. How Ari would be buried with military honors next to Alamid." It was hard to repeat, even in summary. My hands clenched on my thighs. "So…I'm going to leave tonight. I came here to save my gryphon's life, and I'll leave to do the same."

Sharde held up a hand. "Wait a minute. The Commandant would've met with you more than once to discuss your performance if that were true. You don't just fail. I would know." Anyone except for Ari and me would just repeat the year until they passed, just like Sharde and Puzzlebox.

"Yeah, but you didn't have the king meddling in your records," I pointed out.

"That doesn't matter. It's the Commandant's decision, and he hasn't indicated that you're failing. I don't think he can simply fail you," he argued.

Valentic cleared his throat. "I have an idea. Look, there's a way to make the Commandant look *really* bad if he were to declare you unfit to be a second year. Did you know that there's a rule that states if a Cadet-Commander is unable to march his flight, he can temporarily choose one of his first years to do it in his stead?"

"That's a regulation," Ellie murmured. "Anyone have their cadet handbook around?"

My brow furrowed as Weslecker got up and went to his room. "Like, I call the flight to attention and march them in the Pass in Review?" I asked.

"Yup. It happened last year to one of the flights and made Cadet Callan look really good when he stepped up." Valentic punctuated this with a roll of his eyes.

"And what will you be doing during that time? Won't it hurt your rank?"

"If it saves Ari, it'll be worth it," he replied.

Weslecker returned with a pristine copy of the cadet handbook, and Ellie rattled off the particular rule that stated any cadet could be promoted to a leadership position in a time of crisis.

"And my crisis will be…" Valentic tapped his chin. "Well, I could mysteriously get the flu."

"That's hard to fake," I pointed out.

He winked. "I have my ways. Don't worry about that, but please…stay. Trust me, nothing's worse than deserting. There are going to be a lot of people outraged if you don't graduate tomorrow after your win today *and* you leading a flight in a formal Pass in Review."

I glanced around at the nods of agreement from the rest of my flight-mates and finally dipped my head. "All right. Now, did someone say something about a celebration?" I invited, taking another sip of sweet lemonade.

"Kite Flight!" Biggs exclaimed.

"Whoosh!"

CHAPTER 33

LEAP OF FAITH

"Sorry, Sarge. Cadet-Commander Valentic has the flu," I told Sergeant Kobarn the next day as we lined up at the front of the first-year flights.

He looked over me skeptically and shook his head. "That's a shame, Cadet Walker. I'll let the Commandant know."

No one else hassled us, not when the Pass in Review was mostly about the graduation of the third years, who'd returned to be part of this formal ceremony. They'd announce the Ace and his accomplishments, pass out a few awards, but more importantly, the king would knight them, and they'd move on to formal positions within the gryphon knight corps.

Then the second years would have their ceremony and promotion, and finally I would learn whether the king was bluffing me. I sweated in my formal uniform. Only trust in my flight had kept me here to take this leap of faith.

My father and a few of the other Commanders were here too, either to welcome their new recruits or to watch family graduate. They'd be shuffled to the back, as the king and High Command were also here for the formal event. We'd practiced Pass in Reviews every month, but this time, it was the real deal. All those important eyes would see me at the head of Kite Flight because of Valentic's sacrifice.

Hopefully it was enough.

The call to form up came, and we started marching. *"It's just one loop around the Green,"* Ari assured me. He marched with grave formality at my side, his beak tilted up at a proud angle.

"The most important walk of our lives," I replied.

The line slowed as the third years began presenting arms to the stage where the king and ranking military stood. Flags and formal banners were waved. Sharde carried our standard, bearing the blue field and black toy kite. He was most adept at presenting arms with it; it was cumbersome, especially with a breeze.

Before I knew it, the last of the second years were passing by the stage and it was our turn. I bellowed for us to present arms and turned to salute. The king stood front and center, his sneer visible. Flanking him were the Commandant and Paragon Hughes, leader of the gryphon knight corps. The king turned and muttered to the Commandant, while a hint of a smile touched the Paragon's face. I could feel their attention on me until we'd passed them and returned to marching and finishing the loop around the field.

Three long rows of chairs were assembled in the middle of the Green for us to sit. Third years in the front, first years in the back. I had to crane my head around to see the stage from here, spotting a Tulari handing the king something. His voice was suddenly amplified over the field as he greeted High Command first, then the Commandant, the watching Commanders, and finally us cadets.

Ari yawned. *"Wake me up when he's done."*

I should've known we were in for a long speech, yet I was hyper aware of every word the king said, turning them over for hidden meaning. He didn't insult me directly, but he did refer to the crowd several times as "a group of fine young men," which I assumed meant I was exempt from his praise. He outlined the four core tenants of the Academy individually and why they were important. I knew courage, loyalty, discipline, and integrity were vital, but every major speech I'd endured this year followed the same format.

"Is it the same speech each time?" I asked.

"Sounds similar," he grumbled. *"Congratulations on making it this far. Don't die tomorrow as fresh knights. Everyone else, get some well-deserved rest."*

I shifted in my seat, wondering if I was going to melt from stress as the knighting ceremony began with torturous formality. The new knights were called up by rank from lowest to highest, meaning we wouldn't know the Ace until the last name was called.

They walked to the stage alongside their gryphon, kneeling to be christened by the king's sword as the Commandant read out a list of their accomplishments both as cadets and as squires for their last semester apart from the Academy. Then, their new flight was announced, and we applauded.

Repeat that thirty-seven more times.

I nudged Ari out of his nap once the Ace, a burly man named Karos Seaworth, was announced and knighted after a lengthy recitation of what he'd done in battle as a squire. *"That guy killed three rozash on his own,"* I informed my gryphon.

"Sounds like he survived a disaster," he snarked.

"Help me stay awake," I practically begged.

The second years were called to line up next. *"This one's fast. No knighting, just shaking the Commandant's hand,"* Ari told me. They were called up again by rank, and I was keen, at least, to hear where a few of the boys placed.

Valentic, still absent, had sent Birch to accept his rank of tenth place. The speckled gryphon wouldn't leave the stage until the Commandant patted his head.

"And in spot number one, Cadet-Commander of Falcon Flight, Victor Callan," the Commandant announced to a smattering of applause. I sat in stony silence along with half of the other first years, my arms crossed. It wasn't necessarily a surprise that Callan was the Ace-to-be if he continued his performance next year.

Still, it was *him*. Slotting another victory into his belt, no matter what it took to get there.

The first years were called to line up in front of the stage next. We stood at attention as the Commandant said, "This group of cadets has been noteworthy. It's the first time in many years that our underdog flight has come to succeed above all others despite their disadvantages."

"Kite Flight," Biggs whispered out of the corner of his mouth. Sharde didn't say "whoosh" but did blow out a breath.

"There have been many struggles this year, but I've watched this crop of cadets get up, dust themselves off, and try again time after time. I'm proud to announce that no cadet will be held back this year," the Commandant continued. Ari pressed in to steady my legs as I felt lightheaded with a sudden influx of relief.

"I told you," Ari said.

Gods above, he had. From the moment the king had bluffed me, Ari had known, but I'd fallen for it and nearly ended our lives by making a foolish mistake. *"You did. I need to buy you a salmon. Ten salmon."*

He clicked his beak in consideration. *"I'll take two."*

"...in order of rank. This is the first time we are ranking the cadets based on their performance this year," the Commandant was saying. He consulted his notes. "Cadets, when your name and rank are called, come forward to receive your shield and then sit in order of your rank. We start with the cadet ranked thirty-five of thirty-five—"

Sharde was already starting to walk forward.

"—Cadet Sivana Walker."

He paused, then took a few steps back. A few puzzled looks followed me as I came forward to a hail of polite applause, following the motioning soldiers as they ushered me up the steps. The Commandant shook my hand first, saying quietly, "Congratulations, Cadet Walker."

"Thank you, sir," I whispered back. He placed a hand on my shoulder and steered me to where my father waited, holding a shield.

"Your first shield. May it serve you well," he said, offering it over. Its lacquered blue surface gleamed as I shook my father's hand formally. With both of us in uniform, I wasn't about to hug him with all the excitement and nerves buzzing in my chest.

But I wanted to. Instead, I took my shield and went to sit in the first space in the empty row, and it was a long walk all the way to the end. Once seated alongside Ari, I turned my shield around to really look at it and deflated knowing I was the lowest-ranked cadet. *"Hey, we're still in this,"* I said to Ari, trying to be optimistic.

My gryphon was fuming, his talons plucking up clods of grass. *"Thirty-five of thirty-five! After all that?"* he demanded.

"That shows how close we were to not making it," I admitted. Ari quieted next to me with a huff. *"So, I'm happy. And this shield is beautiful."*

"It hasn't seen battle yet."

That might be so, but the wooden kite shield I held was new and vibrant with fresh paint and varnish. It had the blue field and black toy kite but with the silver strip separating Kite Flight's symbol with my personal one, which was supposed to resemble a silhouette of a closed gryphon eye. Part of it looked like a crescent moon, and it was painted in silver rather than the yellow I'd asked for. The artist must've made a mistake.

Still, I loved it. Soon we'd be flying back to Kaiamear for a long, well-deserved break. I looked forward to leaving the Academy and its competitions behind, especially when I glanced down the row to see Sharde right next to me as thirty-fourth...and way at the other end, Prince Mateo with his white and gold Altarian shield at first place.

Ari and I still had a long way to climb if we wanted to sit close to the prince.

CHAPTER 34

HOW WE ARE REMEMBERED

In a corner of the third floor, past all the classrooms, was a door I hadn't opened all year. As a bustle of cadets returned to the fortress to pack and made plans to head to Kaiamear for the yearly graduation ball, I took Ari to the Hall of Graduates.

It was about the size of a hallway where Ari and I could stand side-by-side, just barely brushing either side of the room. Open slatted windows poured sunlight over the treasures hidden here. Dividing the hall in half were a series of tables, the first bearing a bust of the gryphon knight corps' founder, the first King of Altare.

Under glass, a piece of the first gryphon knight's lance was immortalized. Next to it, an old cushion bore a couple feathers from a beast named Glorium. Even now, his feathers gleamed with an iridescent rainbow caught within the filaments. Glory, indeed.

But that wasn't why I'd come here. The true treasure, I thought, were the plaques lining either wall. One side bore lists of names, from the first graduating class to the most current, which had yet to be hung. Running parallel to them were plaques listing when each rider died and the manner of their death.

I ran my fingers over the ancient history stored here, seeing such deaths ranging from a peaceful passing at rest to a brief, heroic recounting of their last moments in combat. A few names were scrubbed off completely; such was the fate of traitors, to be forgotten.

Ari sensed my solemn mood as I toured the graduation side first, coming to a stop at my father's year. Immortalized forever as number one, the Ace of his year, "Nathaniel Walker" was engraved just above "Valtora, Wild-Caught Female." I had to move to the next plaque for my fingers to rub over a familiar name.

"Alamid Maros" was engraved as the third-place graduate of his year. Right underneath his name was Ari's. It seemed the Academy only noted the wild-born beasts due to their more difficult nature.

"Third place," I said, turning to Ari now and smiling. "That's incredible."

"We were close to first. You'll find that that's what it's like every year. The top three or four are nearly indistinguishable," he replied.

"I sure hope that means someone's going to unseat Callan," I remarked, crossing to the other side of the hall. Alamid's name and date of death were newly engraved, the third man from his graduating class to pass away. The other two had their gryphons listed, but blank brass shone underneath my old friend's name.

For the first time in quite a while, I let myself cry over his loss. Alamid was immortalized as Knight-Captain Maros forevermore, dying in a border skirmish to defend King Cortes. If it weren't for his sacrifice, I wouldn't be here right now with his gryphon, fighting to give him the second chance he deserved.

Ari nudged my hip. *"What is it?"* he asked quietly.

"I see what could've been," I murmured. There was no doubt they would simply have listed his name and a different date of death here had Ari been executed on schedule. I knelt and held him, and he cried too in soft wails.

I recovered first and simply held him. In that time, another person drifted through the open door, his hands behind his back. I shot to my feet like I'd done something wrong upon seeing the Commandant in full formal dress.

"At ease, cadet. I was hoping I'd find you before you left," he said.

"Sir?" I said, confused.

"When your father was a cadet, he spent a lot of time in here. On the side you're on. He would read over the deaths." He shrugged, his gaze darting over the plaques. "It's not unusual for all of us to spend time here and reflect on how we are remembered."

I kept a nearly fearful silence as he turned to make sure the door was closed behind him. "There's something I wanted to tell you," he said, lowering his voice. My heart pattered, thinking this was about the king's threats. "There is a way to join Final Flight straight after graduation. You just have to ask for it after you finish your squire period."

Whatever I thought he was going to say, it wasn't that. I already knew that. "Are you saying I should ask to join Final Flight, sir?"

He looked me straight in the eye with his serious Commandant stare. "Yes. If you could request it now, I would send you off with the mail tomorrow."

Ari's hackles raised. *"We've come too far to retire!"*

I shifted uncomfortably. Retiring young to deliver mail was Sharde's dream, not mine, but it would be rude of me to come out and say it. He probably read it off my expression, though. "Cadet Walker, I appreciate the enthusiasm and grit you and your gryphon have shown this year. I am not saying either of you are incapable. You have true talent, and Ari has already proven himself to be a beast the caliber of the First Gryphon Flight."

I waited for the "but" since I could hear it in his tone.

"But Ari is blind now. You may succeed at every task and challenge put before you *eventually*, with enough time, practice, or chances at it, but our country is at war. The Gryphon Rider Academy trains its cadets for combat."

He took a deep breath, shaking his head. His tone softened. "I'll answer to the Gatekeeper if you two are ever sent to a battlefield just to die. I will assign you the bottom rank until you are safely graduated to Final Flight, young lady."

"Sir, that's not what either of us wants," I finally protested.

He wet his lips as he considered me and the gryphon by my side. "There are forces at work against you that even the Academy cannot shield you from. I would prefer to send you on a mail route so the country forgets you. But..."

He shook his head slowly. "Perhaps the country should not forget your story, no matter what else it changes in the process."

"Yes, sir," I murmured. There was that word again: *change*.

"I'll see you in a couple months." The Commandant nodded to me and turned to leave.

"Thank you for the advice, sir," I said as neutrally as possible. Soon Ari and I were alone again, and I deflated. Would it really be better for us if we retired out of the public's eye?

"Am I really your best friend?" Ari asked out of seemingly nowhere.

My outburst against the king felt like it'd happened ages ago, not yesterday. But I could tell it'd been on Ari's mind. *You'd kill my best friend without hearing what I have to say?*

"Absolutely. I came here for you," I said. "More importantly, you've been by my side ever since. We've shared emotions and thoughts in a way I'll never be able to with another human. We've been through so much together already, and I think if we truly change things around here, we'll be legends ourselves one day."

Where words would've taken time to explain, I turned to emotions and memories, sharing like a gryphon does. I thought of Commander Davis pushing Ari into more and more uncomfortable situations and how we'd overcome each one with a little ingenuity. I shared the great well of respect that'd been building from the moment my gryphon had ordered me onto his back even though he's blind. How much trust he must have for me to be his eyes.

Ari bowed his head, butting my chest affectionately. He opened his mind too, filling my chest with a warm love. I put a hand over my heart with a gasp.

"Thank you for my second chance," he said.

SIVANA AND ARI'S **adventure will continue in Gryphon Rider Academy 2: Chosen!**

INTERESTED IN MORE? Join my newsletter as one way to get access to a bonus scene from this book! Sign up on my website.

STAY up to date with Gryphon Rider Academy and the Altare world by joining my Facebook group: People of Altare! In this community, we'll talk about fantasy book releases, share fun posts, and have the occasional giveaway.

. . .

PLEASE REMEMBER TO REVIEW! Reviews help other readers find stories they may love. Consider leaving a review for Gryphon Rider Academy 1: Second Chance on Amazon and other websites.

ALSO IN THE ALTARE WORLD

ROYAL SPY INSTITUTE

Join an unlikely crew of five misfits and a mouse as they strive to become one of Altare's newest elite spy teams. Heists and adventures await!

The Gilded Wolves meets Six of Crows in this YA fantasy series in which a former thief uses her skills to become a spy. If you like clever heroines, strong friendships, and found family, then you'll love Royal Spy Institute!

- See Royal Spy Institute on Amazon -

ABOUT THE AUTHOR

Elise Hennessy is an author of young adult fantasy full of adventure and found family. She holds a master's degree in journalism and enjoys crafting unique stories. When Elise is not busy writing, she's trying to reduce her prodigious TBR list. She lives in Texas with her family and is owned by two cats.

Find out more about her books at: www.elisehennessy.com

www.ingramcontent.com/pod-product-compliance
Lightning Source LLC
Chambersburg PA
CBHW061643190726
48289CB00006B/1724